PRAISE
THE FLOATING GIRLS

"Lo Patrick's *The Floating Girls* is a powerhouse of a Southern novel. At once a poignant coming-of-age tale, a murder mystery, and an evocative tribute to the marshlands of Georgia, this lush and mesmerizing debut has a beating heart of its own. Lo Patrick is a standout new Southern voice."

—Andrea Bobotis, author of *The Last List of Miss Judith Kratt*

"Fans of *Where the Crawdads Sing* will love this immersive mystery set against the salty air of Georgia's marshes. In Patrick's atmospheric prose, the water and its characters come to life. And many Southern women who just couldn't seem to do right and fit in will recognize themselves in twelve-year-old Kay; I know I did."

—Lindsey Rogers Cook, author of *Learning to Speak Southern*

"The Georgia marshes hide a compelling mystery in *The Floating Girls*, but nothing can hide from the astute gaze of twelve-year-old Kay Whitaker. Kay is the smartest, funniest, most curious young narrator I have come across in some time. Her voice stuck with me long after I finished reading. If I met Kay on the street, I'd beg her to be my best friend."

—Tiffany Quay Tyson, award-winning author of *The Past Is Never*

the
floating
girls

the
floating
girls

a novel

LO PATRICK

Published by Sourcebooks Landmark, an imprint of Sourcebooks
P.O. Box 4410, Naperville, Illinois 60567-4410
(630) 961-3900
sourcebooks.com

Library of Congress Cataloging-in-Publication Data

Names: Patrick, Lo, author.
Title: The floating girls : a novel / Lo Patrick.
Description: Naperville, Illinois : Sourcebooks Landmark, [2022]
Identifiers: LCCN 2021042275 (print) | LCCN 2021042276 (ebook) |
(trade paperback) | (epub)
Subjects: LCGFT: Detective and mystery fiction.
Classification: LCC PS3616.A8725 F56 2022 (print) | LCC PS3616.A8725
(ebook) | DDC 813/.6—dc23
LC record available at https://lccn.loc.gov/2021042275
LC ebook record available at https://lccn.loc.gov/2021042276

Printed and bound in the United States of America.
VP 10 9 8 7 6 5 4 3

For Rone. I'll see you on the flip side.

Bledsoe, Georgia

The first foot of water is hot like a bathtub. Heavy, even though it sits at the top. Water is like air: the heat's up above, the cool down below. But in the marsh it's all shallow. It's all warm. It's a hothead, a mean streak, a fever.

The water's full of what's fallen in and what's growing out. The bottom feels like old bread—old bread that's sat under a leaky hose. It pulses from all the life inside; a person can see the heat. It has its own vibrations coming off of it like a drum on a hot plate. You can cook and bang at the same time. The flies don't feel it; they can walk on fire down here.

It happened twice—the coming upon of somebody else's

secret. There was a man and a woman before, a long time ago. They were the first to be found back that way. He'd lay her down in the marsh like he was introducing her—slow and precious. Her hair hit the surface and made the bugs scatter in a hundred different directions. She was soaked from head to toe when they were done. Him too, but he didn't have long hair like an oil spill. It didn't matter anyway—nobody can tell if you're sweating or swimming in Bledsoe, it gets so thick outside. Who'd have said anything about them being wet? People spend half their lives like fish. The town is hardly on land at all.

There were people watching them. Two women: one who cared and one who didn't. The one who didn't would look out the window of her slack-jawed house—its deck half on and half off, sliding into the water, dislocated—and pull the curtain closed. If you live back that far, you're prone to minding your own business. Trouble comes looking for you if you're not careful. It finds just as easily as it's found.

But there was somebody else back there too. If it weren't for the trees, the sawgrass, the thick brush of reeds and the sticklike plants swaying in the damp, they would have noticed the other one, standing there in a fog all her own. The one who cared. She was watching, like a light on in a dark room. She could have been an egret with the point of her face, always in the direction of the man and the woman with the long black hair. The watcher's face even twitched birdlike. She was only wet to her knees; no one dipped her down to cool her off. No one else was around. She might sizzle if submerged. She might pop.

The breeze gave a good shout at the grass, and everything did its proper song and dance but went back to stillness, like rehearsing for a play. Those things with roots took their place, and the hot air from God's own mouth stopped blowing at the ground. It was hushed again, but never silent. The water tripped over itself and bumped into things. The birds dove and sang, jumped and pecked, floated and swarmed right along with the bugs—a whole wall of them. In the wrong light, a person would think they were looking through a screen. There was almost as much water in the air as in the marsh; you could barely see through it even in a hard squint. It was a thick gauze for wounds not yet felt but begging to heal.

That was a long time ago. It was different water in the swirls now, different insects, different birds, different boys and girls, but the same light on in the dark—the distant egret woman who wandered upon something she didn't want to see, again. And again, she watched.

This one didn't dip his lady in the water like pouring cream on silk. He didn't pull her back up with her legs around his middle like the other two. When he put her in the water, she didn't move anymore. Suspended. Floating.

CHAPTER 1

We moved into the house on Hack Road when I was a baby. I don't remember anything about being a baby or moving to Hack Road, but it's where I lived my whole life. My father built the place with his own two hands and "no help from anyone else!" It wasn't even true—he had lots of help, but this was the Whitaker way. I laid claim to good deeds or impressive projects that took no sweat from my brow too. I once took credit for cutting steel for the Walton Waterway Bridge that led to denser land across the bay. I wasn't even born when it went up.

My family didn't live close to the road, but addresses were hard to come by in Bledsoe, so we said we were on the road anyway. We chose our own address: 1234 Hack Road. All options were available. Imagination was also hard to come by here.

We were a ways back, hiding under a large oak tree that my mother called a Spanish moss. A fragile woman, she was not so eagerly corrected. *It's an oak*, no one seemed willing to tell her. *Live oak*. We kept quiet when she was wrong; she might shatter.

We were a solitary type of family without a lot of people around to tell us the right names of trees or other useful things. My mother was the quietest woman my father knew; he used to say it all the time. "Sue-Bess, you're the quietest woman I know." She would nod silently, hoping to keep her title.

People don't really give their children names like Sue-Bess anymore. Those were simpler times meant to be complicated by hyphens and awkward combinations. Now, we're one-named people, except for my sister, Sarah-Anne, who got extra because of her hair. Blond hair has always made a favorable impression on my mother. One name was not enough for hair like that. My name is Kay—mouse hair gets only three letters.

My brothers are Peter and Freddy. My sister who died was Elizabeth. I was almost two years old when it happened. Sarah-Anne was coming up on four. Elizabeth died from being born too early. I came the day I was supposed to. If only I had known what would happen if Elizabeth tried to pop out before her time, I would have told her to stay put. Elizabeth was my parents' last, best chance. There were to be no more Whitakers after we went to her funeral in the yard outside our house. Under the oak. Under the Spanish moss.

We lived in Bledsoe, Georgia. It's a place and a culprit. I know there were seasons, but all I can remember is heat and rot and people sitting, just sitting. Inside, outside, under a tree, in a tree, with cold drinks sweating in their hands, wet cloths on their sweating heads, their feet in a bucket of ice water (my father's favorite), or just lying half-dead-like, roasting like a pig on a spike. Begging God for a cloud.

Grown-ups love to talk about weather, but in Bledsoe, the kids joined in too. The heat gave us a whole new vocabulary and a lot of passion to use it. When I heard the grown-ups go on about it being warm and needing rain, or "we're flooded," or "the trees'll fall over," or "the roots'll dry up," or "the dust'll choke us to death," or this and that, I was compelled to join in: "Woe is me! Hotter than the dickens!" "I'm on fire out here!" "Soles of my shoes turning to butter today!" "More sweat than sense, I'll say!" I did say it was "hot as shit" once, but I got popped for that. I could feel it in my jaw for a long time after. It kept me honest. Honestly quiet. My daddy did the popping while my mother set the good examples.

It took a solid six minutes to run from Hack Road to our house. I timed myself once with a stopwatch that my oldest brother, Peter, got for Christmas. For a while there, he timed everything—even how long it took him to go to the bathroom, both ways—but my father put a stop to that and wiped the watch down with a wet cloth. I was eight years old when he got the watch, ten when I timed myself running from Hack Road to our house, and twelve when I timed myself running from our house to the house I never knew was there, which was exactly nineteen minutes from Hack Road and thirteen minutes from my house.

"I'm just gonna see how far I can run without stopping!" I called out to Peter one afternoon.

"Suit yourself, but don't die of heat exhaustion."

It was August. This is when things got a little dire. Typically you made it through July by pretending to like the heat and wading in salty marsh water with its slimy bottom. "This is nice!" I'd say to no one in particular. "How refreshing! Heat's good for the soul!" Sometimes you just sat down in the creek that went all the way to Dune River and let water run over your privates, which are definitely the hottest part of the body besides the head. By August, none of that did any good. You were as hot as a firecracker, and even the night didn't cool you off. We lived on miles of shoreline, but there were no beaches—just dirt vanishing into liquid. There was no white sand in Bledsoe, and no one came there for vacation. The ocean was for fishing and isolation only.

Freddy was a year and a half older than me, so we were a little too close in age to like each other much. Peter was almost four years older and always a good influence. Sarah-Anne was in the middle of the boys. My parents must have been busy for a time. We were very close in age and proximity, and we didn't have a lot to occupy us in such barren lands. There was a good deal of rabble-rousing. Whenever we got going, my father told us to cool our jets and sent us outside, so that we wouldn't disturb my mother, who was in a near-constant delicate state. Sarah-Anne wasn't included in group punishments—probably because of her hair.

"I'm goin' out for track next year," I said as I did some warm-up stretches before my timed run.

"Middle school track is a joke," Peter said. He played basketball at school, which was not a joke. We watched *Hoosiers* at least four times a week. Peter had said he wanted to walk down the aisle at his wedding to the theme song.

"But the dad's a drunk!" I had argued.

"Lotsa people are drunks, Kay," Freddy had said. Freddy liked to read more than most people and, because of this and other character flaws, was a know-it-all. He knew how to either rile you up or calm you down with his knowledge. No, you couldn't die from holding in your pee; yes, many people have a fear of being kicked by a horse; no, an overbite wasn't a serious medical condition; yes, alcohol could kill you if you drank it like a pig at the trough; no, Sarah-Anne wasn't a mute.

Fear and loathing of alcoholism was a common topic in our home. My mother grew up in a house with a "buncha drunks," so we heard a lot about what the bottle can do to people with the few words she spoke to us. I was so convinced that booze was at the root of all problems, I even got to telling people that the neighbor's dog was a drunk. "Dog's drunk!" I would holler when that obnoxious mutt got going full throttle at six o'clock in the morning.

My father had ordered me to keep my voice down. The neighbors lived almost a mile away, but their dog liked peeing in our weeds. He was over a lot with his leg lifted and his mouth open like he was choking on something. Even if he was a total pain in our ass, my father didn't want me yelling at the neighbors' dog. One of the brothers next door had an AK. My father said he heard it banging when they thought we weren't home.

"I'm never gonna get drunk," I had promised often and loudly. My mother wore a pleased expression along with her sundress whenever we made promises to avoid evils.

I took off at the sound of the small beep that came from the stopwatch. Peter said "Go!" and watched with fierce concentration.

I ran quickly but not at full speed. I knew to pace myself as I planned to go for at least a half hour. Bledsoe is as flat as a table. It goes and goes and goes, but there's no view. The most a person can see is the low-lying brush in front of them. Most of our land had sand for dirt. There was a spot to the left of our house that had good soil, peach-and-blueberry-growing dirt. The farther you went behind our place, the closer you got to the marsh lands. That's where the running got a little tricky. A boy in my third-grade class, Martin Brown, had a waterbed that we used to take turns rolling around on while at his house. He'd invite all the kids over and give us frozen Butterfingers from his parents' fridge like he was paying for our time. When we were done licking our hands, and there weren't any more Butterfingers to give away, we'd play on his bed.

I had a hell of a time getting up from that thing; no matter how much I pushed, I just sank deeper. That's how it felt running in the marsh. Your foot would take forever to find something solid to press down on, but the deeper you went meant it was harder to get your foot back out and onto the next step. I had a feeling quicksand was a lot like Bledsoe. I did try to run on Martin's bed once. It was like trucking it over a half-full inner tube with a tear. Damn near impossible, and I was right—it felt the exact same as the marsh behind my house.

We rarely wore shoes in the summer, mostly because of the heat, and because if you went far enough from our house, you'd end up in the water. When we were small, we were deathly afraid of alligators (common, according to Freddy—the fear of them, not gator attacks), but as we got older we knew that if we just kept running, they'd leave us alone. It's when you stop and stare awhile that you give your weakness away—our weakness being flesh and bone. And blood.

I was always in a dress, Sarah-Anne too, which was my mother's doing. She wore them as well. My mother could sew only one thing; we had dozens of dresses with an identical cut but varying fabrics. Obviously my mother's were larger than mine, but Sarah-Anne and I wore the same size. She didn't grow like a weed the way I did. She grew like a frightened potato—back into the soil with all the other potatoes, afraid to show their faces. I never could understand why we ate dirty roots. Sarah-Anne was the mole child.

I kept on running for what felt like an hour and then started to wonder how Peter was going to know to stop the watch when I got to where I couldn't go anymore. It was pure marsh under my feet. My mother and father said we shouldn't go wandering out into the swamp because of snakes, bugs as big as your hand that nobody knew the names for, and briers that could take your toe off with one wrong step—*and* because we didn't know who lived back there. They emphasized that last part. It was in their nature to think that strangers were worse than wildlife.

It was getting deep, and the bottom half of my dress was soaked. I stopped to catch my breath, figuring that a few seconds to adjust my clothes and pull my underwear out of my bottom wasn't necessarily cheating. I could hear what sounded like a broken violin being played not too far from where I was standing. I froze.

"Peter!" I yelled. The music stopped immediately, and I remained very still knowing that I'd both heard something and then not heard it anymore. "Peter!" I called again. There was some rustling and then the sound of splashing about twenty yards from where I was standing. At first, I saw nothing there but a large gathering of high seagrass. Standing in front of a thick blade was a boy about my age. He'd blended in at first, but as my breath slowed down, I was able to make out his shape. He looked at me with a shit-eating grin on his face. If I hadn't known better, I would have said he was expecting me, but his smile evaporated a little as he took me in. I hated to disappoint someone so keen on standing in the water, so I waved. He took a few steps backward and sat down on a ragged stump before reluctantly lifting one of his hands in a half-hearted greeting. He was holding a guitar in his other hand; his feet were in the water. I waved again, not sure what else to do. He didn't look a bit familiar. We knew everyone in Bledsoe one way or another, so this was curious enough.

"What's that?" I asked, pointing at the guitar. I knew full well what a guitar was, but I felt like asking what he was doing with it out in the middle of the marsh.

"Guitar," he said, shrugging. He looked over my shoulder for a second.

"Right, but what are you doing with it way out here? Don't seem like you're playin' it right. Got a rotten sound." He looked behind me again. "I'm on my own," I said. "Nobody else comin'."

He shook his head a little, like he was setting himself straight. "Missin' some strings," he said lifting the guitar as he pointed to his left. "I live out here." I turned to see a small house on stilts, like a lady in heels, sitting right there in the middle of the reed grass. Beyond that sat a thick group of mangroves—my mother hated them fiercely. She said it was against nature for a tree to grow in the water. I usually shuddered at the sight of them, in direct imitation of my mother. She could shudder the wings off a ladybug. It didn't seem like he was going to say anything else, as was common in this weather. Words were few and far between in late August without air conditioning or a hope in the world.

"Well, that's a strange house," I said to his index finger.

"You're awful sweaty," he said, smiling. I thought maybe people who lived this far back in the marsh didn't have manners—I knew I didn't have any, and I lived up on the road.

"I've been running like the dickens," I said. "At least five miles." I actually had no idea how far I'd gone, but five miles sounded like reason enough to sweat. "Anyway, it's mostly water back here. You're livin' in a buncha water."

"So?" He shrugged again. He was a shiny boy, like a good shell. His hair was the same color as his skin, light brown. I noticed his eyebrows were almost white. I'd long known that was a sign of too much sun, when the hair on your face goes whiter than your skin.

"No shade here," I went on, without directly mentioning his eyebrows. "I mean over in the trees, but it might be deep over there or..."

"So?"

"What? Is that your favorite word?" I put my hands on my hips in small fists pressing against my bones. Freddy called me "bone girl" on account of my thinness. I called Freddy "fuck bucket" when I knew he couldn't hear. I had a thing for cursing. It was like I was born with curse words in my mouth, just dying to come out with my first breath of life.

"No, but you're tellin' me a bunch of stuff I know. Don't matter."

"You don't go to school with me, do you?" I asked.

"I don't go to school no more. Anymore."

14

"Why not?"

"We moved away but we came back, and I just never started again." He shrugged and gave me another knee-buckling smile.

"My sister doesn't go to school no more neither," I said.

"Okay."

"But she don't play guitar."

"No," he said like he knew anything about it.

"Where'd you go? When you moved away?"

"California."

"California?" I almost shouted. "That's on the other side of America!"

"Yeah." He nodded.

"So you went to California and when you came back you didn't have to go to school anymore?"

"Looks that way." He'd stood up during all the pointing and saying "so" and now shifted his weight on his feet. We were standing in about two feet of water that was rising and falling with the sound of the breeze rattling the saw grass. I saw an ibis beyond his left shoulder. The bird cocked its head in a curious gesture. There were a million birds in the marsh, but I never got tired of seeing their funny movements. "I've gotta get home now," the boy told me.

"Where do you live?" I asked, hoping to delay him further.

"There." He pointed impatiently. "I told you."

"Who do you live with that doesn't make you go to school?"

"My dad."

"Where's your mom?"

"She died when I's little. Listen, I gotta go." He turned and took off at a clip with his small guitar clutched in his hand.

"What's your name?" I called after him.

"Andy!" He kept on running through the water splashing up around his waist before disappearing behind a thick mess of cattails and on to the high-heel house. He had to climb a ladder to get to what I figured must be the front porch—a space no bigger than a candy wrapper. The house was a perfect square. I didn't see anyone else, only a small boat with a fan for an engine—the kind the police took out to find people who might have drowned or to track down evidence somebody was trying to hide. People dumped drugs in the intracoastal every other month it seemed. It was the only thing going on within a hundred miles.

"Andy," I said to myself as I watched him disappear into the little pill box on heels. I couldn't shake the feeling that he'd been waiting for me there. Me or someone else.

CHAPTER 2

I was tired enough to lie down and go to sleep, but I turned around and started running back to Hack Road, determined to prove I was cut out for the track team and to tell my brothers all about our new neighbor and his funny house. I kept on through jagged breaths and a pounding in my chest like a hammer on hot cement. The water finally started to disappear, and I was up on sand again, which slowly turned to grass and weeds, then wildflowers and sharp stalks of cat grass. I pumped my arms and continued to run, the burning in my lungs more like an axe trying to split an iron. It was all banging and scorching in a girl's head this time of year.

"God damn!" Peter hollered at me as I came around the corner next to our house. "How far did you go?"

"I met a kid who lives way back there, like a hundred miles into the marsh." I screeched out the words between swollen breaths.

Peter went a little crooked eyed. "Who?" he said after a long beat of thinking.

"His name's Andy," I said. "Their house is thataway!"

"Stop yellin', Kay." Peter paused; he sure was giving himself a lot of time to contemplate. "You shouldn't be goin' back there anyway. Stay away from strangers."

"Like hell I'll stay away! How long did I run?"

"Real long time," Peter said. "A kid our age?"

"More like my age."

"Right, yeah."

"Livin' with his daddy."

Peter frowned like he was thinking about square roots or the capital of Russia or something tricky like that. "Right."

"I won't lie. I didn't run the whole time, because I met Andy, and we got to talking, and my underwear was givin' me a tear in my butt. He was playing a guitar, and he lives with his daddy 'cause his mama died. They're from California." I was speaking in breathless, violent spurts. Peter looked annoyed, or worried. I couldn't really tell which, because my family was always one or the other, and it left the same expression on our faces.

Sarah-Anne was standing in the yard not far from us, like a small sapling trying to get light under the thick canopy of bigger trees with longer branches. She stared at me, keeping quiet as she was known to do. She was like my mother but not exactly. I turned away, never having enjoyed being looked at hard like that. Her blond hair was pulsing in the sun, but her eyebrows were dark. That was another strange detail; she was full of them. Sarah-Anne always kept herself close to the house and in the shade. She said something under her breath. I tried not to bother with it.

"Don't talk to strangers," Peter said, looking at his stopwatch and pressing buttons that made it beep in either short, small bursts or long, annoying streams.

"He's not a stranger. He's our neighbor."

"We don't have neighbors." Peter shook his head before walking up the porch steps and to the front door.

I followed him into the house and ran out to the back porch as fast as I could. Even with how much I'd already been running, I still had gas in the tank. My feet and bottom half of my legs were soaking wet and covered with grass, small twigs, bits of dirt, and pine straw.

"You're dirty!" Peter yelled after me.

"That's where Andy lives," I said, pointing out back. I pressed the screen, making small squares of bright red and pearl white on my fingertips.

"I said you're dirty," Peter scolded.

"I don't care." I pointed again.

"Nobody lives back there, Kay." My father spoke from the living room, where he'd been sitting like a lizard with a bug on his tongue. "Nobody." I turned my head around the corner of the porch to see his sulking frame. His shoulders were drawn forward with the look of a man who'd spent his life doing hard labor. Really it was his poor opinion of life that made him slouch; it had nothing to do with toil. Freddy sat in the chair across from him, perched like an annoying bird waiting for something crucial to happen—like the discovery of a giant worm colony.

"Yes, they do. I saw their house in the water. Andy. His name's Andy, and he lives with his daddy."

My dad looked at Peter with his mouth in a tight bundle. His face reminded me of the handles on a plastic grocery bag tied in a knot. "Stay away from them," my father said, leaning back. He sounded more tired than mad.

"Why?" I asked. "I mean…it's him or the guy with the AK. Who the hell do you want me to play with around here?"

"Don't say 'hell,' Kay!" Freddy said, acting dutiful and committed to family rules about cursing. I rolled my eyes and thought of telling him to shove a rake up his asshole. Freddy got under my skin more than anyone else. I had mixed-up emotions about it too. I felt awful that I mostly wanted to kill him. Sometimes I was putting my arm around his shoulder so I could be a real loving sister. He needed it with his glasses and ugly hair and difficulties playing sports, but other times I was pretty sure I'd be happier if it was him under the tree outside and not Elizabeth. I don't have the vocabulary for everything I felt at 1234 Hack Road. Words do fail sometimes—even for me; that's God's honest truth. "Hell's a curse word too, even if it's in the Bible," he went on.

"Keep your facts and figures to yourself!" I shouted.

Freddy had the same personality as a bad butt rash, and I wondered if it was because he was sick a lot when he was a baby. He was at the doctor more than he was at the nipple; Sue-Bess was sure there was something wrong with him—something severe. My mother was always taking Freddy somewhere to be seen, examined, touched, talked about. Freddy was a prized possession to be shown off. His illnesses made him special and important. My mother drove then, her little bird arms bent wide and shaking as she pulled the car away from the house. She'd taken Freddy to the doctor almost every day, promising the nurses he was probably dying. Often, I was made to go with them. I hated going to the doctor with my mother and Freddy. I could tell, even then, that everyone thought she was as fucked up as the day is long. It only stopped because people came to the house to make complaints against her. They accused my mother of a syndrome that made her want sick kids for attention. I remember her signing some papers while my father held her elbow. She had to promise she'd stop taking Freddy to the hospital every time she got in one of her moods. The police said if she kept on, they'd meet her at the hospital and take her and Freddy somewhere else. This was the start of her deep quietness.

Sarah-Anne always seemed the sickest one to me, but no one

took her to the doctor, not even my mother with her syndrome. I can only assume she thought Sarah-Anne was too far gone to help with the miracles of modern science. And anyway, after Elizabeth, no one with a stethoscope was ever to be trusted again. I got Vaseline and pills from Walgreens when my going got rough— "nothing a Band-Aid won't fix" seemed to be the house motto.

Because of Freddy's butt rash personality, he had a bit of a cruel streak in him. He did a lot of get-under-your-skin stuff just so he'd have more of a reason to explain things. We had a freezer like a coffin out behind the house, plugged into an outlet that looked like it was hanging on for dear life from our mint-green clapboard. Once, when my father emptied it out to get rid of all the food too old to eat, I got in and closed the lid. It felt so good inside, being that it was early September and like an oven in our yard, but the suction mechanism made it hard to open from the inside, and then Freddy, thinking himself funny, sat on top of the freezer, so I was banging and pushing and then started crying. He finally jumped down and opened the lid. He saw how upset I was and said that I couldn't have died in that short a time.

"You weren't in there near long enough to die from a lack of oxygen," he said. I think I gave him the bird and silently swore to dip his toothbrush in the toilet when he wasn't looking. He may not have caught my mother's syndrome in the womb, but there was still something rotten with him as far as I was concerned. Poisons don't usually leave the body—not entirely.

"Why the *HECK* can't I hang out with Andy?" I said to my dad. "What the *heck* is the reason? I'm not tryin' to give him *heck*, just be his friend." I stuck my bottom lip out and lowered my eyelids at whoever was looking.

"Because I told you." My father lowered his own eyelids for one irritated second before opening them very slowly and deliberately. His discontent was heavy, the sofa damn near buckling under his weight—that or it was about to fall apart, like everything else in our house. "Where's Sarah-Anne?" he asked. She was a good distraction; we all took advantage of it.

"Standin' in the yard like a twig in mud," I said. "Just her style."

"She didn't go back there with you, did she?" my dad asked, just a little too curious.

"Since when does she go anywhere? I's told you… She's doing her twig routine in the yard."

"Okay," he said, turning his attention back to the paper.

I followed Peter into the kitchen where my mother was drinking iced tea at the kitchen table, staring. My mother did little else but stare and hide. Freddy said she got that way when Elizabeth died in the hospital, but Peter said Mom was like that before. He would remember, being that he was nearly seven when it happened. Dying of poor timing can really take it out of a family.

"What's *his* problem?" I asked Peter, trailing on his heels.

"No one lives in the house back there anymore," my mother said sharply.

"Yeah, they do!" I said. "Andy!"

Her face twitched before she excused herself and went into their bedroom, off the kitchen at the side of the house. I figured she was going to stare out the window. Sometimes she liked to stare alone, while other times, she wanted to stare in front of us. I had to give it to my mom—she really knew how to pass the time.

"Are you talking about the monkey house?" Freddy said loudly from the other room.

"What monkey house?" I asked, excited by every new bit of information. It had been a damn-near-thrilling afternoon.

"No," my dad said.

"No what?" Freddy asked.

"God, it's like talking to a buncha chickens who don't speak the same language," I said, shaking my head in dismay.

I walked to my bedroom, done with explaining my excitement and having my hopes of a new friend dashed by every idiot in town. I sat on my bed, peering out at Elizabeth's tree. That was one thing I could stare at for a while without getting too agitated. I even went outside to look at where Elizabeth was buried sometimes, although my mother said we shouldn't. "Let her rest," my mother had told me. "Let her rest in the shade."

I heard footsteps in the hall, heavy and dissatisfied—my dad. "So they're back?" I heard him say around the corner of my parents' room. "Sarah-Anne said somethin' the other day… Is it them?"

My mother answered from within. "Oh, wouldn't that be my

luck?" Her voice scratched somewhere between "my" and "luck."
Sue-Bess never got above a certain volume; it was the urgency that
let you know she was having a strong emotion. "You better hope
that's not who she's talkin' about."

"Who?" I called out from my bed over the loud buzzing of
the refrigerator. You could hear perfectly through the walls in our
house, but not through the Frigidaire. "Who y'all talkin' about?
And what's a monkey house?"

"Nothing, Kay," my dad said just loud enough for me to catch
his drift. His lead feet went through the kitchen and back into the
living room. He was on the other side of the house, but I was still
looking at Elizabeth's tree. Elizabeth was just like my mother; she
sure did like to rest. I heard the door to my parents' room close. I
did not see my mother again that day.

CHAPTER 3

The following morning, I woke up feeling hopeful and rebellious—my most perfect combination of moods. My father immediately sensed my enthusiasm and barked "Eat" at me when I walked into the kitchen. I went to sit down where I could fidget better; constant movement was my most agitating personality trait as far as my father was concerned. "Eat now. No snacking before lunch."

"I hate snacking," I scowled. "I just woke up anyways. Not hungry yet." I scooted in my chair, making a screeching noise on the parquet.

"So eat your breakfast!" He was looking at the newspaper, turning pages and frowning at headlines. He walked to town each day to buy it, refusing to pay the dollar-a-week delivery fee. Recurring payments were against our family's religion.

Summer was coming to a close with the promise and curse of school right around the corner. I liked going to class sometimes, because I'm prone to incurable boredom. Occasionally, though, the thought of trucking it up and down Hack Road every day with my books and my lunch and my lessons running through my head made me feel really low. It hit home hard when I thought about Andy, who didn't have to go to school. I wondered what he did all day.

Sarah-Anne wasn't going to school this coming year—we'd been told over dinner a few weeks before. My father said it like he was announcing his bid for town mayor. It was most definitely an announcement meant to be cheered but not discussed, questioned, brought up again, or talked about in front of other people, not that there was anybody else around.

This wasn't the first time they were taking her out of the public education system—she'd been home before with my mother crying over it and with my father talking about authorities and evil people from the state. I guess if someone from the state ever came for me, I'd have to stay home from school too. It seemed like both a shitty punishment and special treatment all at the same time. People from the state weren't a bit interested in me or Freddy or Peter; they barely looked at us when they came around. It seemed to me all this stuff with people at the door asking about Sarah-Anne had been going on for a long time, but it was all hazy memories inside my head, like I was wearing glasses made of cotton balls. If I was ever going to be a criminal, I would definitely do it around a bunch of little kids; I can't remember shit from before age five—not to save my life.

"I want a guitar," I said while spreading jelly on my buttered toast. "A big guitar."

"What for?" My dad didn't take his eyes off the paper.

"I want to play it."

"Join the band at school."

"They don't play guitar."

"So you be the first one to do that, Kay. Be a trailblazer."

"Yeah." I rose from the table and dumped the remainder of my toast in the trash can, hoping my father didn't see how much I'd thrown away. I'd eaten only two bites. He hated waste and paying for newspaper delivery, among other hateable things, like jobs and wives who talk to you. The *Bledsoe Local* was a joke anyway—not worth the paper it was printed on. There wasn't a person in all of Bledsoe worth reporting on. Even if there was a murder, most people said good riddance, he had it coming, whoever he was…probably an inbred.

The boys and I played in the front yard all morning. It was shady out there, and the air felt ripe for rain with clouds and a low, wet blanket hanging overhead. We knew we might be stuck inside after lunch, so we made the best of it now. If it did storm, I knew what was coming—a whole afternoon of nothing and Sarah-Anne watching and twitching in the corner.

For the time being, however, I was consumed with the game of kickball we had going. A kid from our school, Cort Hat, was over. His mother dropped him off on her way to the grocery store. She went to the grocery store all the time and for hours on end. When she came back, she was usually flushed and without a whole lot to show for all that time she spent shopping—maybe a loaf of bread, half-eaten in the back of her car, or some milk poured into a red Solo cup like she'd stolen it, not wanting to pay for the whole gallon. Her clothes were twisted and her face and hairline wet from sweat. One time I saw Celia Hat's bra lying on the back seat of her car, but my father shoved me away before I could ask what the hell that was all about. All I could think was maybe she was going to try to trade her bra for some food. People had to get by.

She couldn't have been that hard up though. I caught Cort's mom giving my dad some bills one afternoon when she came back to get him; her ponytail had slid to the side of her face, and her lipstick was up to her nostrils. I figured we were babysitting. From what I could tell, it looked like about five bucks an hour. Cort was the only friend we were ever allowed to have over anyway. It didn't strike me as odd that it was because his mother was paying us to watch him while she made a mess of herself at the store—my parents always needed the money. It made me feel particularly sorry for Freddy, though, who didn't know about the payments. He liked to tell me and anyone else who would listen that Cort Hat was his best friend.

"Hey, do y'all know Andy?" I asked, carrying the ball back to the kickball diamond we'd fashioned from yard debris.

My father was outside too, fiddling with a lawnmower and smoking cigarettes. He looked up and shushed me loudly. "Enough, Kay. Jesus, give it a rest." Sarah-Anne was standing next to him holding a wrench and his lighter.

"What?" I asked, making my best innocent face. I bounced the ball and waited for an answer.

Sarah-Anne tried to keep herself from smiling in that funny way she had of pushing her lips together and squeezing her eyes real tight. There was a lot of funny stuff we weren't supposed to laugh at around my dad, so we had to find ways to look serious even when we weren't. Sarah-Anne liked it when I gave my dad a hard time; you had to hand it to her—as weird as she was, she had a good sense of humor. "Andy," she said to my dad, who pretended to ignore her. She said something else I couldn't make out.

"What?" I shouted again.

"Come on, Kay!" Peter said, impatient to have his turn.

"Just cut it out," my father said. He exhaled cigarette smoke in a thin stream.

"He lives back there." I pointed again. "Andy." I couldn't help but rattle the cage.

"What's it to you?"

The other boys were looking at me and my father, who'd both raised our voices to be heard from the distance between us. Sarah-Anne handed my father another cigarette even though he wasn't done smoking the one hanging from his lip. She looked at me closely. I grinned a little back but didn't want to get into a staring thing with her. That was her only thing—staring.

"Can you get back over here, so we can play? It's gonna rain," Peter said.

I threw the ball at Freddy, who missed it with his foot and shuffle-stepped after it. It wasn't necessarily a kick, but the ball did roll to Peter. We all took position and played defense while Freddy stumbled toward first base. Peter grabbed the ball with the palm of his hand. He had his shirt off; there was hair in his armpits now, and he had a man's chest, like flat boobs. He had a lot of girls chasing after him, which my father said was a waste of time. Whose time, I wasn't sure.

As soon as I was old enough, I planned to chase boys. It didn't seem like a waste of time to me at all. I liked boys and pretended to kiss them while lying in my bed. I wanted to be married at least six times, so I could marry six different types of men, and I already had the first three husbands picked out. One of them was Peter's friend Duke. I thought of adding Andy to the list, because I fancied the way he was all one color, but we had to talk more to see if I liked his personality. I couldn't base my life choices on looks alone.

After another hour or so, the sky started to spit, and then the thunder came rolling in. Cort's mother wasn't back from the store yet, so he came inside with us.

The house on Hack Road was a giant box on blocks with a wooden slab for a front porch. Inside was a mess of rooms around the kitchen and keeping area. I had my own bedroom, the smallest by a long shot, because I was the youngest—at least the youngest living—while Peter and Freddy had to share. Sarah-Anne lived in the hall, where she slept on a day bed. It was on the side of the house, an in-between space just like Sarah-Anne was an in-between person— half in, half out. I used to wonder if she was an alien living on earth for research. She sure picked the wrong place to spy; Bledsoe couldn't have been the least bit interesting to the mother ship.

Peter liked to complain that Freddy and I were practically twins and should have to share a room. He thought he should have his own. Anyway, it was Sarah-Anne and Freddy who were nearly the same age. I couldn't figure the math, but it seemed like they had to split the womb. Peter looked down whenever I mentioned the funny numbers. "Yeah," he'd say. "God's timing." Funny numbers were just more proof that my theory about Sarah-Anne being an alien was right anyway. It didn't even seem strange to me at the time that we didn't really keep an eye on her—we didn't think we needed to. Imagine our surprise.

We had a hell of a storm that day. The afternoon stretched out under heavy rain on our tin roof and the drift of clouds, thunder, and lightning over the marsh. The boys were watching *Hoosiers* and slapping each other on the back during the best scenes. I came in at the end during the big game and plopped down on the cot that lined the left wall of the screened porch. My family didn't have the television channels you had to pay for, only a VCR for movies. Ours had to be the last VCR on earth. I'd said something to a friend at school about rewinding tapes, and he laughed at me, saying nobody rewinded anymore. "Rewound," I corrected him. I asked Peter later that day why people didn't rewind their movies anymore.

"Because they use DVD players. They don't even make VCRs now." I never mentioned our VCR or collection of worn-out tapes to anyone again; it wasn't anything to brag about apparently. I found out later my father had picked up a box of VHS tapes left by someone's trash can on Miller Highway. That was the entirety of our collection. According to Peter, my dad had removed the porn before bringing the box home.

"I love this part," I said.

"Quiet," Peter reprimanded me.

"Jeez," I said more loudly.

"Go away, Kay. You always come in at the end of the movie. It's really annoying," Freddy said.

"You're such a killjoy, Freddy," I told him, lifting my feet into the air and moving them around like flags in the wind. I saw Cort looking at me, but he didn't say anything. I always got the impression he just really wanted to leave.

"That's annoying," Peter said.

"I hate brothers!" I yelled. I was going to add that I also sort of hated brothers' friends, but I felt a little bad for Cort, sitting there like a prisoner. If his mama needed the Whitakers' help, then things at their house must be about as dire as a plague. I got up from the cot and went into the kitchen, where my parents were sitting at the table talking quietly, with mean voices and lowered eyes. My mother had her book in front of her, ready to shut us out behind the spine when she'd had enough of whatever it was that got her so fed up.

"I'm bored," I said as I walked in the room. Neither of my parents responded; it was like they couldn't hear me. "Super bored!" Still nothing.

People in our house didn't hear a lot when they didn't want to; we also didn't see what we weren't supposed to either. I knew someone from the state had been at the house the day before, but no one mentioned it after the lady was gone. People came to the house about Sarah-Anne all the time. I knew they came for Sarah-Anne, and only Sarah-Anne, because she was the only one of us who had to hide when they showed up. Peter, Freddy, and I could walk around like head peasant on a potato farm, but Sarah-Anne had to disappear. Out back. Out of sight.

I'd seen the car and the lady with her papers, her hair in a braided bun. I saw my mother go into her room and my father run out to the gravel to talk to the woman before she could get too close to the door; he'd told Sarah-Anne to go to the bathroom with Peter. Sarah-Anne didn't need help going to the bathroom. Peter took her to the one in the hall because it was the only room in the house without windows. I really wanted to say something about all the oddities I was starting to notice, but Freddy and I had a single, important duty in our house: to act like we didn't see these things, these people. When we were younger, we used to play spy, but my dad put a stop to that after Freddy and I played spy when people from the state were lurking around on the front porch with notebooks and pens behind their ears.

"Spying is *very* bad manners and could get you in a lot of trouble around here," my dad had said in his troll-under-the-bridge way. He could make himself small and mean—a little firecracker about to be lit, hunting for a match with a hunchback and a sneer. "No spying," he said with his hand raised. You could get popped for a lot in our house, even bad manners. After that, I became a professional at being just out of earshot. When you've been ignoring important details about your life for long enough, it's actually harder to start noticing them. Playing dumb is like a cough you can't get rid of after a full month of the chest rattles.

I didn't like to think about any of that, even when I was mad at my dad for not letting me be friends with Andy and live a mysterious life in a high-heel house. I kept trying to put it in a box with a tight lid, but there was a leak in my head. When someone showed up at the house, and the wind chimes got going from the sudden movement, I'd be five years old again, back in the car with my mother driving me and Freddy away, and my father carrying Sarah-Anne on his back, wading into the water behind the house while Peter sat on the front porch in nothing but a pair of ripped jean shorts, pretending he was a lot older than he was. Sometimes it was

Peter who had to talk to the people with the city clothes. I only got to look at them through the back window as we were pulling away from the house. My mother's eyes would dart to the rearview. Freddy would sniffle in the seat next to me; he often got really sick right when someone showed up at the house. We'd be hightailing it out of there to the minute clinic while Sarah-Anne was smiling in my father's arms, her head hanging down like a soldier shot in the ass as they disappeared around the back of the house. It sometimes took me three deep breaths and a real long, deliberate eye squeeze to get all this out of my head, and sometimes that wasn't even enough.

"I'm bored," I said even more forcefully, trying to get someone to acknowledge my existence. I shook my head a little after saying it. The kitchen was about as uninspiring as *Hoosiers* for the hundred and seventieth time that year. "Jeez," I said to make sure I was getting my point across.

"You're always bored," my mother answered. She picked up her book. My mother did even more reading and staring after someone from the state came to the door; I knew there'd been trouble when she could stare off into space and read at the same time, a real feat. Sue-Bess was a little like Andy—all one color. Pale with light eyes, she always looked like she was caught somewhere between sleep and waking; a dream-like quality to her left most people wondering whether she was there at all. Maybe that's why the wound left by Elizabeth wouldn't stop bleeding; any hole is too big in a person like my mother.

"I know," I said. "But I don't know what to do about it. You know last week, I went outside and sat on the grass to drink a glass of water? I couldn't think of anything to do, nothing at all, so I got a glass of water and sat outside to drink it. It took four minutes. Then there I was with the rest of the afternoon. I couldn't think of anything else to do. I really couldn't." I emphasized my plight.

"You could read one of your library books," my mother suggested, and I knew this meant the conversation was over. My father drove us to the public library once a week where we were allowed, or told in my case, to get ten books each. Freddy was in charge of getting my mother's—she liked bodice-rippers and Jack the Rippers, nothing in between.

My mother read to Sarah-Anne but not to me or anyone else. Although I think I was the only one who still wanted to sit in her lap. When I fussed about this unequal treatment, my mother said, "I enjoy it…reading to her."

"I'd enjoy being read to too," I said, but it was like no one heard me—again. My voice did not penetrate Whitaker eardrums. I was obviously not the daughter my mother wanted. I thought Elizabeth would probably have been her best friend. It's easy to be the dead sister; everyone thinks you would have been perfect if only you had lived.

"If it stops raining, I'm going to Andy's house later," I said, more as a threat to my father. "Yeah, I'm goin' back to Andy's to hang out…" I sat back in my chair with my legs splayed. My mother was looking at my father very closely, like she was expecting him to admit he knew how to split the atom.

"You're not to go back there again," my father said after a beat of thick silence. "Do you understand me?"

"Yeah, but why?"

"Because I said no. Stay away from that kid and keep off their property."

"But their house is up on stilts; it's not property, you know?" I was consumed by this detail.

"Quiet," my mother said over me. "Please." She was still looking at my dad and gripping her book tightly.

"They don't have property," I said again, making my final and most decisive point. "It's not on land or..." My father rolled his eyes while my mother held her book in front of her face with her left hand. Her right hand lay on the table. She made it into a tight fist and squeezed. I watched as it went from white to red around the creases.

"Please," she said again.

"I'm so damned restless!" I said. "I get it from you!" Neither of them answered me or looked up. My mother's book was called *Sins of the Flesh*. Imagine wanting to read that garbage more than wanting to talk to your kid.

For lack of options, I went outside and stood on the cement slab by the back steps. It was still coming down in buckets, but the thunder was gone, having made its way past us, tired of our complaining and our simple outlook. I could smell the cool air moving in in its place.

I looked back inside the house and saw that my dad was talking to the boys, who were still on the screened porch. He said something about fountain Coke. Sometimes when my dad was feeling charitable, he drove us to the Texaco station, where we could get an ice cream, a slushie, a soda from the tap machine, maybe a candy bar, or a pack of Skittles. This must have been one of those days, but I was too hell-bent on seeing Andy again to get distracted. Being told to stay away from Andy was like an invitation to a girl like me.

I yelled something to my dad about a sore throat through the half-open door. My father waved a hand at me, like he was glad to hear I was going to sit this one out. I usually complained a lot in the car, because I had an ass and a foot on all sides of me; this was enough to make me raise my voice to shrill peaks. Some things can't be helped—asses and feet in close proximity really get to a girl after five minutes on a gravel road. I yelled to survive.

Sarah-Anne didn't go to the gas station; she was like my mother and absolutely never left the house. Del Dickson, who owned the Texaco, would go on a spell about many topics on which she just couldn't converse. Del made her nervous—she was too shy for small talk about clouds and economics. Me too, but I would push my nervousness away for a slushie any day. I would just nod at him and say, "Hmmm, that's right." Sarah-Anne would turn around and hide her face in her hands. He was always giving her a peculiarly interested look—just a little too interested if you know what I mean.

I wasn't worried about her seeing me leave out the back of the house. I figured she was over on her bed, going through her drawer. She didn't ask questions about where I was going anyway. She barely said anything at all.

I heard my father and the boys go out the front door, still talking about fountain Cokes like they were made of liquid gold. The door slammed back into the frame with a bang, which was my all-clear signal. I took off my shoes and started off through the backyard, to the sand, and then into the marsh. The rain had let up a little but didn't quit. The sky spits on traitors in Bledsoe.

I just didn't know it yet.

CHAPTER 4

I t took me a lot longer to get as far back as I'd been the day before; I was a little turned around and not sure I was heading in the right direction. I started to sweat between the thick, pear-shaped raindrops. The sky was going black again and I could hear rumbling in the distance. "Well, I'm as dumb as a big pile o' shit," I said to the rain sliding down my face.

I was about to get upset with my own personality when I heard something just out of range of my best senses. It was the sound of the fan on an air boat. Not an uncommon noise for these parts, but since I thought I was getting close to Andy's, I hoped it was him. The noise stopped, but I continued to move in the direction from where it came.

My dress was completely soaked from the waist down. I knew

my small breasts could be seen through the soggy fabric. I tried to adjust the cloth on my skin, so you couldn't see my chest or my underwear, which was an unfortunate shade of bright pink. I didn't wear a bra yet. My mother said I was being silly when I asked. Sarah-Anne had a bra though. My mother washed it by hand in the sink, and sometimes when it was drying on the line, I grabbed it and put it on for kicks. I needed more than fried eggs to fill one of those things out, but all I'd had so far was unanswered prayers about my chest. I didn't know what God was waiting for, but I was ready for some real knockers. I figured my time would come in high school.

I kept walking and finally saw the house on heels, although it was not exactly where I'd thought it would be—about thirty degrees off my mark. It was a lucky guess, though, and I'd ended up close enough.

I saw Andy standing on the deck. He was in the same clothes he'd been in the day before, next to nothing. I waved, but he wasn't looking at me. It seemed he was tying the boat to a pole in the water. There was a man, who I figured must have been Andy's father because they looked like twins from different decades, tying the other end to another metal pole some seven or so feet away. Ropes were tied to rings on either side of the boat, but it looked like something had come loose; there was a gash on one end. The fan was hanging from a hinge, like the boat had a lazy tongue.

I ran, lifting my knees as high as I could, splashing wildly in the hopes of being noticed. When Andy's father finally did look in my direction, he frowned but went back to what he was doing. He turned the boat's fan on and off, trying to nudge it forward. I could barely see his face on account of his faded blue baseball cap pulled low on his forehead and the thin sheet of rain between us.

"Andy!" I called out. Andy turned to look at me from where he was standing up on the deck, but he didn't return my wave or seem to care that I was running through three feet of water to reach him. Andy and his father finished doing whatever it was they were doing with their busted boat by the time I got close enough.

"Hey," I said to Andy specifically. I was smiling as big as I could, believing they would catch some of my enthusiasm if I was just excited enough. My eagerness was as contagious as the flu—at least I hoped.

"Boy, you must like to run," he said to me. The rain was really coming down. I was desperately hoping they would ask me inside.

"We need to go in," Andy's father said to him, like I wasn't there.

I heard thunder clap a few miles away and started to breathe a little heavy for fear that they were going to leave me standing outside in the middle of it. Just when I thought I was done for, Andy made a swirling motion with his hand. I followed, walking up the ladder that led to the small porch of their slanting, toaster-shaped house.

"How does it stay above the water?" I asked, while on the fifth and final rung. Neither of them answered me. We lined up and went inside, like kids heading for the water fountain after PE. The house was one giant room. I could hear the rain, loud as knives banging on a tile counter, just like at our house. "This place is nice," I said again mostly to myself.

Andy handed me a towel that was hanging on a hook next to several other towels. "Where do you go to the bathroom?" I asked. Andy nodded in the direction of the boat. "You do your business in the boat?" I was yelling to be heard over the sound of the rain on the roof.

"No, we go out in the water, or in town, or wherever."

"I'm never swimming out here again." I pulled at my soaked dress and self-consciously wiped the strands of wet hair from my face.

"Animals do it, and anyway, usually we're in town…and there's a lotta land around here. Little islets and all that."

"I don't know what an islet is. We have islands where I come from." I stopped talking and looked around. There was Andy's father staring at me like I was a fish he wanted to hook. I was uneasy and took a step backward, catching my foot on the edge of the front door—still open. "Sorry," I said to no one in particular. I had the idea that leaving was the best thing I could do, but I couldn't make myself take the necessary steps. The rain was like a wall, and it was a long way home. I adjusted myself under the watchful gaze of Andy's father, who was very tense and focused.

"You can stay here 'til the rain stops," Andy told me. He went to a corner of the room and pulled down his shorts. He wasn't wearing anything underneath, and other than my brothers' private parts, it was the first time I'd seen a boy's penis. Andy didn't care a lick that I was looking at him and proceeded to put on a dry pair of shorts, cut-off jeans almost identical to what he'd been wearing before—no underwear. "Want to borrow something dry?" he asked me.

"There's nowhere to change."

"Yeah." He shrugged before holding up a T-shirt and a pair of green sweatpants. "It's clean. We do our laundry at the 'mat."

I wanted them to at least avert their eyes so I could change. Andy's father must have read my mind because he gave a little grunt and motioned for Andy to turn around. They walked to the back of the house, where there was a small window, and looked out. The sky was black as night.

"I didn't think it was gonna be this bad today," I said while pulling my dress over my head in a hurry. I wanted to remove my underwear something fierce, but I didn't know what either of them would think if they saw it balled up with my clothes, which I planned to leave by the front door in case I needed to make a quick exit. My mother would forgive a lot of things but not me losing one of her prized dresses. If I ran, it would have to come with me.

"I mean," I said nervously as I was scrambling to get the clothes over my still soaked body, "I think we steal our electricity or whatever you do when you don't like monthly bills, but I gotta have running water. My granny didn't have it for so long at her house, and there was an outhouse thing with a hole in the ground with all the poop. I just…I can't even talk about it. She lives in Meridian, but just so you know, there are bad houses in Meridian too. It's not at all better than here. We have two toilets. My daddy put 'em in himself. One's in the hall. Not like in the hall, like…it's in a bathroom in the hall." I kept on about the plumbing and all I knew of it, just talking away to fill time and space. I was happy to be inside with all the pounding going on above me. "I mighta died out there," I said for some drama.

Andy and his father stayed looking out the window and mumbling one thing or another about crabs and shrimp. I tore my panties off in a flourish and balled them up inside the dress, again wishing they weren't bright pink. The clothes from Andy smelled like detergent, so I hoped that meant they were clean. I liked wearing something that belonged to Andy. I'd already decided I wanted him to be my fifth husband and greatest romance. He was even more handsome today than he had been the day before. He took after his father but was a good stretch chattier.

"Okay, I'm done," I announced like I was giving away a prize. No one had addressed my near-death experience, but all was forgiven. I was in this strange water house, with two very attractive men, and their light hair, and California ways. I felt special; it was something I was constantly seeking—that one little thing to set me apart.

I waited for them to turn around, convinced they were holding their breath in anticipation of seeing me again and in dry clothes. They proved me wrong by taking their time to finish their conversation. When Andy was done murmuring something I couldn't hear, they slowly turned to face me and then walked over to the couch. There was duct tape holding it together—not an uncommon sight in Bledsoe.

"We can take ya back in the boat when the rain lets up," Andy's father said. He sounded deep Southern the way most of us do. The only time I can hear an accent on a person is when it comes from the swallows, and Andy's father was from as deep down as a person can get and still keep their head above the ground. Mud mouth or soup tongue—there's lots of ways to describe it. I knew I had it too. Whenever we went to Volmer or Blaisedale and had the occasion to meet someone from someplace else altogether, they looked at us funny, like maybe we weren't all there.

"Are you from California too?" I asked Andy's father.

No one immediately answered. I was still standing. I looked around the room a little more closely now. There were two beds, both singles, on the right side in an area that felt separate because of the paint color on the far wall—a cornflower blue that spoke to my soul. I wondered who thought to paint a ramshackle place like this. We painted our house one winter, but it was because there was mold inside. The paint was supposed to keep mold off the walls; it wasn't decoration. I thought to ask my parents if I could paint my bedroom a light blue like Andy's room. Mine was off-white and uninspiring. No wonder I didn't want to spend any time in there with such a dull color. I thought maybe Andy could paint it for me. I made a mental note to find out if they had mold paint in cornflower.

Along with the two large couches, there was also a long table with several mismatched chairs around it. I saw Andy's guitar lying on the floor next to the smaller couch. Its finish was peeling off in little flakes, edges chipped and worn—no wonder it sounded so funny. The roof was pitched and high and had wind chimes hanging from hooks fastened to the middle beam. As far as I could tell, it was dumber than stupid to hang wind chimes inside, but these were two men living alone. A woman has to teach this sort of thing—I knew all about it; I had two brothers and a dad.

"This place is a card," I said.

"What does that mean?" Andy asked.

"Just..." I said cautiously, "like, funny."

I felt sick for a moment, maybe from the way the house was rocking or because I knew that if these were bad people, then I was about as smart as a stump for being in their house all alone in a squall. I'd done some dumb things in my day: an unfortunate occurrence left me without a chunk of my hair on the right side (caught in the wheel of a bike—we had the cycle upside down on its handlebars and were moving the spokes with a stick when I leaned in too close after a forceful spin); I had to have stitches on my knee (climbed over a barbed wire fence, not knowing what barbed wire meant after Freddy repeatedly told me, "That's a barbed wire fence! That's a barbed wire fence!"); I lost my shoes on a railroad track ("What the heck did you think was going to happen to your shoes if you left 'em on the tracks? Trains come through here," Peter scolded me. My mother was so mad about that I went for two months without shoes at all. My feet were hard like real roofing by the time she felt sorry enough to get me new sneakers); a hammer incident that left a hole in the screen on the porch (details surrounding this event are still in question); and so on. I was only trying to make life more interesting. I couldn't help it if it left me battered and bruised—a good time comes at a price.

There were magazines all over the place, on every surface. A few books, but they looked like books of maps. All of the magazines had either a fishing pole or a gun on the front. Their pages were curled at the edges from use and the saltwater in the air.

"We don't have TV either," I said to seal our bond. "I mean, not stations or anything. I don't think you can run TV wires to our house, 'cause—you know, it's like a pile of wood or whatever. I don't think stations go to woodpiles or—" I really wanted to stop talking, but I was nervous and excited. Motormouth was my body's natural reaction to handsome strangers. I looked at the couches, deciding where to sit. I opted for a chair at the long table. "Does your dad talk?" I asked. It was either change the subject or keep going on about wires and wood and a bunch of other stuff I didn't know a damn thing about. "Not sayin' much," I said.

They both laughed before Andy's father responded, "I just don' know who ya are."

"I don't either," Andy said, still laughing. "But I can't leave a girl out in a squall."

I frowned. "We met yesterday."

"I know, but that doesn't mean I know you."

"I'm Kay Whitaker. I live in the house that way." I pointed toward where I thought Hack Road was. "1234 Hack Road."

"I'm Andy Webber. This is my dad." Mr. Webber's face slid a little to the left, and I wondered if he knew me after all.

"How'd y'all end up here? I mean…I've lived off Hack Road my whole life, well, since I was two, and I never knew this place was back here. Never even knew it."

"We're closer to Route 54," Andy's father said. "'Bout a mile that direction. We're not really back anywhere."

"Oh." I felt foolish for thinking my family's house was the measuring stick. "Well, I mean…whaddya do out here? What's the purpose of livin' in such a place?"

"Crabbin'," Andy said. His father was still giving me the hairy eyeball. Handsome fella, I thought. That's what people said about my dad. Young and handsome. I think my mother used to be a beauty herself, but she'd gone tired-looking, which was a trip since all she did all day was sleep and say she was about to.

"Crabs and oysters," Andy said to clarify. "But we've only been back in Bledsoe for a few months anyway."

"Oh. Yeah, anyway," I said.

I hadn't known crabs was a profession. My father had worked on a fishing boat for a time. He said it was the best job he ever had, but then he quit on account of the early mornings. My mother had a hard time in the morning. I think that's when she thought about Elizabeth the most. My father had to leave at 5 a.m. when he was working the boat— that meant my mother had to be up and at 'em. She couldn't. That was the reason we were given at least. He said he had to make us breakfast and get us off to school—even though he quit during the summer.

"Are you from California too?" I asked Mr. Webber.

"No, we're not from California..." he began suspiciously. I'd already asked him; it was clearly working his nerves to have things repeated.

"I didn't say we was *from* California," Andy said quickly. "We lived out there."

"Right." His father gave a nod.

"What happened?"

"Andy, the rain's letting up. I think we can take her back home now. Or as close as we can get. Can you walk from the edge a' the shore?" his dad asked me.

"But your boat's broken," I protested. I wasn't ready to leave.

"It's not broken, just banged up," Andy said. "We didn't tie it tight, and it flew up against the house. Got beat to shit."

"Oh," I put my hand over my mouth. No matter how many times I did it, cursing still made me feel the need to act shocked.

"It's fine to ride in," Andy said.

"Yeah, so we should get going." His father stood up and walked toward the door. He bent down to pick up my clothes. "I can put these in a bag for you..."

"No!" I darted from my seat at the table. "I can get 'em." In my mind's eye, the only thing I could see was my hot-pink underwear falling to the ground, and Andy's father lifting them up with two pinched fingers.

When we got in the boat, I felt instantly beautiful and enchanting, with the slight drizzle coming down and the rough, stormy wind blowing my damp hair around. Andy's father started the engine on the fan, which he had quickly reattached to the edge of the boat with a screwdriver he'd pulled from his jeans pocket. After Andy had untied the ropes, and we spun around in a tight circle with the boat on its backside like a break dancer, we tore through the wax myrtles, zigzagging our way deep into the marsh. Andy's father picked up speed just short of the sandbar that I'd run over earlier. It occurred to me that everyone in my family would be paralyzed with worry as to what became of me during the storm, but all I really wanted to ask was if we could keep riding in the boat for a little longer. I was having such a nice time and could imagine the way we all looked sliding over the wetlands like butter on hot toast, with our eyes narrowed to slits like we had important matters to attend to. I turned to look at Andy. He was smiling with his elbows on his knees, leaning over with the wet air slapping his face. *This is the life*, I thought. Suddenly school didn't seem like any place I wanted to be. I wished the summer would last longer, as I now had new things to consider.

Andy's father, who I found out was called Nile—because Andy called him that instead of "dad" like me and everyone else I knew— got the air boat all the way to the last sandbank. We could just barely see my family's house from where Nile sidled the boat up to the land. I noticed that there were all sorts of stickers covering the boat's wooden seats. Most of them were about wars and being the marines and God Bless America. I liked to think about brave soldiers and what became of them after they survived battles. The idea that Nile might have been in Vietnam, or wherever else he might have gotten good scars, made me like him even more.

"Well, thanks a lot," I said, after the boat had come to a stop and was buzzing at the edge of the sand. "I hope to come for a visit again soon."

"Maybe not in a storm," Andy chuckled, but his father said nothing. I was fully aware that I was still wearing Andy's clothes, but I didn't mention it as I hopped out of the boat—no one else did either. I'd rolled the pant legs up so as not to soak them walking through the water to dry land. Hanging on to Andy's things gave me an excuse to come calling again. I even thought, after waving at them as I walked toward my house—having easily climbed out of the boat and onto the land like I was born to do such moves—that I would take the items back one at a time so as to guarantee two visits.

It was misty out but not raining anymore. My skin was damp and my hair still soaked. I ran all the way back to the house with a smile on my face, feeling rather pleased with myself and satisfied by the day I'd had. Most importantly I wasn't killed or hurt. That seemed important as I considered the anger and questions I was sure to face at home. I went up the front steps, making as much noise as possible, and opened the front screen with a bang.

"I'm okay!" I called out.

"Where were you?" Peter asked, sounding altogether unconcerned.

"I didn't run away. I'm here."

"I can see that. We got you an ice cream. It's in the freezer."

"Okay. Well, I'm fine," I explained.

"I can see that," he repeated, "but you're in boy's clothes. Better not let Mom and Dad see you like that."

"Oh, right." I flinched. I'd left my clothes on the floor of the boat, rolled into a wet log shape that I'd put my feet on while we cruised the marsh. My mother would surely ask about the dress. She kept a close watch on everything she made, except me perhaps. I was a little on the unnecessary side for her—she liked it crucial. I instantly felt sorry for her, knowing how it would hurt her to hear that I'd left the dress somewhere. She'd probably shuffle quietly to her room where she'd sulk for an hour or two before emerging to eat dinner with us, in silence, all the while sighing heavily and making pained expressions like she was about to speak but couldn't bring herself to.

"Don't run off in the rain like that," my father called out from the living room, where he was, again, reading the paper. I walked in to face him, maybe hoping for a tussle. I did so enjoy getting on everyone's nerves. "What are you wearing?" he asked upon seeing me.

"I had to take shelter in that boy Andy Webber's house, and my clothes were wetter than the day is long, so he gave me some of his things to wear."

My father's face pulsed from something he was thinking but not going to say; then he said the other thing he was thinking. "I told you to stay away from there. I told you that, Kay. I didn't ask. I *told* you."

"I went for a walk," I said quickly, "'cause the rain let up, and I just went too far. They were home messin' with their boat, 'cause the fan broke, like clear off, and they told me to come inside until the storm passed. And anyway, no you didn't say to stay away, or at least that's not how I remember it."

"You've never before walked to their house, and now it's two days in a row you just happen to end up out there. I'm not going to say it again, but I want you to stay away from that kid and his dad." He was leaning forward with his legs spread wide—what he did when he was about ready to pounce.

"But I have to give them the clothes back," I explained.

"I can't imagine how you ended up in his sweatpants, and I don't want to know, but *I* will make sure he gets everything back." His voice changed, going from the low growl I was used to arguing with to the disturbed stutter he only got when he was pissing-fire mad. "You are *not* to go back there. Do you hear me? I'm not going to tell you again."

"Do you know them or something? You're awful sure about their bad intentions." I cocked my hip out. I was about to explain that I was a better judge of bad intentions, having had so many of them myself, but my father was on the warpath.

"Do you hear me?" he shouted.

"Oh, I can hear you all right, but Dad, do you know Andy's dad? Nile. He calls him Nile."

"Kay! I'm not going to tell you again!"

I was considering pointing out that my dad was repeating a lot of things he said he wasn't going to say again. "I think they're cool," I said instead.

"They're not," my father said as if in defeat.

"But they lived in California."

"Yeah, well, that was because…" My dad shook his head a little like a grumpy horse trying to get a fly off his ear.

"His mother's dead. Andy's mama."

"Well…" My father exhaled. "Just don't talk to them."

"But why?"

"Because I said so!" He put the paper down on his lap with a crack.

"I think they're nice people, and they have a boat with crabs and all that, and I think I might want to be a crabber when I grow up, so…"

"They're not the only people who catch crabs and oysters around here, Kay. If you want an after-school job, I can hook you up with Ollie Bragg. They'll work you 'til your hands bleed."

"I'd rather work with Andy and Nile."

"Kay!" My father raised his voice, signaling that he was done with the conversation.

"I just don't see what the big deal is."

"The big deal is that I'm your father, and I told you to keep clear. You keep going and doing what you want all the time, then you can go live where you want, and eat what you want, and pay for it all how you want, 'cause I'll be done with you. Done!" He said that last bit like he was trying to kill a fly with his tongue. "You're gonna listen to me!"

My face was burning. "Yes, sir," I said reluctantly before bowing at the waist like a servant. I have always been excellent at faking respect. I'm not even sure I ever really knew what the word meant.

I went into my bedroom and sat down on the bed. I had a lot on my mind. I smelled Andy's shirt and wondered what he was doing at that moment. It occurred to me to ask my dad, when the flames had died down a little, how far the Webber house was from Route 54. I'd been down that road a hundred and fifty times and never seen it before. It had to be a lot more than a mile. Straight talk was another thing that was hard to come by in Bledsoe—people never said it like it was. *Mile, my ass*, I thought to myself as I stared at the ceiling with Andy's shirt pulled up over my mouth.

I was just getting to the middle of a good daydream about me and Andy on a motorcycle in California (without helmets) when I heard the back door slam and my dad say in his best ogre voice, "Now why are *you* all wet? Where'd you go?" I figured he was talking to Sarah-Anne, because I hadn't seen her when I came in. Of course, she'd decide to go outside in the rain; if it was a beautiful day, then she'd be holed up on her bed, hiding from the good weather. "Where were you?" I heard my dad ask again, a little louder this time. I don't know why he was getting fired up at her; Sarah-Anne barely talked, and she sure as hell never got in trouble—my mother saw to that. I smelled Andy's shirt again and tried to get the vision of the motorcycle back in my head. My dad raised his voice, and I thought I heard Sarah-Anne say Andy's name. I rolled my eyes—she was like a little kid. Such a copycat.

CHAPTER 5

School started back, and despite being told that he did not go to school, I looked for Andy the first day. I knew he was my age, twelve to be exact, so he'd be at least in the sixth grade unless he was an idiot or a genius. I asked Freddy as slyly as I could if there were any new kids. He said no but that Aria Grant was back at school. She'd been out the previous year with a headache that sent her to the hospital in Jacksonville. It was a tumor, but now she was back and okay. Freddy told me some facts about benign brain tumors, but I'd tuned him out. I only cared to think about Andy, and we all knew Aria Grant was doing just fine. She'd been at the indoor skating rink all summer wearing hats while her hair grew out after her brain surgery. Everyone wanted to know if she liked Jacksonville, but she said she didn't see much but the inside of the hospital. My brothers and I went skating once in July—in a moment of weakness, my father said he'd take us. He sat in the car the whole time and forbade any snack or soda purchases, even if we had money left over after we rented skates. He was still mad about the time Freddy used all of his arcade coins on Twizzlers.

I tried to listen to Freddy, who was talking a mile a minute—still about tumors—but it hit me that I knew Aria was named after a guitar and that she also knew how to play. I wondered if I could get some information about Andy from her, being that they both played guitar. Aria's mother taught her when she couldn't even talk, and now she played at every school assembly, accompanying her strumming with her whiny, high-pitched vocals. She was going to be a famous roller skater or singer when she grew up. We were all certain of it. I knew she too would have a BMW just like her mother—the first of its kind in Bledsoe. Freddy said her mother's was used, but all I could say to that was "So what?"

"Can you still play the guitar?" I asked, interrupting Freddy. "After you have a tumor?" We were walking to Bledsoe School on the second day. Peter walked with us too but ahead a little on account of his age and wishes to be his own man. Sarah-Anne wasn't with us, but that wasn't unfamiliar. She'd barely gone the year before, or even the year before that. I always lost track of years when I was thinking about Sarah-Anne. She'd been the same for so long, a person started to forget there was any difference in the time she was alive. I only knew they asked about her sometimes at school, like everyone was so concerned. I never knew what to say. She was at home. That was where my parents thought she belonged. When I asked Peter why she didn't go to school, he told me not to worry about it.

"Like," I went on, "would Aria still know about the guitar, or did her brain get messed up from the surgery?"

"Sure, you can still play." Freddy shrugged. "If you had to have something removed or if your nerves were damaged from surgery or…there are reasons why a person wouldn't be able to resume their life. Yes, I guess you're right that her hands are connected to the upper vertebrae, so that actually makes sense, But no, I think she can do everything now. She's playing guitar at the Welcome Back assembly. She announced it when she told us about her tumor and all the treatments and all that." Freddy shrugged again, still trying to answer my question, which hadn't been asked out of concern for Aria at all.

"Okay. I'm going to talk to her. See ya later!" I scurried off to my new locker.

"Yeah," Freddy called after me.

In the seventh grade, we were given our own lockers and no longer had to share cubbies with a friend. I put a sticker on mine with my name on it. I'd decorated the sticker all summer, adding glitter, paint, other stickers, shapes cut out of construction paper, and then further decorated a couple of newspaper advertisements of women in fancy clothes, and one of my own school pictures. It was now as big as my hand. I looked quite pretty in the picture I'd chosen of myself. I was showing my naturally straight teeth that were also naturally white and well placed in my unfortunately large mouth, framed by large lips that I would not learn to appreciate until later.

I was distracted and agitated at school. I didn't feel capable of keeping up with all of the learning I was supposed to be doing. I could read and felt this was more than enough to get by. It seemed we were always looking at charts of elements with abbreviations or putting stickers on maps while in class. Day two, and I was ready for a break. There wasn't anyone worth marrying in the seventh grade; I'd known all the kids since I was knee-high and had tired of both their looks and their personalities. I had Andy on my mind. Him out there in that boat on the water with nets of crabs all around had me thinking the periodic table was a complete waste of time.

The boys and I walked home from school together too but came from different directions. It was a hot day for our trek, the kind of day that makes the trees look thirsty and tired. I was sweating bullets by the time we got to our house. It was a tragedy that I knew it wouldn't be any cooler inside. I dropped my backpack on the front porch and lay down in the grass. All I could set my mind on was riding around in the air boat and how much better that sounded than anything else there was to do that afternoon.

"Peter," I said. He'd lain down beside me, also miserable. "Who sells crabs and oysters?"

"What?" he asked, then answered anyway. "Sho Nuff, Ollie's

place, but that's a lot of fish. Or I don't know, there's the market off Route 54."

I sat upright with a jolt. "Where's that?"

"Off Route 54. Like I said."

"How do I get there?"

"In a car."

I was quiet for a moment. A warm breeze whirled through the branches of the large oak. The moss dangled and seemed to weep with gratitude for the cool air. Little did Peter know that I knew how to get to Route 54 without a car.

"Where is it on 54?" I asked.

"Jeez, I don't know. If you want oysters, go to Ollie's place. What money are you going to buy them with anyway? And since when do you like oysters?"

"I've always liked 'em," I said, rolling onto my stomach. "I'm gonna take a walk." Freddy was sitting on the front steps with his nose in a book. Peter looked at me a little too seriously.

"You know Dad doesn't want you going back there," he said.

"Going back where?"

"To that kid's house. He told me to keep an eye on you."

"I'm not going there. I want to go buy some oysters on Route 54."

"Why?"

"Because I heard oysters are good for your skin!" I stood up frustrated that I was asked to explain myself at every turn. My family had nothing better to do than get on my case.

"They're an aphrodisiac," Freddy offered.

"We can go over there, but we'll have to swim a little," Peter said. Just as bored and hot, he was looking for any excuse to have something to do. "Dad's gonna be pissed."

"Oh, let him," I said, annoyed. "He's al'ays pissed. I mean, come on…what's new?"

"I'm dying to get in the water," Freddy said agreeably. I had been hoping Freddy wouldn't come. His annoying personality turned to rot in the wrong environment, like food left outside on a hot day, and it was damn near hell hot.

"We'll walk most of the way," Peter corrected. "But we have to swim across the lagoon to where Hobbs' Market is."

"How do you know anyway?" I asked. "And is that really a lagoon?"

"I'm older than you," he said. "Hobbs' Market's been there for a hundred years." He didn't say anything else about the lagoon.

"I never heard of it," I said.

"We don't go over there. Just 'cause we don't do something doesn't mean it doesn't exist." He took off his shoes and suggested we get going.

"I'm thirsty," Freddy told us.

"Well, get something to drink and let's go!" I said.

"We should all drink something. The walk from school's over a mile, and now we're setting out again. It's over ninety today. You could end up with dehydration." Freddy sniffled a little—he sniffled all the time. It was a disgusting habit.

Freddy poured lemonade into a mason jar with a few ice cubes and told us he'd carry it the whole way.

"Suit yourself," I said. "Seems damn heavy."

Peter led the way. It was always hotter just before the sun set, like it was letting out one last wail just so we'd know who was boss—and who would return the next day to punish us again. I turned back to look at the house as we began our trek. I saw Sarah-Anne's face in the side window, looking at us like she was studying the bone structure of human children for her presentation on the spaceship set to return her to her home planet. "Jeez," I said about the chill going down my spine.

"What?" Freddy asked.

"Nothing…just Sarah-Anne."

"She can't come with us," Peter said in a hurry.

"I don't want her to."

"She doesn't leave the house," Freddy offered like we didn't know and needed to be told all about it. "Well…" he paused.

"Don't talk either," I said. "Just stares atcha. Gives me the creeps." Sometimes I remembered that Sarah-Anne used to talk, but it was like the memory of a dream. I couldn't quite put my finger on it.

"Not her fault," Peter said, lowering his head and pressing on.

I put my hand over my eyes like a visor and trudged first through the sticky grass, then through the sticky sand, then finally into the salty water. We were going a different way than I'd gone when I found Andy's house.

We were melting until we hit the water. I let myself fall in face first and practically took a breath. The salt stung my nostrils and the edge of my lips. I floated on my stomach with my mouth shut tight and waited to drop a few degrees in temperature. I felt the floor of the marsh and clawed through the slimy sand with my fingers, pulling myself forward. When I finally came up for air, I looked ahead of me to where Peter was floating on his back with his eyes closed.

"How far we got to swim?" I called out.

"I don't know…not too far. You can see the road from here."

I squinted and saw a small car cruising the landscape. "That must be it!" It was farther away than I'd expected.

"Jesus, Kay!" Peter stood up in the water. "Stop yelling. Yeah, that's it."

Freddy wasn't saying much because he was drinking all of the lemonade and trying to find a good place in his shorts to put the mason jar. He'd won the Science Star and Math Whiz awards just the year before, but he sure didn't look like a math whiz trying to ram a full-size jar in his underwear.

"Ain't gonna fit," I said. "Don't need to be a science star to know you don't got room in your drawers."

Freddy ignored me and continued shoving. "We're swimming over there?" he asked Peter.

"Yep," Peter answered over his shoulder before diving back in the water with his arms raised in a point over his head. He swam in the direction of the road.

I followed with my dress dangling between my legs and slowing me down. I then twisted to my back, where I found it easier to float. My dress was still vying for all the attention and swarming around my legs like a boa constrictor, but I could move slightly more freely.

When I was younger, I just took my dress off and swam in my underwear like the boys, but now all of us had our clothes on—it was making things more difficult. About halfway to shore, I started to get nervous that I wouldn't make it. Peter was yards ahead of me and Freddy surprisingly close on his heels. Swimming was the one thing Freddy did well. I thought to myself that this was a bad idea, but that it had been all my idea, and now here we were swimming out to Route 54. Once there, we'd have to swim back. That was how things worked.

My mind got to thinking about Andy's sweatpants—one of my favorite topics. I didn't know what had become of any of the clothes I'd taken from him. My mother hadn't yet asked about the dress with the yellow trim, but I was sure she'd wondered where it went. I knew Andy's clothes were washed and hung to dry, but they disappeared after I saw them on the line outside. I figured my dad took them—it was clearly his plan to make sure I didn't have another excuse to go back to their house. I sometimes thought he was determined to make sure we were as unhappy as he was—a father's love.

Peter made it to where he could stand a lot faster than I

expected and a long way before the road. I sighed with relief while still swimming as fast as I could. I was tired and ready to be out of the water. Freddy stood up with the mason jar in his hand. It made me both mad and proud that he'd been dumb enough to try to carry it the whole way, and that he'd managed to do it. I put my feet under me and found the ground was not as far down as I'd thought. I probably could have stopped swimming sooner.

We trudged up the small beach off Route 54 and into the back of the market. It was an open-air type of place that sold fresh fish, mussels, oysters, crabs of all varieties, shrimp, and so on. I'd heard of it, but we didn't shop there—or anywhere except the discount grocery store with the plentiful day-old section.

The market on Route 54 was closer to Blaisedale than Bledsoe. Blaisedale was a bigger town with a real beach—there were people there with money, unlike in Bledsoe. Volmer was the other town in our midst. A lot like Bledsoe, but with a Walmart and a few restaurants. There wasn't much else to say about the place, but at least they had their Walmart. We had nothing. Two traffic lights and a small pile of stores—grocery, convenience, pharmacy, and the place where you got your hair cut. Meridian was the best, but it was far away and looked down its nose at all of us. I longed to be the kind of person who could look down their nose at anyone.

The reason a person moved to Bledsoe was that you didn't have any money and needed cheap land. Most of the houses were homemade, ramshackle numbers on cinder blocks or with dirt floors if you were up high enough to guarantee your home wouldn't fill with water on a bad day. Make no mistake, though—guarantees were hard to come by in the flood plain. Blaisedale was a real place. They had stores and big gas stations with car washes and a Chick-fil-A.

We didn't have a dime to our name, so there was no real reason for us to be at the market on Route 54 other than to scope it out. Naturally, I was only interested in looking at the boats pulled up at the dock a few yards away from where we swam in. I saw Nile Webber's air boat with the stickers on the seats and felt a swell of excitement. Seemed I was always in a soaking wet dress whenever I was to see Andy; today would be no exception. I'd told my mother I wanted to try some new clothes, but she acted confused and sewed me a dress with gray fabric and purple lace trim. Apparently I was not permitted to wear shorts or a shirt that stopped at my waist. I figured I would ask again when I was thirteen.

After discovering the Webbers' boat, I surveyed the scene with an electricity I usually reserved for sports day at school or a fight with Freddy when I was tired or bored. There were dozens of tables set up under umbrellas, all covered with chests of ice that were filled with various dead things. A few dozen people milled about: marsh people like us—poor, lost, and lonely. I did not feel out of place.

Peter was sitting on the small beach, staring back at where we'd come from, while Freddy was filling then emptying the mason jar with seawater. He might have been completely unaware of the market or any of the people standing next to the road.

"Have you ever been here before?" I asked Peter.

"Nope." He rolled onto his stomach. "Why don't you go over there and get yourself an oyster? I'm not sitting here all day."

"I don't have any money."

"I'm sure someone there'll let you taste somethin'... Just stay away from the Webber kid."

"But why?" I insisted.

"Kay. Jesus. They're bad news is why. The mom died and they ran off. You don't need to know everything all the time. Just do what you're told for once in your damned life. It's for your own good."

I didn't like being told what to do, but it was Peter doing the telling—he wasn't nearly as fun to argue with as my dad, so I listened and appeared to consider what he said. I decided that I wouldn't go looking for Andy, but if I happened to see him I wouldn't be rude—bad news or not. The problem was, however, that my natural inclinations were to go looking for Andy, so I went off and found him, unintentionally of course. He was sitting on a closed cooler when I spotted him. His father sat on top of another larger ice chest, also closed. They talked to each other sideways; their mouths hardly moved at all. Andy didn't see me at first, but after I circled their post a few times, he finally caught on and smiled. His father was not as excited to find me at the market. His sticky grin left my stomach a little turned over and put on ice—the kind shaped like pebbles that you get at the 7-Eleven.

"Hey, Kay," Andy said when I walked up. Once again, my dress was stuck straight to me like glue on paper. "You're always wet," he said, laughing a little.

"We swam here. It's like flames out. Too hot to walk." I shrugged.

"Gonna buy anything?" Andy asked.

"No money. You just sit here all day waitin' for people to buy your stuff?" I wiped a strand of wet hair from my forehead.

"We sell most of our crabs to restaurants, but this is as good a place as any to sell the rest. Oysters, too. You can have an oyster." He began to stand so he could lift the top of the blue cooler. "Slow day. We're gonna have a lot left."

"I can't pay you for it, and as a woman of principle, I don't feel right…" I began. Nile Webber laughed.

"Don't be standing on principle on our account," Mr. Webber told me. "You can have as many oysters as you want." He was smiling in that peculiar way I'd noticed the day at their house—like he was thinking about me very carefully. "Are you here alone?"

"No, Peter and Freddy came too. They're my brothers. Sarah-Anne's back at the house. She's my sister. She's off."

"Do they want anything?" Andy asked. "What's 'off' mean?" He was messing inside the cooler, looking up at me every few seconds. I looked around and thought this did seem like a better way to spend your time than at school. Andy got to chitchat away with the local color and sit on a box all the time. I was almost jealous.

"I'll bet we could take a dent out of that pile of ice if nothing else," I said. "I don't really know what it means. Sarah-Anne's always been off. When you meet her, you'll get it. Just off her island a little. Don't talk."

"Not talking a lot's okay," Andy said.

I wasn't sure if this was a dig at me, so I narrowed my eyes and nodded, but just a little. If Andy liked people who didn't talk all the time, I would have to learn to communicate in other ways. "Mmhmmmm," I said. I took a fistful of ice and raised my hand to my mouth.

"You can't eat that. Could be tainted." Andy reached for my hand, but I dropped the ice before he had to do anything about it. He began to shuck the oyster in his hand using a tool that he'd had in his front pocket. He still wasn't wearing a shirt, but I'd stopped minding. If every time he was going to see me, I was wearing a wet sack for clothes, then I guess I could let him go without a shirt in peace.

"But if I'm eating the stuff that was sitting in it..." I started to argue but decided against carrying on and trailed off. "Sorry I still have your clothes." I changed the subject instead.

"Yeah, we washed your stuff for you. Gave it to your dad." He leaned over the cooler to get another oyster. He'd put the one that he shucked on a small tray resting on a table behind him. On the table was a cash box and a clipboard. There was a piece of paper with some writing on it—prices per pound. I saw a scale sitting on the ground under the table with plastic bags and twist ties. It wasn't much of a set-up, but I had to suppose they had everything they needed.

"My dad?" I asked.

"He came by with my clothes." Andy smiled at me before throwing an oyster in his mouth. He reached for the tray and held it out to me. I popped it in my mouth, wincing a little. Raw never suited my fancy.

I turned to look behind me where I'd left Peter and Freddy. They were still on the beach and didn't appear interested in moving.

"Whaddya mean, my dad gave you your clothes back?"

"He came by."

"In what? We don't have a boat."

"Naw, he came to the market on Monday," Andy explained like I should know. Nile Webber shifted on the cooler where he'd been sitting and loudly cleared his throat. "Yeah," Andy said before sitting back down on his own ice chest. "Do your brothers want one? I didn't e'en know you had a sister. Lotsa kids around here don't talk much."

"Maybe," I said, not sure what he was getting at. I talked enough for a dozen people—my dad said so all the time. I shook my head and looked down, still thinking about my father coming to the market with Andy's green sweatpants and the T-shirt with the roadster on it. He didn't tell me he was doing any such thing.

I had a mind to give it to him when I got home. "Okay then." I frowned trying to think of a reason Andy would or wouldn't know I had a sister. I was worried he was thinking there was better crop in the field than me.

"Don't worry about it," Andy said, tapping me on the arm. I grimaced a little. He wasn't older than me; I didn't want him acting like he was. The dresses always threw everyone off. I was mistaken for a girl three years younger all the damn time.

"I'm not worried." I took another oyster from the tray that I could clearly see was dirty. Here he was lecturing me about the ice, but he'd let me eat food from this filthy tray. "I just didn't know he'd be able to find you is all."

"Not hard to find." Andy looked at his dad, who had stood up.

"We're packing up here in a few minutes," Nile said. "Time to get home."

"Y'all do everything together. Don't you get sick of each other? You could come over to my house and see how it is to have a buncha brothers and a sister. There are neighbors dropping by when their mama's gotta run errands to the store that sells milk in cups. You're invited anytime. We're not all that interesting, but since you don't go to school, I'm sure you get lonesome to play with kids or talk to somebody besides your daddy." I had been overcome with powerful urges ever since I met Andy—before too, but they were even more powerful after—and seeing him again wasn't making things any better. My daddy gave me a good smack and shove at least a couple of times a week, but I couldn't shake the feeling that I was on borrowed time if I kept this up. I was going to get a lot more than smacked or shoved; I may not live to see thirteen.

"Yeah, we'll see," Nile said.

"Yeah, we'll see," Andy repeated.

We swam back the way we came, but not after I put up a fight that we could walk in the water up to our armpits. I needed a longer rest—I'd never properly learned to breathe by turning my head, so doing freestyle full throttle all the way to the market had near done me in. I had to come up for a gulp between every few rotations; it was so tiring I didn't think I'd make it all the way back if I had to swim the parts where my feet touched the sand.

"Gonna take us forever," Peter argued.

"Not more than five minutes," I snapped back. We walked with our arms above our heads for about a hundred yards before we were too deep to keep walking. I was tired from water trudging and found it hard to get myself going, but I refused to admit my mistake and swam as fast as I could, taking gasping breaths every few strokes. I ended up in front of both the boys at the other end of the water; stubborn pride has its advantages. I stood on the bank and waited for them with my hands on my waist, feeling victorious and jittery. Freddy swam with only one arm, using the other to hold the jar. It took him a while to reach us; his face was redder than usual when he arrived.

"I think you coulda left that," I said of the jar. "You didn't share anyway."

"I don't litter," he said, giving a sniffle.

We ran the rest of the way home. We'd been gone for at least a couple of hours. It might have been wishful thinking, but I had this clear vision of my mother standing on the porch with her hands clasped in despair, because she couldn't find any of us—me especially. I'd expected as much when I went out in the storm the week before, but it didn't seem anyone even knew I was gone. Now that I was with Peter and Freddy, maybe my parents would be concerned—the more prized possessions missing, the deeper the lines on the forehead. I'd barely caused a crease.

CHAPTER 6

I could hear Sarah-Anne when we got close to the house. Because she hardly ever made a peep, when she did it was so surprising, like a car alarm gone off in the middle of a funeral. I knew because I went to my cousin's funeral where a car alarm went off for the better part of six minutes during the eulogy. Corley Taft dove into the shallow end of a pool and broke her neck when I was seven—she was nine. It was the kind of thing they warned us about, and that you never thought would happen to you, but Corley went and did it. I barely knew her—I found out later she was a second cousin anyway. I told everyone at school about her accident and then her funeral, which had been silent (other than the car alarm) and fragrant. The kids in my class asked me if I was scared it would happen to me, but I said no. I'd never been to a swimming pool. It didn't seem I had anything to worry about.

"They's back," Sarah-Anne said. "Hurryin.'" Her voice was raspy from lack of use and very small. It couldn't fill a teaspoon, but I heard it loud and clear.

"They better be hurrying," my father said.

They were all on the front porch when we came around the corner, wet as the morning dew and with exhausted faces. "Where the hell were you?" My father stood up from where he'd been stewing. He looked younger when he was mad. A boy-man, he had never seemed fully grown-up; different parts of him aged but never at the same time.

"We went swimming. Was so hot," I said in a sing-song voice meant to lighten the mood.

"Like hell. Where did you go?"

"The market on Route 54," Peter said somberly.

My father looked at me, spit on a porch plank, and walked inside, letting the screen door slam.

"I carried the mason jar all the way there and back." Freddy showed my mother, who smiled approvingly before putting her hand on Sarah-Anne's shoulder. They were unified against us.

"We should eat dinner," my mother said. She was standing at the rail and turned to walk inside the house like a little lost cloud following the rain.

Sometimes my mother used my father's anger as a way to

perfectly display her superiority. She didn't yell or slam doors or storm around like my dad—this was the better personality as far as she was concerned. I agreed, even though I hadn't inherited any of it. I was a bull like my daddy. I was born mad. My mother liked to contrast her serene waters with his stormy seas. She thought we liked her better because she didn't threaten us with violence or raise her voice. The way she tiptoed around usually made me want to bang the drum louder and get into more mischief. I knew she thought she was proving me wrong somehow. But she never did. My father said my rebellious nature was born of the water, which has been rebelling against the land since the beginning of time. It would be so much easier to love him when my father said things like this, if he weren't so moody all the other time. Just when you thought you were getting somewhere with him, he'd find a reason to be mad as hell again. Or depressed. Or lost in unfavorable comparisons. Feeling sorry for yourself is about the most useless thing to do with your time as far as I can tell. I lived with some professionals—I knew all about it.

We followed behind my mother's slight frame and went to our rooms to change out of our wet clothes. I saw my dress and pink underwear from the day at Andy's house lying neatly on the bed and went red as a beet. I vowed that I would no longer wear panties, period, when swimming in the marsh. The sight of them cleaned and folded on my bed in my parents' house, when my own mama hadn't done the cleaning and the folding, was enough to make me go off underwear altogether.

"Come on," Freddy said, peeking around the corner of my barely open bedroom door. "We don't want to upset Mom."

"Oh, yes, let's not upset Mom." I rolled my eyes a little.

I'd already changed my clothes, but this intrusion on my privacy was enough to make me throw a sock at Freddy, which he darted from before pushing my door open further and turning to go. He walked backward toward the kitchen with his face blushing true crimson. This only served to annoy me further.

"Can you please knock next time?" I called out after him. My hair was wet and still in the ponytail I'd worn to school. I stomped into the kitchen in my clean T-shirt and cotton shorts—my sleeping clothes; the only time I wore anything but a dress was when I was unconscious. "What are we eating?" I asked.

"I've had enough of your disrespect," my father said from where he already sat at the table. Peter and Freddy were also seated, with forks in hand. My mother brought pots and pans over from the stove in silence. "You don't come in here and demand to know what's for dinner like some monarch eating grapes and being fanned by your workers. Sit down and thank your mother for cooking dinner for you. If I was in my right mind, I'd send you to bed hungry for disobeying me again."

"I didn't disobey you!" I snapped. Cursing and lying to save my own hide were bad sins as far as I could tell, but I was able to forgive myself for them. The one time we went to Sunday school at my Aunt Christy's church, the lady teaching the Bible class said that to get right with God we have to forgive ourselves and others. I saw it as an either/or kind of a thing and always picked myself.

I sat down in my chair and noticed we were having peas and beef. I hated beef and especially when it was served with peas. My father would have been doing me a favor by sending me to bed without dinner. Brown and green were awful colors for food—I'd told my mother this a hundred times.

I'd stashed a Snickers bar under my bed the week before; my mind went to that while looking at the food on the table. Clarke Milton, who worked at the Texaco, had given me the candy bar a week earlier. He was thirteen and under my spell. I had accepted. I was not usually one for gifts given with expectations, but I love Snickers. I couldn't see the harm. I saved it for a special moment when I could eat it in peace—Snickers being the only brown food I approved of. I pouted and tried not to make eye contact with my dad.

I considered faking illness so I could go back to my room, but my father was in one of his moods that were specifically aggravated by me. I figured if I just kept my head down, the moment would pass, and we could all live in forced tranquility again.

"Are you listening to me, Kay?" my father asked, pounding his hand on the table.

"Yes! But what do you want me to do? Just forget Andy exists? He doesn't go to school and only has his daddy for company. I can't just pretend he's not there. I've never even been to the market before; it was so interesting, fascinating even. I was fascinated!" My father rolled his eyes. "We were so hot when we got home… Dad, that's a long walk from school, and it was just so hot, we needed somewhere to swim. Why can't I be friends with him? It's so boring all the time, and no one new ever comes around, 'cept Cort and his mom, and the neighbor's got that awful dog. What do you want me to do with myself all day? Just sit and be quiet? I want to be able to visit fascinating markets some of the time at least!"

My father took a breath and began to speak, this time with a little more restraint. "Kay, I don't care what you do with your time, but when I tell you not to do something, I expect you to listen to me and not do it."

"But you're big buddies with them… Why can't I be?" I moved my fork around on my plate. It made scratching sounds that were both irritating and pleasant—because I've always found it pleasant to be a little irritating.

My mother looked up from her plate where she was carefully cutting her food. My father noticeably swallowed and shook his head. "I'm not big buddies with them…with anyone."

"You went and saw them."

"Kay," he said, like spitting my name at me would be enough. Peter and Freddy were stock-still. The only one moving at the table was Sarah-Anne. She crossed her legs up under her on the small chair that squeaked and moaned with her every shuffle.

"Kay what? He said you went out there to the market with his clothes. How'd you even know what they looked like? Did'cha just walk around with the sweatpants on your head and hope somebody claimed 'em?"

"I know what they look like; they used to live back there!" He pointed over his shoulder with a jerk. He had a looney grin on his face. My mother watched him closely. I wondered if she was even breathing with how tight she had her jaw clamped. I could see her small muscles pulse from under her tissue-like skin. She was probably nervous I was about to end up with a bloody lip or worse with the way I was arguing. We all knew she didn't like my dad knocking us around so much, even if she never did anything to stop it. "But I don't want..." he went on, not really able to get ahold of what he was saying. "I've told you that I want you to keep away from them. It's not..." He stammered and stuttered for a couple more seconds. His mouth seemed a little out of his control—this was my cross to bear as well, so I couldn't judge him too harshly for the way his words overtook his faculties; that happened to me a good ten times a day. "We keep to ourselves," he said finally. "And it's gonna stay that way. I don't want people comin' around here. And they don't either. Anyway, can't you play with the kids at school?"

"I hate them!" I said angrily. "And we don't get to play at school. We have to work on math and science and all that other sh—" I stopped myself just in time.

"You hate who? You don't hate anyone." My father ate a pea and looked around like he was doing us all a favor. Setting me straight while eating my mother's bland meals was his best work.

"Can Andy come over here then? That way I wouldn't have to go to his house or to the market for oysters. He doesn't have any friends or anything."

"No, he cannot come over here," my dad said. My mother nodded a little. Finally he'd said something she was comfortable with. "We're not having anybody over here."

"'Cept Cort." I wanted to mention the fivers but was more in the mood to sock it to my dad than hurt Freddy's feelings.

"How do you know he doesn't have any friends?" It was Peter hammering me this time.

"He doesn't go to school." I put a pile of meat and gravy on my plate and tried not to sneer. There were baked potatoes too. My mother made potatoes too often. I was beginning to think she'd forgotten how to boil rice. "Is there sour cream?" I asked.

"No, just butter," Mom answered softly.

I sighed in frustration. "Pass me the salt. Gonna need a lot of salt to make it taste good." My father shot me a look like a dart and I piped down. "I don't think he has friends," I said, "because he doesn't go to school."

"That doesn't mean he doesn't have friends," Freddy said. "I go to school and I hardly have any friends." It was like the music stopped. We all looked at him, forks hanging from our hands like limp spaghetti. "It's true," he said. "I don't have hardly any friends."

"Sure you do, Freddy," I offered. I was glad I hadn't mentioned the payments. I thought about Freddy always trying to high-five

84

Cort or show him some damned science experiment with pennies and lemon juice and Cort just going along with it, always with this look on his face like he was serving hard time. "You got a lotta friends." I was trying to convince myself more than anyone.

"No, I really don't. I don't have a lot in common with the kids at school." He shrugged.

I couldn't think of anything to say, so I looked at Sarah-Anne who was arranging the peas on her plate in a semi-circle. They looked like a green necklace. She'd eaten all of her potato, including the skin. It was Sarah-Anne who loved potatoes. I had her to blame for many of my problems.

"That might change when you get older," my mother said to Freddy. She ate her peas one at a time, perhaps mimicking my father's flair, and had only two bites of plain potato before putting her fork down. I didn't see her touch the beef, which was gristly and overcooked. I was grateful for the oysters I'd eaten earlier. I could tell it was going to be one of those nights when I couldn't get my fill on account of the poor-tasting dinner. I'd lain awake many a night with my tummy grumbling while my pride prevented me from begging for scraps. If I were a raccoon or a dog, I'd have been long dead by now.

"Not if I stay in Bledsoe," Freddy answered.

"Where else would you go?" my father said.

"I'm just making the point that no one moves here. I'm not going to meet different people, and everyone eventually drops out of school, so there won't be many of us left—there's only twenty kids in the senior grade. Mom said it would change when I got older, but..."

No one responded for a while. I put some more beef in my mouth and chewed like a cow on cud. "Hard making friends," I said to ease the pain.

"I did talk to the counselor about going to school in Richmond Hill. They have a program there for kids interested in science. You don't have to be from the area," Freddy said.

"Richmond Hill's an hour from here," my father said like this was the end of the story.

"I know."

"So is the counselor going to take you to and from the school in Richmond Hill?"

"No, she didn't say that." Freddy was getting frustrated. "But she told me about it, because she knows how unhappy I am here at that school and...you know."

"No, I don't know. Does it cost money to go to the place in Richmond Hill?" My father was really on one and didn't appear to be letting up. First it was me trailing around after Andy, and now Freddy wanted to go to school practically in another state.

"Mrs. Chalke didn't tell me how much it cost or who would drive me there or anything else! She just said it was for kids like me, really interested in science. You can do a whole course on meteorology, so that's it. I don't have friends here. I don't like the school.

I don't see why I wouldn't want to go to Richmond Hill. I'm just bringing it up." I thought he might cry.

"It's worth a thought," my mother said at the top of her very small voice so for once we could actually hear her. And with that, the conversation was over.

After dinner, my brothers and I helped clear the table. Sarah-Anne rinsed the dishes in the sink after she'd dipped and scrubbed them with a dish brush. We used Palmolive. I caught Sarah-Anne licking the cap. She smiled when she did it.

"Boy, that girl is seriously off," I said to myself, but loud enough to hear. I put the damp dish towel through the handle on the refrigerator and shook my head.

My mother said she was feeling tired. But she didn't need to tell us; we knew, because that was her only mood—exhausted. She excused herself to go to her room; we wouldn't see her again until morning. She walked past the refrigerator but turned around for a split second to look at me.

"You know she drowned," she said softly. "They found her under the house. Dead. Caught next to one of the stilts. His mother…"

"What?" I said at three times the volume.

My mother looked at me very closely. "That's why you should stay away from them." She glanced over her shoulder to where my father was sitting, watching us from the couch in the living room. He had the paper near his face but not directly in front of it. I froze for a moment, not sure who was messing with who—it was often too hard to tell. "Everybody thought Nile did it—the dad."

"Okay," I said, absently wiping my hands on the towel even though they were already dry. I could hear the blood in my veins as it made its way through my head and back to my heart, making a pit stop in my stomach where it did a flip. Sarah-Anne was just beyond my father standing very heavily with her belly sticking out behind the couch. She had her legs spread and her chin down. She looked like the letter A—if it had swallowed a beach ball.

"You're tired, Sue-Bess," my father said firmly. He had moved the paper down to speak then back up again.

My mother glanced at the ceiling; her eyes were wandering to the heavens. "She'd been floating there for hours before they found her. Just floating. Hours."

"Is she talkin' about Emily?" I heard Sarah-Anne ask in her peculiarly forceful whisper. "Emily," she said again. My father looked at me too hard while my mother slipped into her room, her leaving practically unnoticed.

CHAPTER 7

Who the hell is Emily?" I asked the boys the following day, while walking to school in the red, dusty heat. I kicked a rock that went flying at a dying bush.

"Emily?" Freddy said.

"Freddy, you are normally such a fuck-bucket know-it-all. Emily. Sarah-Anne and Mom were talking about her last night. Who is she?"

Freddy's face flushed as he slowed his gait. "I don't know; maybe it's her imaginary friend or something."

"Jesus bless." I put my hands in my pockets and walked on. "Sarah-Anne said something about Emily. Who's this Emily? I never met her. She's *not* imaginary."

"Isn't Emily Andy's mom?" Freddy sounded exasperated.

I spun around, and so did Peter; he'd been walking ahead of us the whole way to school, ignoring my questions. I figured he was mad at me about the market and getting in trouble with Dad. Peter didn't like our parents any more than I did, but he was a lot more concerned about being out on the streets. He took the threats about getting kicked out more seriously. I figured I could just go to the police and tell them about my parents' strange habits and all the running off when cars came to the house—I had ammunition that secured my place under their roof.

"Freddy," Peter said sternly.

"Last night was the first I've ever heard that name," I said. "Since when did you know anything about it?"

"Emily was Andy's mother," Peter explained. "The one that drowned."

"What?" I interrupted, stamping my foot. "How the hell does Sarah-Anne, and Freddy, and YOU know about Andy's mama, and I don't? Motherfucker!"

"Kay, stop it. Come on—we have to get going." Peter started moving again at a quicker pace. "And it's 'cause we're older than you, and Mom talks to Sarah-Anne all the time."

"She sure as hell don't talk to me."

"That's 'cause you never shut up long enough for anyone else to say anything," Peter said with his back to me.

"Why do you want to hang out with those guys anyway, Kay?"

Freddy asked innocently. "Who cares about... I mean, they're living in a... It's worse than our place. It's like...end of the line."

"Yeah, and that's a tall order," I said. "Tall as the sky to get further down the block than us. I mean...how come Sarah-Anne knows Andy's mama? How come? And what does it matter that you're older than me? Do you remember them? Do you remember what happened?"

"Stop talking about it," Peter said. "And Sarah-Anne doesn't know her; she's just heard Mom talking."

"I'll talk about whatever I want," I shouted.

"Yeah, me too. I can do..." Freddy tried to catch up with us but stumbled a little. "I don't care," he said. I thought he might really need to go to the science school in Richmond Hill, because his personality and constant sniffling were about to do me in. Although Richmond Hill wasn't far enough away, is what I really thought. "I can say what I wanna say," he sniffled.

"Oh, yeah?" I said, mostly thinking that nobody was listening to Freddy anyway, no matter what he said. Except maybe now I would listen a little closer to him and Peter since it seemed like they remembered Andy from before he skipped town. I pressed my fingers into my temples trying to jog my own memory, but I came up empty-handed. I'd never before known these people existed, and here my whole family was on a first-name basis with the lot of them. That was about as odd as finding Andy standing in the middle of the marsh with his guitar.

Instead of concentrating on my schoolwork, I made a plan to wander back behind the house when I got home that day. I would walk in the right direction and make myself conspicuous enough to be seen from a distance. I was wearing one of my brightest dresses—red with gold trim.

I got through the day and was able to enthusiastically participate in PE, even though I was tired of the heat and the sweaty kids and the sun so close to us like an iron overhead, pressing down with the steam button pushed hard. I used my frustration with my situation—constantly in the dark and living with a bunch of secretive lunatics—to fuel the fires of my basketball game. I scored nine points and pulled a foul off Ginger Graves. All she ever did was double-dribble and yank on people's clothes anyway.

When we got home from school, I told Peter and Freddy I was going for a walk in the water, which was understandable given the devil temperatures. My mother and Sarah-Anne were sitting on the front porch when we arrived but didn't speak to any of us. Sarah-Anne was sitting in my mother's lap like a small child. I went inside, straight through and out the back door. No one seemed to notice me—I didn't give a shit. My mother hadn't come out of her room in the morning before we went to school, so I hadn't had a chance to ask her about the Webbers. About Emily. She would pretend she forgot what she said anyway. She always pretended she forgot the important things she told us, like when she said that my dad was in jail when Freddy was born. She'd been talking to me and Peter.

"Jail," she had said. "For the birth." I tried to bring it up again—Peter too—but she just stared off into space and acted like she didn't hear us.

"In jail for what?" I said more than a few times.

"What?" Nothing.

I walked in the direction of the Webbers' but veered a little off the correct path in the hopes that if I was caught, I could say I really was just going for a walk. I didn't put it past my father to take off after me, desperate to catch me in the act of disobeying him. Pressing buttons was my calling card.

My adventure did not disappoint. I didn't have to wait long for my dress to work its magic. I'd only been standing back behind the house, killing time by acting out scenes from *Hoosiers* and *The Goonies* (another favorite on the porch), for about an hour when Andy and Nile came around the corner in their boat. I waved at them with wide-stretched hands, knowing I would be more easily spotted the bigger I made myself.

Nile saw me first and pointed without conviction. Andy waved back, but like he was trying not to get caught, as the boat sidled up to the land where I was standing. "Hey," Andy said.

"Hey yourself. Do you want to come and play at my house?" I asked. I was immediately embarrassed, because people don't say "come and play" after the age of ten. I forced a laugh and tried to pretend I'd misspoken. "I mean…just come over and hang out."

I was wandering into dangerous territory; I had not been given permission to invite Andy—or anyone else for that matter—over to the house, but here he had a drowned mother named Emily who my whole goddamned family seemed to know about except me. All I wanted to do was give the kid some company.

Andy looked at his dad, who looked at me, squinting in the sunlight, and I didn't know who I had a bigger crush on. Andy didn't have but a few buzzed hairs on his head, but his father's was tousled and filled with salt and sand the way a good marsh rider's should be. Their skin was just about the same color, though— like different flavors of the same good soda. It was only the years between them that had me able to tell them apart at all—that, and their hair. I reached for my own long, limp, brown ponytail and gave it a twist. I smiled and stuck my hip out; my hair may have been lame, but I had other perks.

"I'll be back here in two hours," Andy's father said to him. Andy smiled and stepped out of the boat without another word to his dad. We started to walk in the direction of the house. I turned and looked behind us several times to see the silhouette of the boat and Andy's father disappear into the horizon like a cookie being eaten by the sun.

"You okay?" Andy asked. "He's not coming back."

"Oh, I know," I said. I was nervous for a second. I'd paid too much attention to Mr. Webber. "I just like the boat. We don't have a boat."

"Yeah," he said.

"Where's your guitar?" I asked.

"Back at the house. Out of tune. Needs new strings."

"Who taught you to play?"

"My dad and his buddy, Cole, out in California. I don't really play anyway. Just when I'm bored."

"Did you like living there?" I was glad I hadn't invested a lot of time and energy in guitar lessons, as it appeared this was not the way to Andy's heart after all. "How long was y'all out in California anyway?"

"Naw," Andy said. "California was okay I guess. I thought it was cold all the damn time. Doesn't get good and hot like here." He didn't answer the part about how long they'd lived there.

"It's too hot here." I put my hands in my pockets. All of my dresses had pockets—big ones right on the front, just below my privates.

"Never too hot," Andy countered.

"You walk home from school at three in the afternoon every day in August then…"

"No thanks. I don't like the cold any more than I like school. I'd rather sweat."

"You kinda hafta go to school," I said, tired of talking about the weather like a couple of old folks. "You're the only boy I know who doesn't hafta go to school none."

"You don't have to go to school no more once you know how to read."

I didn't say anything at first, thinking hard on the wisdom of his claim. It was true. I didn't know a single adult who used their learning for more than reading a book now and then, or going over a form for something with their kids.

"Yeah, but you have your fishing," I said. "That's your trade, so you're not like the rest of us. I need to have a lot of skills, so I can get a job when I'm older. No one in my family works, and we're poor as dirt 'cause of it. I want to have a nice house someday." I looked sideways for a moment. Andy's house on stilts was fine and all, but no one would have accused it of being a nice place. We kept walking over broken branches and grass flattened by the weight of water and sand. Collapsing ground cover was the only sound.

I wore shoes but Andy was barefoot. He said the bottoms of his feet were like shoes anyway. "No need for any of that stuff," he told me when I asked if he owned sneakers for running. "Get along fine without 'em." Like the weather, I decided I wouldn't talk any more about shoes with Andy. We had to have more in common than feet and the sun. Andy's mother and her body floating under the house were on the tip of my tongue for at least half a mile, but I knew better than to ask him about it. He had that way that suggested he liked to come up with the topics for conversation, and not the other way around—kind of like my daddy and Peter. We kept on in silence while I tried not to say the name. *Emily.*

"You know there's a lady out here who has monkeys, like… living in her house," he finally said when I was just about so uncomfortable with the silence between us I would have kissed a snake to have something to say.

"What?" I squinted, trying not to feel like I had any idea what he was talking about. A strand of hair had fallen over my eye. Andy flicked his head to the side as if to help me move it. I used my fingers and brushed the hair away. He smiled.

"Monkeys?"

"Yeah, like…if you…" He pointed to his right. "Go over that way for a while, she's there with one running around on the deck a' her house. Maybe two. I dunno how many."

"Does she have a house like you? Like, in the water?"

"Yeah."

"So it's not just y'all livin' back here by your lonesome?"

"We're fine," he said. He smiled at me again. I felt like a little peanut coming out of its shell the way I was popped open. The view was better on the outside. "I'll take ya to see the monkeys someday."

"Yeah, I'd like that." I smiled, but more to myself. "I never seen a monkey, 'specially not one living on stilts."

Peter and Freddy were out in front when we reached the house. They were throwing a football back and forth.

It was getting on to six o'clock, dinnertime. I hadn't really thought of a plan for what to do with Andy while we ate.

"Hey," Peter called out to us as we rounded the corner of our house and came into view.

"This is a nice house," Andy said.

"It's okay." Freddy threw the ball to Andy, who wasn't really looking but managed to hold on to it after fumbling about for a moment, trying to get a grip.

"Jeez!" I called out to Freddy. "Make sure he's lookin' at you!" I was about to add that his mother was murdered and died right there under their house, but I didn't think that was good ball-throwing conversation. I figured it was something we could talk about while we were kissing in the moonlight. I could surely help him lick his wounds with my deep and sincere love.

"Sorry," Freddy said, wiping his nose with the back of his hand then putting that same snotty hand in his pocket.

"Can't catch the ball with your hands in your pockets," Andy said, tossing the football in the air, waiting for Freddy to ready himself to catch. Andy threw a spiral in Freddy's direction that Freddy caught with great determination—snot-covered hands and all.

"Gosh, Andy," I said. "You've got a good arm." I winked, trying some new looks on for size. I'd investigated my face just the week before in the bathroom mirror. I did some winks, a few lip pouts, a kiss face, and a half-smile that I thought looked mighty steamy.

Peter rolled his eyes, caught a pass from Freddy, and threw the ball at me. I caught it and tossed it up in the air the way Andy had done. We went round and round like this for a spell; no one said much of anything, but I thought we were having fun enough. Normally, this kind of thing was boring, but I had a shirtless boy to look at who wasn't my brother—I decided to enjoy myself. I didn't really think to introduce Andy; I had a pretty good feeling that Peter and Freddy knew who he was, and anyway I guess they'd known him before even though Peter said they were all too little to remember.

"Where's your sister?" Andy said.

"I don't know," I said. "Prolly off bein' weird. What's it to you anyway?" I tried not to scowl.

We continued throwing the ball, not talking about anything in particular, when my father came outside with a cigarette in his mouth. I was all nerves as I saw him take in the situation. He noticed Andy and immediately looked away. I thought he might run over and grab me by the neck, but he stood still. He was a little too calm—a way he only got when he was quitting his job or just about to.

Peter was watching my father closely too. We all knew I'd gone and done it. I'd been going and doing it for some time now, but there had to be a limit. I crossed my fingers behind my back, hoping this wouldn't be the straw that broke the camel's back. I hadn't forgotten that my mom said it was Nile Webber who killed his wife—which would have been a good reason to stay away from him, but I just told myself that wasn't Andy's fault. He couldn't be held responsible. I was doing God's work by being his friend.

I could see friction in the air, coming directly from my father's mouth as he exhaled a stream of smoke. I thought he might be smiling, but a mean smile like the kind kids have when they smash an ant pile with their shoe. No one in our house smiled—not even halfway—unless they were trying to play a trick on you. Something was up for sure. My father took a long pull on his cigarette and told us dinner was ready.

"I better be getting back then," Andy said.

"You can stay for dinner—right, Dad?" I spoke loudly. Peter looked at my father, who continued to smirk like he smelled something we didn't.

"I don't think I should," Andy said. "I don't have a shirt."

"I've got something you can wear," Freddy said. I wondered if my father was able to see how lonely we were for friends. We were made to live so far off Hack Road that we were practically invisible. There I was tracking the-kids'-tragedy-left-behind down in their stick houses and inviting them to dinner.

We waited for my father to answer while the Spanish moss swayed from the rickety branches of the twisted oak hanging over our heads. I thought it might be God telling me to cool it. I didn't know much about God, but he had a way of talking to me that rolled over like distant thunder. I was pushing limits, and I couldn't stop. We were all sweating from the thick evening heat slowly flowing out of the air after a long day of fighting with itself, bumping into other hot air and then the falling sun. My skin felt like sandpaper. I looked at Andy. His brow was dry as a bone.

"Come on in," my father said, making a cup with his hand.

He then looked at me completely without expression, his face an empty dinner plate about to break in two from the force of my revolt against him.

"Come on then," I said to Andy as quietly as I could. "He don't want to make a scene."

My mother was already seated at the table. In front of her was a pot of potatoes and, to the left of it, fried chicken. I almost skipped with excitement. If my mother did one thing well, other than her dresses of course, it was her fried chicken. She fried it twice the way you're supposed to and soaked it in buttermilk, like a proper woman. I grabbed a leg before sitting down. My father smacked my hand and I dropped the piece on the table. He picked it up and put it on Freddy's plate. I looked at my dad but said nothing—he was as mad as he'd ever been. I was lucky it was only the chicken leg that got smacked.

My mother put another piece of chicken on my plate, but it wasn't a leg, and said something about having guests. I wondered how long a time would pass before my parents would speak to one another again. It usually began with moments like this. First my mother stirred the pot with something she half-said, like the thing about my dad being in jail during childbirth, then my father did something that my mother didn't like—like smack one of us in the face or drink himself silly and throw all his cigarette butts on the ground outside their bedroom window, then she closed herself off, and he leaned over her like a half-dead tree with too many branches at the top. A person had to wonder how they had five kids—including poor Elizabeth. I looked at Sarah-Anne, who was peeling the skin off her thigh. Stupid girl, I thought. She always wasted the best parts.

Andy too kept looking at Sarah-Anne like a weasel at a bird's nest—my mother said weasels ate unhatched young when they got real hungry. I had a nightmare that night that a weasel crawled into my mother's stomach, through her girl parts, and ate Elizabeth right out of her. As far as I knew, Elizabeth was unhatched young. I asked Freddy about unhatched young the next day. He said that meant eggs. Elizabeth hadn't been an egg. It wasn't a weasel who took her.

Sarah-Anne, who never really looked at anyone—only stared—looked back at Andy. I thought there was something between them, a lot like an unhatched egg. Something waiting to be born. Something now hidden. I cleared my throat loudly, like a lawnmower on glass, just to get the attention away from whatever they were thinking.

"Jeez, Kay," Peter said. "Excuse you."

"It's not like I ripped a big fart at the table," I said. "I got crud in my throat." I watched Andy closely. He smiled a little. Sarah-Anne was smiling too. She always laughed when someone said the word *fart*. That and *dick*.

"Watch your mouth," my father said crossly. I closed my eyes and nodded. I had a mind to get a chicken leg before dinner was through. I needed to cool it.

Andy ate with a healthy appetite. He took some cucumbers from a dish where they sat under a heavy snow of salt and pepper. He smiled at my mother. "I like these," he said. My mother nodded in approval. Freddy and Peter were strangely quiet, while Sarah-Anne did more trimming and fussing over her food than she did eat it. Her white hair hung around her shoulders, like a curtain about to close on the mystery of her inner being. I didn't want to solve that mystery—leave well enough alone.

I was normally hell-bent on talking at dinner, trying to hold the conversation together, keep everything moving, but I was too frantic on this evening to ask dull questions, or make comments about school friends and the food. I was afraid I'd ask Andy if his mama was murdered, and what was up with his daddy? To avoid utter foolishness, I stayed quiet—having never trusted myself in stressful situations.

We finished dinner and were left staring at one another again. No topic had taken hold; the conversation had been like splitting nails and chewing on them. Freddy was reading a paperback with tattered pages throughout the meal, and Andy didn't seem to know how to speak—I'd suspected as much. His father appeared to suffer from the same ailment. I went from sitting nervously quiet to rattling on a mile a minute about my teacher, Mrs. Clancy, and my homework that I didn't understand, and my foot that itched since yesterday, and that we used to have a dog named Elkie, but she died of the worm. I spent my whole wad in about ten minutes of fast-talking and exaggeration. No one said a word after my last comments on the state of the gravel road past the school, which was kicking up more dust in the hot weather than a sandstorm in the African desert.

"We can't hardly see our math equations," I explained of the air quality. "The wind got going something serious the other day, and I just about choked during Social Studies. We're learning about World War I, and it's a lot of reading, so this kid, Samuel, opens the door and walks in with a cloud of gravel dust, and we almost had to evacuate. They wore those masks back in the day, so I suggested we do the same, but the school's on a budget. That's why we don't have a paved road back there."

Freddy nodded after sighing loudly. My mother looked like distant fog. Andy smiled like I was speaking a foreign language that he thought sounded like pigs giggling, and that was that.

"Anyone want some ice cream?" Peter asked. "My treat if I can take the car."

Peter wasn't yet sixteen, soon enough, but he was occasionally allowed to drive the car on his own when my mother needed help with something or my father was feeling too tired to go into town.

My mother said that Peter could drive to the Texaco. Andy turned to me and said he needed to be getting home. I'd hardly noticed that he sat at the dinner table without a shirt. That wasn't allowed in our house, but I figured we were giving the kid a break, because he was living out there in the water with his handsome but silent father, and his mother was dead under their house—water in her lungs.

His skin was the color of maple syrup. I wanted to touch it. I caught Sarah-Anne looking a little too closely at his caramel nipples. She reached a hand but pulled it back. That was another thing that happened—a couple of kids at school complained that Sarah-Anne was touching them the wrong way, like a pervert. I frowned, preferring to think about Andy and ice cream rather than how Sarah-Anne didn't go to school anymore on account of her terrible troubles.

"You gotta stay to have ice cream," I told Andy as we all got up and walked around aimlessly in the kitchen, and then the living room with its creaking wood floors, and then the screened porch where Freddy suggested we once again watch *Hoosiers*.

"I really oughta go," he said, putting his hand on my shoulder and then his arm around me, walking toward the back door like I was his girl. My stomach dropped out of both embarrassment and excitement. The two emotions, experienced at exactly the same time, were a rush of blood to my cloudy head. I felt like I was on the gravel road outside my Social Studies classroom, breathing heavily without the aid of a wartime mask. "But I like having dinner with you." He leaned in and kissed me on my cheek. I saw my dad's face over my shoulder; he pressed his lips together and didn't blink.

I walked Andy, in Freddy's company, to the edge of our yard and then let him go the rest of the way on his own. My mother made a weak suggestion that someone should make sure he got home okay, but Andy told her not to worry.

"It ain't even dark yet," he said. "And I wouldn't want Kay walkin' back by herself."

"He could call us when he got home," I said too eagerly.

"No phone." He winked.

Freddy didn't mention the kiss nor Andy's dinner visit at all as we crossed over the back edge of our land and returned to the house. He was busy talking about a girl in his class who had headgear and braces.

"I don't want braces," he began and then went on at length about how cruel it was for parents to force children to be "so ugly!"

"Damn, Freddy, who is this girl? Don't call her ugly like that. She's probably feeling awful about herself anyway."

"But who would do that to their kid?" he asked.

"Ugly people procreate all the time, and God knows what they're thinkin', but I don't know if it's child cruelty."

"I just can't stop looking at her face," he went on, "with this big thing on it pulling at her teeth. When you were saying that nonsense about the gas masks at dinner, all I could think was that Charlotte Reins has got a big gas mask on."

"She can come sit in my classroom if she wants. She'll be the only one of us who's safe. Yeah. Can you believe Andy kissed me plain as day like that?"

"Yeah, he's kind of high on himself, isn't he?"

"What's that supposed to mean? And I wasn't talkin' nonsense at dinner anyway."

"I don't know. I guess if I didn't go to school and went around in a boat with my dad, who may or may not have killed my mama, I'd have a way about me too."

"You *do* have a way about you," I told him, "but it's not that way, and whatever... His daddy didn't kill his mama. That's crazy talk." I tossed my long ponytail around my shoulders for effect. "Did Mom tell you that?"

"Maybe." He shoved his hands in his pockets and kept on with his head low. "I don't remember."

"Woman's full of stories. For a person who never leaves the fucking house, she sure knows everybody's business." I glanced sideways, blushing. God, I loved that word, but it did make me feel a little guilty to say it in front of Freddy. He didn't seem to care— for once. "You know Andy told me there's a lady back here with monkeys?"

"Yeah." Freddy nodded.

"You know her?"

"No...but I heard of her."

"I'll bet, like who the hell in Bledsoe has monkeys?" I said. "He kissed me right there in the living room."

"There's ruins from a fort." Freddy nodded distantly, ignoring what I'd said about the kiss.

"What fort?"

"I don't know. A fort from a long time ago, like maybe even before the Revolution. Like from Marco Polo."

"Yeah, he likes to kiss me, I think."

"Okay, Kay."

Peter was in the living room when we got home, sitting in silent frustration with my father, who was also glaring. Peter had an open carton of coffee-flavored ice cream in his hand and had clearly just finished saying something offensive. I didn't want to get into their trouble, because I had Andy's kiss on my mind. I thought it would be nice to go to my bedroom and dream of him for a bit, with my knees grasped at my chest and my lips in a pout.

"Hey, there's a fort back in the water," I exclaimed upon entering the room. My dad looked up at me but didn't speak.

"There's a fort out here, like maybe some time somebody conquered this place, or even gave a crap about it, you know. Like…maybe Bledsoe was important back in the day." I nodded excitedly. I was just about to remind them that Andy had kissed me, because I didn't think anyone had made a big enough deal out of it, but Peter interrupted.

"Yeah, it's a stone fort, but that's all fallen down now. We used to go back there… It's mostly underwater."

"Did you see the monkeys?" I asked.

"Yeah, but it's just one monkey. The other one died." Peter looked at me then went back to glaring at my father.

Freddy opened his mouth as if to explain something, probably about Marco Polo or how stones were made, but I announced my departure just as he was about to speak. "Well, good night, all! What a fabulous evening if I do say so myself!"

My father looked at me from his chair. His head and eyes were at an angle, but a slightly different one, so it appeared as if he was on one side of a sway. I thought he was smiling a little, but it was that same kind of smile I'd seen before—like I didn't really know what was going on.

I was smiling in my own suspicious way—I too had something to hide. I decided that I liked being a suspicious person. I walked to my room and shut the door. Peter called out to me that he bought butter pecan. I called back to give me a minute. I stared at the ceiling and determined that I would only get married once, and only to Andy.

The next morning, my father told me over cornflakes that if I ever did "that" again, he would kill me.

"What's that?" I asked like I couldn't hear death threats.

"I'll kill you," he said.

"Isn't that nice…" I said nervously.

"Kay," my father began but paused.

I heard the door to my parents' room open—a small crack of sound and then a little slip of air. My father glanced up. I knew my mother was watching us.

I was scared for a moment, but it was old fear, forgotten fear about forgotten experiences—a thick memory caught in the fence of my thoughts where it stayed, in limbo, like a reflection behind my head in a mirror I couldn't find.

Sarah-Anne was sitting next to me at the table. She tipped her bowl of cereal over and watched the milk run like a white river over my dad's newspaper. She smiled at the table. It did not smile back. "I'm gonna kill you," she whispered.

CHAPTER 8

The kids at school were on to me, or rather they were on to Andy, who'd been highly visible riding in his father's air boat along the road every afternoon with his shirt off. The Webbers had nets and hats like Indiana Jones and caused quite a stir in their shirtless glory. I was not the only one who'd noticed them.

"I heard they ran off to Mexico to escape the law," Mary Winger told me.

"California," I said. I was about to explain what had happened with Andy's mother when I decided to keep my mouth shut.

"Why'd he come back here?" a girl named Maddie asked. "I'da stayed in California."

"I think he's in love with a local girl. Very beautiful and interesting," I said before excusing myself to the restroom, where I looked in the mirror and said over and over again, "Shut up, you idiot!" I wanted it to be true though. I wanted that story to spread like wildfire, very specifically about me.

I was trying to make myself scarce around the house. My mother was eyeing me with particular interest, like she couldn't wait to get something off her chest and throw it at me. The afternoons were quiet with no adventure awaiting. My father had made himself clear about going back to Andy's house, what with the promise to murder me and all. Cort's mother didn't need milk or didn't have any cash to give us, and Sarah-Anne was absorbed in her collection of thimbles; she spent hours each day stacking them, then unstacking them, then realigning them from large to short and back again. I tried to talk to her about them, but she didn't answer my questions. "What's this one here?" "I like lilac... Is that lilac?" "I can barely get my finger in here...too tight!" Nothing. That was the thing about Sarah-Anne—she would always look at you, right direct in the eye, but she wouldn't talk. The only person she talked to any was my mother; this was the kind of thing my mother had been hoping for her whole life: someone for whom she could be the entire world.

For lack of anything better to do, and because getting to the bottom of all things related to Andy was my only interest, I dared to ask my mom about Andy's mother.

"Did you know her?" I asked. "Emily. Before she died."

We were sitting at the kitchen table, just the two of us, much like I thought moms and daughters were supposed to do. The boys were out helping my father in the shed; the house was dead quiet. I was about to suggest we get the nail polish before realizing that we didn't have any. My mother didn't go in for polish, or bows, or lipstick. She didn't go in for much. The sun was at a slant out back and in our eyes. Neither of us moved out of its line of fire. She didn't answer me about Emily but instead said I was moving "awful fast for a little girl."

"Huh?" I said, thrown.

"He's gonna get the wrong idea with you running back to his place every hour of the day and night," she said. "Andy."

"*He* kissed *me*!" I argued.

"Right, but I don't want him to get the wrong idea about how you were raised."

I paused, thinking how odd it was that in Bledsoe, mothers were concerned with appearances when we stole electricity, had depression ten months out of the year, and the neighbor may or may not be feeding their dog whiskey with his kibble.

"He won't," I said. "I'm going to be his friend, and when we get older...old enough to get married, then I'm going to marry him, but not until we're of proper age. Then Dad can't stop me."

"Nobody needs to get married anytime soon."

"You got married at eighteen," I said matter-of-factly. "And to Dad, who was a bad seed! And anyway, how was I raised? I don't have a clue how I was raised. I was here, but I don't even know..."

My mother looked at me for a while without speaking then said she was tired.

"Oh, come on, Mama." I slapped the table a little. "Can't we ever talk about anything interesting? How'd she drown out there? Mrs. Webber…how'd she die?"

"Quiet, Kay," my mother said, darting her eyes without moving her head.

"Did she fall in or, like…"

"Why do you think they left here?" she said quickly before standing up. "They've been gone a long time. I'm tired."

"How long?"

"Long time," she said again. "After Emily drowned," my mother said before turning on her heel. She was barefoot and in a long dress, much like mine but down to her ankles. "They found her floating under the house. On her stomach. Her face was in the water. Bricks…" My mother shuddered a little but her mouth twitched with a backward grin. "Most of 'em were gone, but she had bricks in her pockets, pullin' her down. Rest was on the bottom. On the sea floor."

"Who can fit a brick in their pocket?" I asked, looking down at my dress. "Well, I guess you and me. You sure make the pockets big enough." I laughed a little too, even though none of it was at all funny.

"It's hard to swim with bricks in your pockets." My mother put her small, pale hand on the table and stifled something that had bubbled up inside her. I saw her grip the edge of the table with her thumb then release it. I suppose whatever it was had passed.

"Well, that's not Andy's fault—that she couldn't swim with bricks in her pants or whatever. And I want to marry Andy. Plenty of people have dead mothers. Look at Lauren Walker. Her mama died, then her stepmama too. Jesus Lord in heaven!"

"No one needs to get married," my mother said sharply. She stood up from the table and pressed her hands onto her thighs.

"Why'd they say his daddy did it?"

"Oh, people say all sorts of stuff. It was 'cause they left. If you leave, that means you're guilty. Stayin' would have meant he had nothin' to do with it. Anyway—"

"I'm still gonna marry him. Even if his daddy is a killer. Maybe she had it coming. Emily." I tilted my head to the side, feeling very rebellious and willing to say nasty things to my mother.

"Well…I don't know about that." She walked into her bedroom after lightly tapping the refrigerator door with her index finger. She didn't say another word and let the door close behind her.

I sat very still, feeling as though someone was playing a terrible joke on me. I looked out the kitchen window and saw my father. He'd been standing at the edge of our land—at least the part that was solid. He caught me noticing him and flinched. He had a shovel in his hand. He turned around and walked toward the shed with his shoulders hunched.

"Oh, go shove a brick in it," I said with a chuckle, only because he couldn't hear me. I had to watch what I said to my dad, but not when we were on opposite sides of a wall. And anyway, we did have a big pile of bricks in the shed. I thought I might put some in my pockets later just to see. God knows why we had bricks anywhere—our house was made of fake wood and tin, not a goddamned brick in sight.

I stayed at the table a bit longer, mostly pondering marriage and what it would be like to be Andy's wife. I thought I'd leave school right then, leave Bledsoe, leave everything, and run off with Andy in the blink of an eye if only he would ask.

I continued to think deeply, now about Andy's lips on my cheek, when it dawned on me that I'd never seen my father do that to my mother. I rarely even saw them touch. My mother fell once, slipping on the wet floor in our kitchen, which was slanted at a fairly severe angle—the house my father built was not all that well constructed. He helped her to her feet and ran his hand over her head like he was stroking a puppy. She jerked away from him and knocked his hand with her small fist. He pretended to laugh, but like alligator tears, I knew he was putting us on.

I was still sitting at the kitchen table, mostly thinking about Andy and a little about Elkie, our dog who died, when I heard a loud bang on the door, a rat-a-tat that carried throughout the house, like ice breaking on ice. At first I thought something was wrong. I looked at my father, who was now sitting on the screened porch in an old wicker chair on a faded cushion with a level in his hand. He was rocking the level back and forth; I could see the liquid in the little vial at its center move from side to side. When we heard another fist on the door, my father jumped as if being awoken from sleep and ran to the front of the house. He threw open the door with a jerk.

"Oh, Nile!" I heard my dad say loudly but not exactly like he was surprised. I bolted out of my seat and scurried to where my father was standing with his clenched hand still on the door handle. He was breathing heavy with his body stiff as a board. Andy's father stood waiting on the porch. He was clothed properly this time and wearing shoes. My father smiled at him awkwardly; he was clearly uncomfortable or nervous—an uncommon sight, but he tried to appear welcoming. "How the hell are you?" They both extended their hands in the manner of men.

"I'm doin' well, Clay." Andy's dad grinned but spoke very softly as I had come to accept was his way of doing things. "I just wanted to say hello and thank you for having Andy over for dinner. He enjoyed himself."

"We liked havin' him here!" I piped in. I stepped forward, almost between the two of them. "Nice to see you again, Mr. Webber."

"Hi…" He was searching for my name.

"Kay," I told him, not offended in the slightest. "Kay Whitaker."

"Good to meet you."

"We've met, Mr. Webber. I've been to your house on sticks."

"Right, I know." He smiled.

"Kay," my father said sternly.

"Where's Andy?" I asked, ignoring him. I had no interest in improving my behavior.

"He's at home."

"You leave him out there by himself?"

"Kay," my father said a little more loudly.

"They live out in the middle of the water," I said. "I mean, it's literally in the middle of the water."

"Kay, go to the kitchen."

"Not hungry," I said. My father grabbed my arm and pulled me back a little. I frowned and walked into the house, the kitchen, and then to the refrigerator. I opened it loudly, letting the jars and bottles in the door bang against the shelves. I knew this annoyed him and, therefore, couldn't help myself. My father stayed by the front door talking to Nile Webber but did not invite him in. I tried to listen in on their conversation, but Nile Webber was mumbling. My father's voice wasn't any clearer.

Peter had come inside and was sitting at the kitchen table, sweaty and dirty. He smelled like the marsh dipped in teenage hormones.

I'd taken a jar of peanut butter from the shelf and a large spoon from the drawer. "Dad says not to eat 'cause you're bored, but then he tells me to go in the kitchen all the time. What else am I supposed to do in here? Nothing to do in the kitchen but eat. So many mixed messages in this house. I swear. I don't know why Mom always gets creamy," I said of the peanut butter. "Always creamy."

"Because me, Dad, and Freddy like it."

"Me and Sarah-Anne like crunchy!"

"Sarah-Anne doesn't even eat peanut butter," he said. "Who came to the door?" He finally looked up at me. He'd been pretending to concentrate on the apparently highly interesting spiral notebook lying on the table in front of him.

"Andy's dad." I watched Peter for a reaction. He squinted slightly before reaching for his math book peeking out of his backpack, which lay on the floor next to his feet, and sat back in his chair.

"Yeah, seems like the Webbers are here all the time now," I said, trying to get a rise.

"Whatever," Peter said. "You know someone was here about Sarah-Anne too?"

"He's not here about Sarah-Anne. He's here about Andy. Who I'm in love with."

"No, not him. There was a lady from the state here."

"Why? 'Cause she's not going to school no more?"

"I don't know. Mom was crying."

"Where was Dad?"

"He left when they showed up."

"Shocker."

"Right." Peter looked back down at the table.

"I wish Andy was here," I said. "You know I'm in love?"

"Oh, Kay, come on," Peter said, putting his pencil down. "Stop bein' so loopy."

"I don't even know what loopy means." I put my spoon in the sink, still covered in a thick layer of peanut butter. I'd gone off the taste halfway through.

"It means a person without logic or reason who just wants to get everybody riled up."

"That's unintentional," I said, knowing it was mostly true. "I don't know why they don't take Sarah-Anne to the doctor."

Peter closed his eyes and tilted his head back—his body rigid. This was what he did when I'd said too much, taken too much comfort in our conversation. He didn't want to be my friend, and more importantly, he didn't want me to think he was. "Whatever, Kay," he said. "Don't leave a dirty spoon in the sink. You're so freakin' lazy."

It felt like Mr. Webber was at our house for a decade and a half, and that my exile in the kitchen would be permanent, when I finally heard the front door close with a thud. My father turned the lock heavily but didn't move for a few seconds before I heard his footsteps coming toward the kitchen.

"Was that your old friend?" I asked when he made his way toward where Peter was sitting, hunched over his trigonometry book.

"I don't have any friends," my father said sharply.

"Ain't that the truth."

"He wants Andy to stay with us for a while."

Peter looked up, letting his pencil fall to the table. I nearly jumped out of my skin.

"He can stay in my room!" I said. "I'll sleep on the porch."

"Would you just hush up for a minute?" Peter scolded. "What did you say, Dad?"

"I said that was fine, but only for a month 'til Nile gets things together..." He wouldn't look us in the eye. If I'd known any better, I would have said he was a man with a guilty conscience. I wondered if he felt bad for Andy and his daddy. Clay Whitaker never felt bad for anyone but himself, and we didn't help other people out. But it was to be a year of firsts.

"Dad," Peter said, "should we really—"

"I gotta do something," my father said, interrupting. He was talking more to himself. I looked at Peter, but he didn't respond.

My dad patted the doorframe lightly and then walked back to the bedroom where my mother was in retreat, quiet and withdrawn. Sometimes, when I saw a turtle, I thought about my mother. She wasn't born with a shell though, so she had to find places to hide.

"Where's Andy going to sleep?" I called out. My dad didn't answer.

I looked beyond the living room; there was Sarah-Anne on her bed, staring out the small window above her pillow. She was looking at the marsh, toward Andy's house.

CHAPTER 9

I got small pains in my stomach that were like good pains, but pains nonetheless, when we talked about Andy coming to live with us. We were told that Nile Webber was in a bad way financially and had to go out on a big boat for a while so they'd have more money. I wondered why my dad didn't do the same—it seemed we always needed money.

"It's gonna be so fun," I told Peter and Freddy on the way to school the next day. I was in a sweater for the first time that school year. The boys didn't have to wear old, pilly sweaters. They had windbreakers—better in every way; it's always paid to have a penis. I was thankful for the relief but a little concerned that with things cooling down, the water was going to get downright unbearable. My first concerns were always of Andy—especially when it came to weather and him out there in that house on the water, but I didn't have to worry too long, because Andy was coming to our house. I wouldn't need to swim to see him or fret over him falling under his stilt house and dying of hypothermia. God has mysterious ways that my mind has never understood. It was such good timing with the cold and all that. "So fun!" I repeated.

"I don't know about that," Freddy said.

"I do," I said. "And anyway, we have to look out for him. You know Mom said that his mama drowned, so I mean…" I watched Peter for a response.

"You can kill someone by drowning them," Freddy said.

"Jesus," Peter said, annoyed. "Shut up with his mother dying."

"She had bricks in her pockets," I said. "And here I thought I was the only one with pockets big enough for bricks." I laughed too enthusiastically.

"Mom told you that?" Peter asked.

"Yeah!" I shrugged and smiled. "How old was Andy then anyway…I mean, how long ago did she die?"

"I don't know," Freddy said.

"He was little," Peter answered.

"Did you know them?" I asked Peter.

"Not really—it was…like ten years ago or something. Just leave it alone."

It was quiet for a while. I figured someone was trying to think of something to say that would change the subject. It didn't matter if we were talking about dead mothers or drowning or anything—so long as we were talking about Andy, I was in good spirits.

"That woman's coming back today," Freddy said. "The woman who came to get Sarah-Anne...I heard her say she was coming back."

"What's that got to do with anything? Sarah-Anne's got poop marks in her underwear," I said with a small, angry laugh. "Can't even wipe her own ass right. Is the woman a professional ass-wiper or something?"

"Shut the fuck up, Kay!" Peter growled. It caught me off guard. "They're gonna take her away and all you can do is make fun of her." His face was as red as Freddy's after a short, slow jog. "They're trying to take her away."

"Sorry," I said sincerely. We kept walking while I tried to think of something else to say. "Why are they gonna take her away?"

"I don't know!" Peter threw his hands up. "I don't know what's going on, but Mom and Dad are in trouble. That kid shouldn't be coming to stay with us."

I frowned at the *that kid* remark. "His dad's in trouble too," I said.

"No, he needs money," Peter argued.

"What did Sarah-Anne do?" I asked.

Freddy sniffled loudly and cleared his throat. "There was an officer at the school yesterday too...about..."

We all stopped walking at the same time. "But Sarah-Anne

doesn't go to school," I said. A strong breeze blew up the sides of our faces. I had chill bumps on my arms—I wasn't sure if it was from the weather or the strange news.

"Welty," Freddy said. "Officer Welty."

"From the police?" Peter asked, head tilted so far down, I swore he couldn't get any air through his windpipe. It was like he was trying to control something that just wasn't going to be wrangled. Ever.

"He came to talk to me," Freddy said. "I got called into the counselor's office."

"The weakest link," I said.

"What?" Both boys looked at me with their shoulders drawn— their eyebrows were in one long line. We started walking again.

"I just mean—" I started to say but stopped myself. It was awfully easy to make fun of Freddy. Too easy sometimes.

"What did he want?" Peter said after a few pounding steps.

"He asked me to get Mom and Dad to sign a paper so they could test my saliva."

"What?" I asked. For some reason Peter was picking up the pace. I was struggling to stay with him. Freddy was uncoordinated as the day was long, but he had sizable legs and was keeping up just fine.

"Spit test," he said like I was an idiot.

"Why?" Peter said.

"I guess the medical records are messed up."

"Like everything else in Bledsoe," I said.

"This doesn't make sense," Peter said before taking off in a trot, with his head still down.

I looked at Freddy, who was watching Peter and not at all concerned with me. "Did Mom and Dad sign the permission slip?"

"No," Freddy said. "But I did." He pressed his glasses firmly on the bridge of his nose and mumbled that he had to go.

"Don't talk to anyone!" I heard Peter yell while he quickly traveled away from us. He was looking mostly at me. I rolled my eyes. I didn't know what else I was supposed to do.

Not a lot of preparation went into Andy's stay with us. I know, because I heard my mother ask about it, that Andy's father gave us some money to cover food expenses. He was going on a fishing boat that would travel all the way to the Panama Canal and back. Andy wasn't old enough to go with him and work too, and Mr. Webber didn't want him out at the house by himself for that long because of "trouble" in the area. I knew all about it from eavesdropping on my parents. They talked circles around my questions and seemed angrier with one another than normal, which was a high bar. "They don't have any friends here anymore, Sue-Bess," my father said behind their closed bedroom door. I was pretending to get something out of the refrigerator and took my time.

"Then why'd they come back?" my mother said in her meek, mouselike way. "Shoulda stayed gone."

"He's a kid." My dad sounded like maybe he was trying to convince himself. "Nile's got nowhere else to put him."

When my dad spoke to me, Peter, and Freddy about it, he used a lot of hand gestures and serious faces. "He doesn't want Andy out there alone. He might fall in with a bad crowd—people without direction," my father told us, like he was explaining the nature of sex. I blushed and looked down. If Mr. Webber was concerned about people without direction, then he shouldn't send his only son to stay with the Whitaker family. "He isn't safe out there by himself, especially not if people know he's there alone," my father said for clarification. "They might try to take advantage of him." I was certainly one of these people who were trying to take advantage, but I kept this to myself. "We need to help each other out now and then," he said to our confused faces. I could tell Peter wasn't buying a word of it.

"Right, Dad," he said. "We're always helping people out, aren't we?"

I, on the other hand, was almost unable to contain my excitement and scurried about the house like a mouse with the shakes, nearly vibrating across the creaky floors. "What blanket is he going to use?" I asked. The porch got cold at night. This was a reasonable question.

"I think he'll sleep in the living room," my mother answered while folding towels at the kitchen table.

"Can he swim?" I asked. She dropped the towel she had in

her hand; it was dark blue, with holes and frayed edges. I never used that towel after my showers, because I knew it was my dad's favorite. He complained if it wasn't ready for him—the king of the castle. Too bad it was a shitty wreck of a towel. Imagine taking pride in that.

"Who?" my mother asked.

"Andy."

"I don't know, Kay. Can he?" She did not look up. I heard Sarah-Anne come into the kitchen; a creak in the loosest floorboard gave her away.

"Can *she* swim?" I pointed at Sarah-Anne. I was on my knees on one of the chairs. I balanced dangerously on the edge and enjoyed the risk of falling.

"She doesn't need to swim," my mother replied.

"I swam all the way to Route 54."

"You shouldn't have. You coulda drowned." My mother refolded the blue towel for the third time.

"Like Mrs. Webber."

My mother's face twitched. "Have to be careful in the water."

I looked at Sarah-Anne, who was watching me closely. She scratched her privates and stuck her tongue out the side of her mouth. "Now you don't go back to their house," I said, pointing at her. "If you fall off the porch, you'll end up fish food just like Mrs. Webber."

"Emily," Sarah-Anne said softly, with her tongue still hanging.

I slid off the chair and stumbled onto the floor—too much wiggling. I'd snagged my tights and heard a thread snap. "I like that name," I said, because I couldn't think of anything else to say. No one bothered to help me up.

My mother looked at Sarah-Anne. "Okay, sweetie." My mother never called me sweetie.

CHAPTER 10

A couple of nights later, during a particularly sullen dinner, I asked, "Can we please be happy while he's here? Please." We were eating baked potatoes and one chicken finger a piece. They were from a bag in the freezer and had the taste of something that sat too long under a layer of frost. We had honey mustard sauce, thank God, or the meal would have been inedible. "We are the saddest lot this side of the Mississippi River, and I can hardly stand it. Andy's gonna tell his daddy he'd rather live out there in the tree fort than with us and our long faces. He'd probably rather get killed than stay here with all this silence and people staring at their forks, like a fork is gonna do something interesting. God, there isn't anything interesting about the floor, or the top of your shoes, or your spoon, or whatever it is everybody's lookin' at all the time. Jesus bless!" I took in the view from where I sat at the table. "Don't look at me like that," I said. "You're making those same faces I hate."

"We're not unhappy," Peter said a little defensively.

"Well, why is everybody so quiet and lonely-acting all the time then?" I still had one bite left of my chicken finger. I was saving it, afraid that after eating the final piece, I would be left with nothing but mealy potatoes for the rest of my life.

"We can talk, Kay," my mother said softly.

"Yeah, but you don't—none of you. You never talk, like it's a disease to have something to say in this house—that can't be right. I get so flustered in this family. No one wants to talk to me, and now we have Andy coming, and he's very loving, so I know he's gonna want to chat, and if people are either mad at each other or being peculiar, then he's probably going to want to run away." I'd been motoring pretty quick and mispronounced *peculiar*. I saw that Freddy was about to tell me—he had that look on his face he got when he thought he knew more than everyone else about a certain topic; he made this face most of the time. "Pick Ewww You Larrrrr!" I said at the top of my voice. "I know how to say it! And anyway, he lost his mother to the marsh—drowning accident." I nodded somberly. "So it's like we gotta be kind to him to help him get through the sorrows."

"I doubt that," my father said, about Andy I had to guess. I caught my mother giving him a harsh look that quickly vanished when she saw me watching them.

"See, that's the thing," I said, pressing on the table firmly and with great deliberation. "Nobody ever knows if they're comin' or goin' with this family. I tell ya, that's exactly what Mrs. Robbins said. 'You never know if you're comin' or goin' with the Whitakers.' She said it, not me, and it's God's truth, I'm sayin'. I really am."

"That's one of those sayings that don't mean anything," Freddy said like an official sayings expert.

"That was Sarah-Anne's teacher," Peter announced.

"I know that," my mother said. Sarah-Anne looked at the table and continued chewing with her mouth open.

"Mrs. Robbins doesn't believe in homeschooling," my mother said, mostly to my father.

"Oh, so that's what we're doing around here? Homeschooling?" This was the first I'd heard of the word.

"Mrs. Robbins has always had it in for our family," my father said.

"Oh, yeah," I said. "Her and everybody else...your mama and daddy, Del Dickson, the people al'ays comin' to the door all the damn time, every Tom, Dick, and Harry"—Sarah-Anne laughed and scooted very abruptly in her chair, almost knocking herself onto the floor—"we ever met has it in for our family. The Whitakers—famous for bein' so tough to squash."

"Mrs. Robbins should mind her own business," my father said.

"Her students are her business." Peter was also looking at the table.

"Eat your food," my mother said, wiping her mouth with the folded paper towels we used for napkins. A couple times a month, when we were low, we used toilet paper squares. "Eat your food," she repeated.

Sarah-Anne stood up and walked out of the kitchen giggling to herself. "Dick," I heard her say on her way out. She didn't have to explain where she was going. I fumed a little thinking how I was never allowed to come and go as I pleased.

It further served to anger me that my dad held the honor of being the only one of us given two chicken fingers. I couldn't figure out why. All I'd seen him do that day was move his lawn chair from one side of the yard to the other to avoid direct sunlight and then, later, to put himself in its path. He was halfway through the second one and eating slowly, I thought, to prove to us that the head who wears the crown is only heavy because it's better fed—and gets the blue towel.

"I'm glad Andy's coming," I said, probably because I knew I was bothering everyone. "'Cause I just don't get enough talking in at school. We don't live near a soul out here, and they hate talking to me," I said, pointing at Freddy and Peter, "so I'm stuck. Stuck in silence. If I was going to write a song, that's what I'd call it."

My father laughed sadly and leaned over to me to rub my back and said something along the lines of "there, there." He was none too far away—we squeezed six people around a kitchen table the size of a lampshade. My mother grimaced a little. I knew she didn't like when he came to my rescue—or anyone else's. After all, he couldn't save Elizabeth. For my mother, it was all about the ones who got away.

I wiped my eyes furiously and tried to stop the wave of tears threatening to spill over. So far I'd only let a few leak. I didn't want to completely melt down. I was half-sad about being so lonely with a backwards family and half-sad that my dad was being nice to me. He had a kind streak in him, but it was rare and went away as fast as it came on. I'd be kicked to the curb again as soon as he started thinking about all the things I'd done wrong in my life. He could switch from hugging to backhanding in a blink.

"Don't write a sad song," my dad said, patting my arm. My mother rolled her eyes. I collected myself and was fuming mad at her for the way she could never seem to care about me. I had a list of uncomfortable topics to choose from when I wanted someone to feel as bad as I did. I thought of mentioning people coming to the house earlier about Sarah-Anne, and then Freddy's spit test, but I kept that card up my sleeve. I'd get to her later.

After dinner, I helped the boys clear the table before heading to my room, where I did some exercises on the small space of bare floor next to my bed. I'd become more interested in physical fitness ever since I was the last one chosen for both soccer and kickball at recess. This was a recent development, as I'd been considered quite sporty until this year. I heard one of the boys in my class say I was too tall and "gangly" to play well. I figured I needed some muscles. I had good endurance on account of my upbringing in the wilds of the marshlands, and I kept up with my brothers, who were always tossing something around that required good hand-eye coordination—well, Peter, not Freddy. Sarah-Anne couldn't even jump rope properly—I didn't want to get lumped in with that well-known fact on top of the way Freddy ran like a go-cart with only three wheels.

I did several sit-ups using my bed frame as a hook for my feet. I did as many push-ups as I could, which was only about seven, and then did frog jumps, which we sometimes had to practice in PE. I was tired and ready to throw in the towel when I imagined Andy in the air boat, and then his father next to him—his distraught face cracked with remorse that he was not able to save his wife from the evil swirling water under their house. In my vision, they were both tanned and fearless having survived something real. I was suddenly filled with vigorous energy to do more exercising. I did the rounds again and then sat down to stretch. I was a little sweaty and breathing heavily.

I walked out into the living room, where Peter was reading a book for class. My father was sharpening his knives. He had several. We were not permitted to touch any of them, only to look at them like the small children we hadn't been in years. My father cared for his collection like one would a premature kitten. He sharpened and polished the blades at least once a week. I sat down on the couch beside him and watched him work with far less wonder than I used to.

"You're sweaty," he said with a smile.

"I was working out. I'm too skinny."

"You're just fine. Most people want to be skinnier."

"Not in this family. We're all a bunch of beanpoles who eat nothin' but potatoes. I'm starving to death half the time." It was an offhand comment that I hadn't meant in any particular way except maybe to complain about all the damned potatoes we were eating, but my father frowned and didn't say another word. A little while later, he went out on the back stoop with a drink in his hand, looking at the stars and listening to the summer bugs, who were moving away or dying due to the chill in the air. They would soon be impossible to hear when it dipped below fifty.

"I think I hurt Dad's feelings," I told Peter before going to bed. He was still reading on the couch. My mother was over at the daybed talking to Sarah-Anne. It was a slow, quiet whisper—the only noise I associated with either of them.

"You always hurt Dad's feelings," Peter said without looking up.

"Somebody's always out to get him," I agreed. "E'en me."

"What goes around comes around," Peter said.

"Huh?"

"Guilty conscience."

"About what?" I asked.

Peter didn't answer.

CHAPTER 11

The following morning my father wasn't home when we woke up. My mother was in their room with the door open, which was unusual; she typically kept us out with the sturdiness of a bull.

"Where's Dad?" I asked Freddy, who was buttering toast. He'd taken to wearing headphones around the house. He got a CD Walkman for his birthday, and you would have thought—after having almost no interest in it for the past six months—that it was now glued to his head.

"What?" he asked, lifting one of the phones off of his left ear.

"I said, 'Where the hell is Dad?'"

"I don't know. The people from the state were here again this morning. He left."

"With Sarah-Anne?"

"No, she's here." Freddy looked down.

"Did you give it to Welty?" I whispered loudly.

"What?"

"The spit stick."

"Quiet." He pressed down hard on his bread, causing it to tear. "Seriously, Kay. And it's Officer Welty."

I picked up another butter knife from the counter and stuck it in the bar of Land O'Lakes Freddy was using on his bread. "Well, that's just great," I said loudly. "I didn't hear 'em. I didn't hear the people from the state! Always comin' round!" If anyone heard me, they didn't respond. "Jeez, it's gonna be a long day."

We took off for school in the chilly morning air. I was wearing tights with my dresses every day now. After hearing a classmate comment that I'd worn the same thing "since the day she was born!" I thought to ask my mother if I could get a pair of pants. The girls in my class were changing—wearing bras, and makeup, and buying their clothes at the mall. I was the same as I'd always been. I figured pants would be a good start to all the changes I wanted to make for myself.

"Gettin' cold," I said, trying to make conversation with my brothers.

"That's why that kid's coming to live with us," Freddy said. He had his headphones around his neck like a tight necklace. "Too cold to live out on the water like that."

"And his dad's got a job," I said. "Like our dad used to."

Peter grunted a little too loudly to go ignored.

"What?" Freddy asked.

"A job is some place you go every day that pays for your health insurance. Our dad's never had a job," Peter said.

"He worked at the stereo store," I said.

"Yeah," Freddy joined in.

Peter took a breath. "Got fired and begged for his job back then got fired again. That's not having a real job, and Andy Webber's dad is the same. You don't go off on a boat every once in a while if you're a responsible person. You hold down a job day in and day out." Peter looked straight ahead and walked a little faster.

"Gosh, somebody's in a bad mood," I sneered.

"I'm not in a bad mood, but I'm not gonna go work only when I'm broke when I grow up."

"Fine, don't. Where did Dad go this morning anyway?" I asked after I got tired of listening to my feet pound the road. "Is it 'cause of the people from the state?"

"I think he's unloading trucks at the grocery store," Peter sighed. Peter too worked at the grocery store sometimes for under-the-table cash; it was true that he couldn't have anything that was his own.

"That's a good job," I argued.

"We'll see how long it lasts." Peter ran his hand over his shaved head, which was growing out in all directions. It looked like a shoe cleaner—the kind they had at the 7-Eleven near where the shrimp-ing boats docked. Earl Beavers, who owned the place, said he was tired of cleaning his floors, so he bought the boot brush. No one thought it helped at all. Poor Mr. Beavers: he was as old as the hills anyway. His hair looked like the strings on the mop he used to get the shrimp guts off his floor, and here Peter was looking like the boot brush. Bledsoe had to be the worst place in the whole world to live.

"Not all of us are gonna go and work for the president of insur-ance or something, Peter," I said. "I wanna be a housewife."

"No you don't," Freddy said. "And yeah, there were people at the house again today." He looked at Peter as if trying to get answers. "Second time this week."

Peter kept walking with his gaze steadily in front of him.

"Yes, I do. I like being at home and working on projects…you know, around the house, and I wanna have kids," I said. "Not kids like…like us or Sarah-Anne, or whatever, but nice kids."

"You hate being at home," Peter said. "You need to be an astronaut or something. Floating around out there." He pointed at the sky, which was clear and pulsing. "I don't know who was at the house. They wanted to talk to Dad, but Mom…whatever." He threw his hands up in some kind of adolescent confusion—the kind that comes from never really knowing what's going on but having to explain yourself all the time.

"I don't care what I do," I replied dreamily. "I wanna be in love for the rest of my life, so I'll get married and divorced as many times as it takes to keep things interesting."

"That's not Christian," Peter said as he walked ahead.

"We haven't been to church since Elizabeth died. Are we even Christian?" Freddy asked. "Is Dad in trouble again? Is that why they keep coming by?"

"What is 'the state,' even?" I asked, irritated. "What does that mean? Do we even know if these people were from the state? What state?" I stopped jabbering just for a second. The space between us needed filling, so I kept on talking at a higher volume. "They were cops who came before. Y'all act like you don't remember, but we had cops at our house before Sarah-Anne stopped going to school. Y'all play dumb, but there was Mama hidin' by the freezer. I remember it plain as day. She even got *in* the freezer with Sarah-Anne. Of course they fit, 'cause Mama's about as big as an acorn. What the hell does 'the state' mean anyway? The state doesn't come to your door—the police come to your door. And it don't matter if we're Christian now. We buried one of God's own angels in our yard. He don't want anything to do with us anymore. We stole from him. Stealing is a sin."

"You say the strangest things," Freddy told me as we turned off Hack Road and toward the school.

"Not strange. Dead people in the yard relieve you of your duty to go to church." I kicked a rock that sent a poof of loose dirt into the air.

"She was a baby," Peter said. "Stop it anyway. I hate when you're like this."

"Like what?" Peter had picked up the pace considerably and was mostly out of earshot. I was, as usual, struggling to keep up with him while talking at the same time.

"So disrespectful. You probably will be married ten times the way you go on. You have no respect." I actually wasn't sure if it was Peter or Freddy who said it.

I spent the day ignoring my studies and instead thought about the way I was talking about Elizabeth and Sarah-Anne all the time like they were garbage to be hauled to the road—no joke where we lived. It took about ten minutes each direction with our old, tore-up cans. I was pretty sure I cared about my family the way I was supposed to, but I didn't know how to act like it.

I took four bathroom breaks during the day—two because I had to pee and two to practice looking concerned and serious in the mirror in the girls' room—before deciding that I was a good and moral person, but I was up against very dire circumstances given the stolen electricity and the way our house looked (and felt) like it was about to fall over in a strong wind. I couldn't help it if Sarah-Anne was so weird they were making Freddy do DNA tests. I didn't really understand any of that anyway. "Gosh," I said to my reflection. "I promise I love you, Sarah-Anne." I also thought about telling Elizabeth that I loved her, but Josie Ringold came into the bathroom and said hello to me just as I was channeling my more calm and caring self.

Peter stayed after school that day, so Freddy and I walked home on our own. I asked him about the spit test, but he didn't answer. "I just want to listen to my music," he said, doing a jerky and embarrassing dance move that I was grateful I was the only one to see. Freddy's body was like a puppet made of cold hot dogs; he just wasn't put together all that tight.

"Must be some song," I said. Freddy only had one CD. It was a compilation of hits from two years previous; it came with the player, bought used at Harmon's Salvage. There were three to choose from; our dad picked the one that came with its own CD.

I was heavy with the day and the impending afternoon while we walked. There was nothing to do with myself; time was my worst enemy, mostly because my head was so full of it.

When we got home, instead of going inside with Freddy, I put my bag down on the ground and walked over to Elizabeth's tree. I lay down next to where she was buried. "Sorry, Elizabeth," I said to the grass above her little body. "I don't mean it."

I rolled onto my stomach and put my hand on the little stone we put to mark where she was resting. I felt a cold breeze and heard one of the oak branches bend under the weight of a chilling wind. I closed my eyes, afraid that if I opened them, I would see my mother standing above me. She had a way of sneaking up on you when you were talking to Elizabeth.

CHAPTER 12

My father got home that night right before dinner. He acted the way he usually did when forced to labor for a long period. He was silent and bitter. My mother passed around the soup she'd made and smiled at each of us in turn.

"What have you been doing all day, Sue-Bess?" my father finally asked, ladling some food into his bowl.

"She made potato soup," I said, widening my eyes. "Imagine that. Potatoes."

My father picked up his spoon and threw it at me, narrowly missing my head. "You're gonna learn to watch your mouth if it's the last and only thing I teach you!" Sarah-Anne bent over and picked the spoon up from the floor then put it right back down. There was an off-white creamy residue left behind.

Freddy stood up, swallowed uncomfortably, and waited for a moment—his conflicted expression suggesting that he was about to say something very important. "I'm going to bed." He chose flight ninety percent of the time. As a result, I associated cowardice with the sniffles for all eternity.

"Sit down!" my father growled.

Freddy sat and looked at Peter, who was humbly eating at his corner of the table.

"Well, excuse me!" I said bitterly. "But she did make the soup today."

"I made the soup," my mother said calmly. "Do you need another spoon, Clay?"

My dad rose from the table and walked over to the drawer where we kept all of our mismatched utensils. "Stop arguing with me," he said as he came back and sat down.

"I'm not arguing with you. You asked what she did all day, and here we are eating this delicious potato soup, so I said…"

"I know what you said." He took a bite and looked at my mother. "It took all day to put this together?"

My mother didn't answer him and looked at the window behind Peter's head. "When does the Webber boy move in?" she asked instead.

"He's not moving in," my father said. "He's coming to stay with us for a while. Next week."

"Yes!" I said, pulling my fist to my stomach in celebration.

"So is that what you did today?" my father asked, his attention still focused on my mother's serene face. "You thought about Nile Webber's son moving in?"

"I'm getting the house ready for him," she said, refusing to engage.

"I'm wasting my life lifting boxes and listening to asinine conversation between these two sixty-year-old idiots who've never been anywhere or done anything." My father sneered and leaned over his elbows, which were pressed into the pine board table. "You know today they had a forty-five-minute discussion about mayonnaise. I thought I'd walk in front of a truck if I could find one. I was on my feet all day with my back aching like someone took a hammer to it, and I have to do it again tomorrow and the day after that and the day after that, and I really could throw myself off a cliff it's so boring and senseless. I'm glad you didn't strain yourself too hard today, Sue-Bess. I'm glad you were able to get the soup done by six o'clock at night."

I took a bite and waited. Nothing happened. We continued eating in silence for a while before Freddy spoke again to ask if he could go to the screened porch to watch a movie.

"Turn on the heater out there," my father said. Freddy gave him a thumbs-up and walked out of the kitchen. The space heater barely worked and was a better fire hazard than anything. My mother forbade its use when my father wasn't home, but my father insisted we plug it in. It might have been a cause of pride that we owned one. Sometimes, he got his confidence in the strangest places.

"Does he get out of dish duty then?" I asked.

"Yes," my father answered sternly.

"I'm going to bed," my mother said. She stood up, letting her napkin fall to the floor.

"I'll bet you're tired," my father said. "Real tired."

"Good night," she said, walking to the door of the bedroom like she was skating on floating sheets of ice. She had an unsteadiness about her that made me think of drunk people leaving Spittoons Bar on Devore Way.

I heard my dad outside the house later that night after a few full glasses, talking to himself—sauced and wobbly, lecturing the air around Elizabeth's tree, explaining the way things were in long, drawn-out sentences with lots of hand punctuation. I'd gone to bed in silence and woken up around 2 a.m. to the sound of Clay Whitaker telling life to kiss his ass, telling my mom to kiss his ass too, although she didn't respond. She was in their bedroom, asleep. I went to my window to get a better look. I could hear him just fine from inside my room—the walls might as well have been made of paper. He threw a couple of air punches and said something about Sue-Bess this and Sue-Bess that. I heard "bitch" a few times and "psycho" a few more. It went on for an hour or so; then I heard the back screen door slam and some shuffling around the kitchen and a "You're gonna get what's comin' to you, fucking bitch" before another door opened and shut, and that was it.

"Goddamn," I said to myself as I got back in bed. It had been a long time since my dad had gotten in a fight with God over a bottle of rum. I'd seen the Captain Morgan on the shelf in the shed the day before. He did his best religious exercises over rum. Whiskey was his thoughtful drink, while rum was fuel for his inner fires. I had inner fires too, and I didn't need rum or anything else to get my blazes going full throttle. "Goddamn," I said again. I sure knew where I got my fondness for cursing from. Thank God we didn't have neighbors so close was all I could think as I drifted off to an agitated sleep.

The next day my father was still home when we woke up for school. He was at the kitchen table with a cup of coffee and the city paper. "Morning," I said.

"Kay." He nodded but didn't look up. I could see that his hands were a little shaky—always an aftereffect.

"Why aren't you at work?" I asked. "Don't you gotta get there by six?"

"I'm going on the ship," he said, still without raising his head.

"What ship? To fish?"

"Yes. We're leaving Monday."

"You're gonna be with Andy's dad?"

Now my father finally looked up. "Yeah," he said and then went back to reading.

"We're gonna be here on our own?"

"Your mother'll be here. And Sarah-Anne, and Peter and Freddy."

"They're not the same," I said.

"You'll make do."

I sat down at the table. There was an open box of cereal in front of me. I went to the refrigerator to get some milk, silent and thinking so hard I thought my brains would bubble over and out my ears. I would be alone in the house with Andy. Freddy and Peter were distracted and watched *Hoosiers* all the time, and my mother spent almost the whole day in her bedroom. Sarah-Anne was on another planet as far as I was concerned. It was my father who was lurking and rule-oriented, and now he was going to be gone. I was both excited and worried. I put my hand on my cheek where Andy had kissed me. I wondered if he would want to do that again, or maybe even on the lips if no one else was around.

"This cereal's stale," I said after pouring the milk and taking a bite.

My father snorted. "So get a job and go buy some new cereal."

"Maybe I will." I paused. "So, did Andy's mama really have bricks in her pockets? Did she, like, off herself?" I put a frosted mini-wheat in my mouth and bit down hard. My dad had told my mother to quit it with the Webber talk, but my mother wasn't at the table.

My father closed his eyes and exhaled. "No one knows."

"You're always so mad about it."

"I'm not mad, Kay—" He continued pretending to look at the paper. It was just ads for bras on the page he had open. I knew bad acting when I saw it. "I'm not mad," he said again—a little more convincingly. "I feel bad for them."

"Me too," I said. "You sure as hell were mad last night."

He winced a little but didn't look at me. "Watch your mouth."

"Mad at Mom…"

"Kay, you're gonna have to learn to mind your own business."

"Seems like it's my business if you're standing outside my room when I'm trying to sleep."

He kept his head down and didn't speak.

"And why's people here about Sarah-Anne all the darn time?" I said.

"Who told you that?" Now I had his attention.

"I'm not blind."

"Then cover your eyes." He turned back to the paper. His face was white. I felt the stale cereal go to the pit of my stomach.

"They're comin' a lot more now," I said.

"That's not your business."

Three days later, Nile and Andy showed up at our house, first thing in the morning, for the long farewell. Andy was just leaving his things before going to the market on Route 54 where he had to work all day selling crabs. He was not going to school while he was with us. My mother looked nervous when this was confirmed. He was still going to crab and get oysters for the family business, so he'd be gone all day—but not every day. The market wasn't open every day.

"Okay then," my mother replied softly.

Andy stood in the driveway with a duffel bag wearing a hooded sweatshirt, ripped jeans, and sneakers. His head had been re-shaven, and his face was perky, like he was expecting something great even though there was little chance of that in our house. I didn't want to be the bearer of bad news, so I didn't tell him the best was not yet to come—at least not while he was living with us.

Nile Webber stood with Andy. They'd taken the boat to shore then walked all the way to our house and around to the front steps, a more suitable place to be received. Peter was going to drive my dad and Nile to the loading dock. They were to be gone twenty-eight days, four weeks exactly.

Peter was to take them and bring the car back so we had a car in case of emergency. My mother didn't get behind the wheel—ever—emergency or not; it would be Peter driving if we had somewhere to go.

I walked over to Andy and took his hand. "Come on," I said. "I'll show you where you're going to sleep. We don't eat a lot of crab and oysters…just think you should know that."

"I don't care," he said. We walked inside together. He put his bag down in the living room and looked around.

"The bathroom's down here," I said rather proudly, reluctantly dropping his hand as we made our way down the narrow hall. "We have a bathroom. Two actually, but only one shower."

"Yeah." He smiled.

"You can go whenever you want, but, like, you have to ask my parents to use the shower 'cause it's in their bedroom, and, like… my mom always hides out or whatever in there. It's fine though." I reached out to take his hand again. To my relief, he gave me his hand and smiled. "When's your birthday?"

"November 13."

"No way—mine's July 13. I'm older than you."

"Yeah." He smiled again. "I guess so."

"You smile a lot," I told him. "But I like it."

"This is a nice house."

"It's okay."

"Let me show you my room." I pulled him toward my door. My bed was made and all of my things picked up and perfectly placed around the various mismatched shelves and furniture.

"It's nice," he said but did not attempt to go inside and take a closer look.

"I just cleaned it."

"Where's your sister?"

"Who? Sarah-Anne?" I paused. "I wouldn't really worry about her much," I said, frowning. "I don't know where she is…probably doin' a whole buncha nothin.'"

We walked back outside to where everyone else was standing. My father's hands were in his pockets, and he grinned sadly, not at anyone in particular but at the house and all that he was leaving.

I went and put my hand on his back. "I'll miss ya, Dad," I said.

I knew he was battling demons. He held on to things with far-reaching arms—our life got him down now and then. Not me; I pushed away bad thoughts like I was using a broom.

"I'll miss you too," he said quietly, if not a little embarrassed.

My mother hugged him and strangely refused to shake Nile Webber's outstretched hand, an aggressive gesture that was unusual for her. I noticed the slight, as did Andy. We looked at one another and then away, back at the cooling scenery around us. The one large oak tree had a tendency to steal the view. Once noticed, it was difficult to look at anything else. Spanish moss dangling, branches outstretched like they were hugging the air—I pretended to care deeply about the tree; anything to avoid watching my mother have a personality.

The wind blew, and my mother suggested we go inside. She wasn't dressed for the chilly October weather. Time and temperatures were moving quickly toward fall and then winter, in a race to get the leaves off the trees. My mother's hair was thin and moving about her head like loose strands of cotton candy. Her eyes were glazed and watery from the cold breeze.

"Come on, Mama," I said. "Let's get you out of the cold. You're not used to being outside." She went with me like a delicate bird with a broken wing that I'd promised to care for.

"Where's Sarah-Anne?" Freddy asked, but no one answered.

My brothers and I had to be at school within the hour, so we went about gathering our things. I saw my sack lunch sitting on the counter with my name written in pencil along the crease—my mother's doing. I always took a peanut butter and jelly sandwich for lunch, while my brothers ate in the cafeteria. I didn't like to roll the dice on my midday meal. Sometimes I bought crackers from the vending machine, and occasionally my mom put a banana or orange in my lunch box. I drank water from the water fountain and was the only one in my class who carried her lunch to school. A lot of the kids in Bledsoe were on the meal plan, whatever that was. It meant they got their food for free. I didn't know if we paid for Peter's and Freddy's lunch—it seemed like if we could get something for free, we took it. I always was the thorn in my parents' side. I just couldn't stomach all of the brown and green food on plastic trays.

"What'll ya do all day?" I asked Andy. "Isn't it too cold for fishing?"

"No, some stuff likes the cold water better." He put on a coat and some thick socks that looked like they were woven by hand. He'd removed the sneakers and shoved them in his bag.

"Do you miss California? I think it would be so neat to live out there."

"Naw," he said. "Didn't you already ask me about that anyway? I haven't changed my mind…" He sat down on our couch and looked like he was expecting something to happen.

"I don't know. Just making conversation. I like to talk," I told him. "I have to go to school now."

"All right then," he replied, maybe a little annoyed. It didn't seem like he wanted to kiss me again, so I went to my room and brushed my hair before putting on a heavier sweater and a scarf that my mother had given me on my birthday one year. It was a strange gift for a summer birthday, but I knew she'd started working on it during the cold months. It took her a while to finish projects, what with all that sleeping.

Peter, Freddy, and I were quiet on our way to school, walking like soldiers in unison, aware of each other but not talking. It seemed life was full of duty.

"I'm gonna miss Dad," I said to pass the time.

Peter hadn't said a word since dropping my father and Nile off at the shipyard. "He'll be back," he said dismissively.

"I know that."

"I'll miss him too," Freddy said before putting his headphones over his ears and dancing a little to something I could barely hear. I didn't have any music to listen to, and Peter didn't seem too keen on talking to me, so I listened to the birds and other far-off noises like cars backfiring and the sound of our feet on the ground. The road was crunchy and crisp like shaved ice. My shoes were getting a little too small, and I needed to trim my toenails. I began to focus on that discomfort, and suddenly the school felt a hundred miles away.

"Don't go messin' around with Andy," Peter cautioned out of the blue.

"What do you even mean, 'messin' around'?"

"Just stay away from him."

"That's gonna be about as hard as asphalt bein' that he's livin' in our house."

"You know what I mean."

"I never know what anyone means," I complained.

"Where's Sarah-Anne?" Freddy asked loudly over the music playing in his headphones.

"Home prolly," I said. "Where else would she be?"

"No, I mean this morning. Where'd she go?" He was yelling to hear himself.

"She went somewhere?" I said.

Peter didn't answer.

"Everybody's al'ays asking about Sarah-Anne," I said. "Makin' me nervous."

"Just wonderin' where she went. Got a funny feeling."

"I always got a funny feeling about her," I said. "A little too funny."

"Andy was looking for her this morning," Peter said.

"What?" I turned my head like a fish with a hook through my gills, jerking to get free.

Peter shrugged.

I was quiet, pieces of a bitter nut stuck in my teeth. "He must think she's real interesting," I said. "That hair's always got a lotta looks."

"Oh, Kay," Peter said, stifling a chuckle. "Don't worry."

"Sarah-Anne this and Sarah-Anne that."

"What?" Freddy shouted again.

"She's like bad news," I said. "And take your headphones off for the love of God! Stop yelling!"

"She's not bad news—don't do nothin' wrong," Peter said.

"Hardly worth talkin' about is what I've been sayin'." I shook my head and widened my eyes to make myself understood. This was important, I seemed to say with all this gesturing—it was important for us to recognize how unimportant Sarah-Anne was.

We never saw her again.

CHAPTER 13

I made it through the school day with a pill of nervousness caught in my throat, stuck there like a rock even the best toilet couldn't flush. I daydreamed more than usual but talked less. My friend Hattie noticed and asked if I was okay. I told her I had a headache. I felt like I would never see her again when she said she hoped I felt better and turned to catch her bus after the last bell. It was like we were saying goodbye forever. I waved and wished I could be her—a person who lived in a neighborhood with a bus route. It was all I could think about, just being jealous and alone. I shook myself out of my state and went to meet my brothers at our usual place after my last class. I was cold and anxious.

"Hey!" I said loudly as I walked up. "Man, I'm off today. I feel like a weirdo."

"Stop yelling, Kay!" Freddy said angrily.

"Oh, you're one to talk!" I was still hot over the walk to school with everybody talking about how Andy was trying to get his eyes on Sarah-Anne. "You're always yelling!"

"Quiet!" Peter said. "Both of you."

I think we could all feel it coming on—the doom. It was creeping up over us like winter come from the dirt. That's where the cold comes from—the heat is from the sky, but the cold gets you from the bottom up.

We walked home in stiff silence, the boredom of the house pulling on me like a magnet. The only thing that kept my feet moving, one after another, was the possibility of seeing Andy. I was just then tossing around my passionate feelings in my mind when Peter abruptly stopped walking.

"What?" I asked, a little annoyed when he threw his arm out in front of me to halt my progress. The dust was still kicking up in all directions, even in this time of true autumn, damp and endlessly wet. Moisture is a real issue this far south. Moisture and lack of progress. I was wrestling all my demons right there in that very moment. It was a long moment, and it stayed with me for a long time.

I looked at the path to our house. I saw blue lights and two police cars attached to them. We'd had the police at our house before—the memory was in the back corner of my mind where I kept things I didn't want to remember.

"Why are we stopping?" I said angrily. "Mama!" I started to

run as fast as I could. I was really getting my knees up and was, apparently, uncatchable—I could feel the boys on my heels, but they never got around me. I turned from left to right a couple of times just to see how far ahead I was, but the movement slowed me down, so I kept my focus straight ahead. I was worried about the police and my mother, but I had a hard time thinking about anything but Andy while I was moving like a race car on a bumpy track. I heard my engine roar as I took the sharp left to the front of the house where my mother was standing with her hands clasped, her eyes bloodshot. She was terrified. So was I. "Is it Andy—" I called out.

"Sarah-Anne!" she shouted. "She's gone!"

One of the police officers who'd been talking to my mother turned around. Like almost everyone in Bledsoe, I recognized him but didn't know his name. I thought maybe I'd seen him with my dad. He watched me closely, his attention briefly caught by my brothers, who were now nipping at my heels.

"What?" Peter asked.

"Sarah-Anne's gone!" my mother said again. Her small hands were twisting each other, trying to break the fingers off the wrist. I stopped running, having gotten close enough to absorb the worry.

"Where?" Freddy said. It was a good question, but no one answered.

The officer looked at me. I didn't say anything. I looked at my mother again. There was something about her that day. Everyone was looking at each other like they might not want to know. I mostly couldn't believe she'd called the police. There was nothing more out of character than Sue-Bess Whitaker inviting law enforcement to her home. And her dress was wet at the hem—all the way around, like she had dipped the bottom half of herself in water; bare feet and a wet dress and talking to the police. I never thought I'd see the day. I never did again.

The police stayed for some time, asking my mother questions. They were talking very deliberately to her. I didn't like being excluded from conversations and tried to give my two cents every chance I could. No one listened to me, or even really acknowledged that I was speaking. I continued to talk, but it was like I was stuck in air that was too thick—I couldn't get through. They eventually left, claiming they would do everything in their power to find Sarah-Anne. I rolled my eyes a little; what the hell kind of power did the Bledsoe Police have? I was glad to see them leave, even if it still felt like we had an intruder. We'd gone inside the house, and I couldn't shake the feeling that someone was waiting for us there. I kept expecting to find someone I didn't know lurking beyond a doorway or in a closet.

"What happened, Mama?" I asked. I never called my mother mama, but I'd done it twice in one afternoon. We were all playing at something; I just couldn't figure out what. "She just up and left?" We were standing perfectly still around the kitchen table.

"I don't know," my mother said. She sat down with her hands in fists, squeezing.

Peter hovered cautiously. "Did she leave the house or…" He paused.

"She's not here," I said. "I mean, obviously, she left the house."

"Alone?" Peter said, annoyed with me.

"Who called the police?" I asked.

My mother turned her head to face me. "I did," she said. "She's been…she's been going…"

"But, like, when did she disappear?" I said loudly and like I was mad not to know. While Peter hovered, I leaned and scooted and shuffled all over the small room. I bumped and knocked and pounded. I tried a few times to comfort my mother—who was always awash in distress—but mostly because I thought I looked like an earthly saint when I did it. If I covered her shoulders with a blanket or patted her loose hair when she was having her struggles, I thought maybe God was watching me and giving me points for my good deeds. "When?" I asked again impatiently.

"When I couldn't find her."

"But what happened, Mom?" Peter said.

"I don't know. I could see her out in the water. She took the—" She frowned, emotion overcoming her otherwise empty face.

"In the water?" I shouted. "What the hell?"

"Did you go looking for her?" Peter asked. He was talking about her wet dress.

"I'm tired," my mother said as she pushed her chair away from the table. "I'm tired of thinking about it." She shook her head.

"Yes, of course." Peter put his hand on her back. I didn't have the strength.

"What the hell?" I said again. "She doesn't go out in the water."

"She does," my mother said nervously. "She has... It's..." She stopped talking. We didn't press her; she might shatter.

The house swayed with emptiness; one less person, and the place was bound to float away from a lack of weight holding it down. Instead of Sarah-Anne, the house had the shadows of my mother's longing. My mother paced about in a strange, frantic slowness, wringing her hands and pressing the front of her dress with her sweaty palms. She stood by the front door then walked to the back of the house with her eyes like saucers and her mouth pulled tightly down. There were squirrels outside gathering acorns; with each brush of their tail or strange squeak from their small mouths, my mother was at the window. She ran like an injured mouse: tiny, frightened, and always looking up for danger. She kept turning over her shoulder with her neck like a screw. I tried to think of something to say to her other than questions that she didn't seem to be able to answer. She was too afraid. Her face was marked with tear tracks; her lips trembled; her feet didn't touch the ground. I stood behind her, just behind, at an angle, and waited to know what to do.

No one spoke anymore; sounds felt like they were a hundred miles away, but right up under your head like a bug flying with a rope round and round your neck.

Andy came home from the market on Route 54 later that evening and could immediately, like a starved cat, sense that he should leave—no food for him here.

"Is something wrong?" he asked after he put his things down on the front porch. He was jittery and sweating.

"What do you mean?" Peter said.

"You don't have to come in the front door," I said. "You live here now. You can come in the back, you know."

"He doesn't live here." Peter sat forward in his chair. We were on the front porch together, in hostile silence. Freddy was inside listening to his headphones and reading his science book for pleasure. "And no," Peter went on. "Nothing's wrong."

"Okay," Andy said, pulling at the sleeves on his sweater. He was right filthy and soaked up to his thighs.

"This is what we do all the time," I said. "Just sit around—uncomfortable and bein' quiet."

"Right."

"Kay," Peter said, giving me a mean glare. I shrugged and was about to tell Andy about the police and Sarah-Anne and Mom crying, but Peter threw an arm out like he was blocking a pass and practically shouted. "There's been some trouble," he said, like we'd lost our best shovel and we were damn near beside ourselves we were so upset about it. "You might need to stay at your house tonight."

Andy looked sorry and tired, not unlike my mother, who almost always looked like she'd lost a child. She didn't have to change her look the more and more things happened—she'd been ready for it for a long time. Her sickly desperation was like a good coat, now worn on every occasion.

"Okay," Andy said. He was wearing high wader boots over jeans. I really couldn't get used to seeing him in shoes—boots no less. They were wet and covered in loose dirt, leaves, and other relics from the old mud we lived on. Even the tops of his jeans were soaked. I figured he had to get out of the boat a lot while using the nets. "Okay," he said to Peter again. "I'll head on then."

"Okay?" I blurted. "You can't kick him out!" My mouth was open wide like a fly trap. "Peter!"

"Quiet," he said in a frustrated whisper. "Mom's trying to sleep."

"She's the only woman I know who can sleep when her kid goes missing." I rolled my eyes and crossed my arms over my chest.

"Who's missing?" Andy asked. He shoved his hands in his front pockets. He couldn't seem to stop moving. I knew the drill, but it was unlike Andy. A more relaxed fella I'd never met.

"You okay?" I asked. "Acting like a grenade without a pin." I crossed my feet in the chair, twisted up like a troublesome shoelace.

"Our cousin." Peter spoke quickly, with his head forward. We were on my dad's lawn chairs. He had a few, one for each sour mood, and then a blue one for good times. He never sat in the blue seat. It was empty on this night too. I looked at Peter sideways but kept my mouth shut. It had been a long day. "He didn't come home from school," Peter clarified.

"Oh." Andy wasn't going to put up a fight. He stepped back on his heel a little and made like he was going to do just what Peter had told him to do—leave.

"Don't you need your stuff?" I asked.

"Oh, yeah." He looked at Peter, who was avoiding eye contact.

"Just come back tomorrow," Peter said with a sigh. "Sorry, it's just…just come back tomorrow. I'm sure she just wandered off."

"He," I said. "You said our cousin, he." I pressed my teeth together and waited for my anger to fade. "I'll walk ya," I said to Andy, rising from my chair.

"No," Peter said. "Kay, just sit down."

"It's almost dark! We can't send him off like this."

"I'm okay," Andy said. "So…she didn't come back?"

"He," I said, winking with my whole face. "Our cousin. He." I winked again. I thought about my mother saying Sarah-Anne was in the water. I was almost going to say something about it, but the wind chimes clattered loudly, like someone hit them with a bat.

"*I* will walk with you." Peter stood up and motioned to Andy. Neither of them turned to look at me. My disappointment was like really bad breath; you didn't have to be very close to me to smell it.

"Do you need to pee or anything?" I called after them. Neither of them turned around or answered. I sat on the porch for a while, then went inside. Freddy had already gone in and was lying on Sarah-Anne's bed; he'd been there all afternoon. He wasn't crying, so I said, "Oh, it didn't take you long to claim your throne, did it?" I didn't know where the anger was coming from, but I was spitting nails.

"What?" Freddy asked stupidly.

"Why are you sleeping in Sarah-Anne's bed?"

"I'm not sleeping."

"Well, what the hell are you doing?"

"Remembering her."

"I'm glad everyone is so sure she's gone. She's too dumb to get lost." I walked away with no particular destination in mind. The house was uneasy, as though it had been lifted off the ground and put on a rotating dish, like a lazy Susan. We never had one, but my mom's sister, Aunt Christy, did. I had marveled at it on the occasion I got to go to her house. I marveled at most things in Christy's house—especially her children with their clothes from the mall and catalogs. I had caught my mother sneaking a peek at one of their garments. Christy had two daughters not very far apart and then another one some years later. They all looked exactly the same to me. I think my mother thought about Elizabeth when she saw them; I don't think I reminded my mother of Elizabeth at all.

I went from room to room looking for clues. Freddy had had Sarah-Anne's drawer open beneath her bed and was rifling through it with his fingers. "All her thimbles got holes in 'em now," he'd said, but I was too mad about him lying in her bed to ask him what the hell he was talking about. "And dental floss."

"We don't use dental floss," I said, walking away. "And no, I don't want to hear about its benefits!" I never looked in Sarah-Anne's drawer—not since she got in trouble about the touching. I frowned and closed my eyes; I hated thinking about that.

There were a lot of things I hated to think about, that I kept kicking out of my brain like a slippery rock. And then there was my father leaving on this very day, this so very important day. I took a few deep breaths, circling our home with my head in the clouds of my disturbed thoughts. I went into the kitchen and could hear my mother crying. She sounded like a child. I wanted to cry too, because that's what a good sister would do, but normally when I cried it was for myself or the state of the house—it was such a shithole it could bring tears to my eyes. The house was a dump, and now Sarah-Anne was gone. Things were really taking a turn for the worse. I wished I hadn't been wandering off to Christy's lazy Susan in my mind, because there, tucked away with memories of spinning it, was a relic I'd longed to forget. My mother in the bathroom. She was bleeding. There was blood down the front of her dress and all over her hands. The bath mat was soaked in it. My mother was screaming for my dad. I closed my eyes.

I went out to the back of the house and thought about walking all the way to Andy's. I might have walked off a cliff if I could have. But there are no cliffs in Bledsoe. I saw one of Sarah-Anne's thimbles lying on the ground next to the back steps. I picked it up, and sure enough on either side of the top—where you stick your finger in—were two tiny holes on opposite sides. It was a gray thimble with small indentations, like a muffin tin. I was thinking it was a little funny because Sarah-Anne never really went out back unless she was going to the shed with my dad. She was a front porch kind of girl. I sighed as heavy as a wet sponge. Things had gotten so bleak for us out there on Hack Road, my big sister had taken to flossing her thimbles—wonders never ceased.

CHAPTER 14

The next morning, my mother was in the kitchen when we woke up. I could tell she hadn't slept. Her eyes were bloodshot and her mouth quivering like she was just about to say something but couldn't bring herself to. She looked at me, but it was in the way of a blind person—she couldn't see anything at all.

"Are we going to school?" I asked.

"No." Peter was in the kitchen too. He was holding his schoolbooks in protest it seemed. He stood over the table without any apparent reason to do so. There was no food out. Freddy wasn't in the room; I hadn't yet seen him that morning. He was always the last to get going on account of his lack of physical fitness. The door to my parents' room was open—unusual enough, but on this day, startling. I could see inside where the bed was made and the curtains were drawn over the windows.

"Peter sent Andy home last night," I said to my mother. "Just sent him on home while you were sleeping." I don't know what I expected her to say, but part of me wanted Peter in trouble. He always thought he was the boss because of his age. I didn't get why people think the more years you have, the smarter you are. Both of my parents were older than me and dumb as stumps. "He's out there all by hisself."

My mother's face clouded over and her lips drew into a thin line. "Okay," she said.

"We were supposed to be watchin' over him, but he had to go off in the dark. Alone." I made my eyes into slits too. Two could play at this game. "We coulda put him to good use and had him go lookin' for Sarah-Anne. He's a real marsh dweller type, but no—Peter just sent him on home in the dark. Sent him on his way, so he could get lost like Sarah-Anne." I stomped my foot.

"It wasn't dark," Peter said. "And he lives out there, so he..."

"No," my mother interrupted. "I think he—" She paused. I always did wonder what she was just about to say; she didn't get to say it. Freddy suddenly burst into the kitchen with his hair on end—a large, uneven, red helmet.

"The police are outside," he squawked. His wild, flailing hand gestures suggested he was about to fly off the handle—hanging on by a thread. We all were. Peter put his books down with a loud clap. Freddy's face was muddled with sleep, waking, and urgency. I wanted to beat the snot out of someone, but I couldn't make up my mind who.

"What police?" I said. I was nervous enough to hear my heartbeat in my ears. "What police?"

"The *police* police," Freddy said, frustrated. "Like, from the police station. There're two cars out front."

My mother sat very still at the table. She hadn't moved at all, only sighed. She placed her hands on her lap and took another breath.

"Did they find Sarah-Anne?" Freddy asked my mother.

"No," she said before I took my turn to talk over her. We might have stopped it then, before it was too late, but we wouldn't let my mother tell us. We kept bursting in the room, shouting above her head, answering her questions for her, stopping her from saying what we didn't think she knew. It might not have been too late then. There still might have been time that day, that morning. Before.

"Maybe they found Sarah-Anne," I said over my mother's timid voice. "Maybe they got Sarah-Anne!"

I'd almost forgotten she was missing. I woke up with a feeling of sadness and worry—not uncommon in Bledsoe—but I thought it was because my father was gone, and Andy had been forced off into the night like a vagrant. I hadn't worried for Sarah-Anne at all. I don't know what I thought happened to her. It dawned on me that I didn't think there was anything I could do about it, like the touching, like her silence, like my mother who wouldn't leave the house, like thinking about the egg after it's cracked—too late.

"Did they find Sarah-Anne?" Freddy asked my mom.

"You already asked her that," Peter said, annoyed.

My mother did not respond; she was caught in the haze of her blurry mind. She was an egg too, born cracked. Her mouth remained a line on her face; her eyes were glassed over—nobody home. She and Sarah-Anne had certainly mastered that look.

"Mom. The police are here," Freddy said again. "What do you want us to do?"

We heard a knock on the front door, but my mother still did not move.

"Has anyone talked to Dad?" I asked. No one had mentioned my father the night before; it was as though Sarah-Anne wasn't his concern. We were to handle everything without him. "Awful convenient—" I started to say when I was interrupted by shouting and pounding, heavy boots, heavy knuckles, heavy business.

"Police!" More noise came from the front of the house. Peter looked at my mother pleadingly, but she said nothing and remained sitting at the table with her hands in her lap. She was like a child, in her dress, with her light-pink stockings. We could have been sisters.

"Mom!" I said.

The front door opened. Peter made a move like he was going to throw the table over, but my mother put one of her hands up like the blade of a fan, and he stopped.

"What do you want us to do?" Peter asked, but it was too late. There was an officer in the kitchen. It was a woman—highly unusual for these parts—and I saw that her uniform was not for the Bledsoe police but for the state. It was always the state at our house.

"Mrs. Whitaker," the woman said to my mother. I sensed sympathy. I looked at the floor, ashamed. Pity was the go-to response for us. It had to be the tilt of our house. Or our mother in her little kid clothes. My hair like ropes hanging from a burnt-out light bulb.

"You are under arrest for the murder of Emily Webber. You have the right to remain silent. Anything you say can and will be used against you in a court of law. You have the right to an attorney. If you cannot afford an attorney, one will be provided for you. Do you understand these rights as I have just explained them to you?"

"Mom!" I shouted again.

Peter ran around the table and stood in front of the officer. She put her hand on her belt right next to her gun. "Sir, I'm going to have to ask you to step away from your mother." She was a young woman with a wise face.

"He's not a sir!" I said through thick tears. I was like a slowly melting sheet of ice. I could feel my face falling and my words coming out as gasps. I realized I was hiccupping—I thought it was such a ridiculous time to get the hiccups. "He's only fifteen!"

"What's going on here?" Freddy asked as if he had the power to stop it. "Did you find Sarah-Anne?"

"No," the woman said. "We have not found your sister."

"What do you mean, 'Emily Webber'?" I asked.

"That's Andy's mom," Freddy said like we didn't know.

"Mom!" I yelled again. "Where's Sarah-Anne?" My voice ricocheted off the cheap kitchen cabinets. I was a screeching owl, trying to rip an unruly field mouse out of its burrow. "She drowned!" I said to the officer frantically. "Mom!" My mother would not look at me. "I thought we were looking for Sarah-Anne! Emily drowned right there under the house! Nobody's lookin' for her no more!"

"No, we are not looking for Emily Webber," the woman officer said calmly.

I was trying to catch my breath and my thoughts. It was no wonder I was so mixed up. I kept having to right my mind and reassure myself that Sarah-Anne did not drown. We were not talking about Sarah-Anne.

"Mom!" Peter reached for her, but it was as though she was moving away from us. She had always been moving away—she only picked up the pace.

I almost yelled out to the woman who was taking my mother away that it was Andy's daddy who did it. I almost said it was Nile, but I stopped myself. Later, I would sometimes think that I had no loyalty at all. That even in that moment, I cared more about Andy liking me than my own mother being locked up for murder. It's in those small moments, the ones that pass very quickly and don't give a person any time to think, that true character is revealed. It depended on the day, but a lot of the time I didn't think I had much character at all.

She went willingly, like a lamb. I'd heard that expression. They put her small wrists in handcuffs and led her to the car by her drawn shoulders.

Peter, Freddy, and I stood in the kitchen together after the police took my mother to the car. We were not permitted to go outside with her. They kept us in the house while they put her in the back seat. We went to the front room and watched from the window there for a moment before we were forcefully ushered back to the kitchen table. She didn't turn around to look at us and said nothing as she was being led out of the house. She wasn't wearing shoes, only her dress and thick stockings. No one mentioned her shoes; it was all I could think about as they closed the front door like the top of a casket. It was a brisk morning; my mom's exit let a mound of cool air into the house. I'd dressed myself for school and was wearing a sweater. I pulled it tightly around my waist and felt for my own dress.

"They're saying she killed Andy's mama?" I barked. "But she drowned! And where's Sarah-Anne?" Peter bit his lip and shushed me. I so hated to be shushed.

I was asked a million and a half questions about this day, about the days leading up to it, about the days that followed. To each of these questions, I said I didn't know. "I don't know," I said over and over again.

CHAPTER 15

A man named Officer March, who'd been standing outside while they put my mother in the back of the car, came inside and sat with us. We hadn't left the kitchen—feeling both trapped there and unsure of where else to go. Officer March said they were waiting for someone from child services to come. We couldn't be left alone; none of us were old enough—not even Peter, who'd been a sir for a split second.

Officer March was thick around the middle and a heavy breather. All I'd heard all day was air going in and out of various people's lungs. I was red hot over it—angry with myself, angry with Peter and Freddy for not being able to do anything, angry with my father for not being there.

"I mean, didn't Andy's mom die, like, a really long time ago?"

I asked. "Did you find Sarah-Anne?" I said to Officer March. "I mean…she goes missing, and all of a sudden, Mom killed Mrs. Webber? I don't get it. What the hell is going on here?" Officer March looked bored, Freddy looked tired, and Peter looked like he not only got, but swallowed, the short end of the stick. "She had bricks…" I started up again. The silence was deafening.

"Shut up, Kay," Peter said. I looked at him meanly; he nodded in the direction of Officer March and then looked away. It didn't seem to me that this March fella knew a damn thing anyway. He was our babysitter. The lady cop probably had all the goods. I thought for a second that it would be awfully cool to be a lady cop and arrest all the bad seeds in town. Too bad we had a bad seed living right under our noses—not that I didn't know. Sue-Bess was too quiet to be on the right side of the law. No one is that tired.

March's lips hung loose from his mouth in a drooping frown. His gums were reddish pink and almost fully exposed. I thought maybe everyone's gums were this color, but we didn't know, because we couldn't see them the way I could see his. His uniform had a stain on one of the lapels. He was missing a button. I had no respect for an officer of the law who could take a person's mother away in such a careless ensemble. I thought about telling him, but the sorrow I felt for myself, for him and his drooping mouth, and for my mother, who was surely not going to make it out of this alive—she'd barely been alive holed up in her little burrow on Hack

Road—kept me silent. It was the medicine everyone had been hoping for. I could no longer speak.

"Why isn't Dad back?" Freddy said as if it had just occurred to him to ask. "Shouldn't he come back?"

"How the hell could Mom have killed someone?" I said. "She doesn't leave the house, and besides…Mom can't really *do* anything, much less, like, kill someone. Didn't Mrs. Webber drown?" The meds wore off, and I was back to talking. I'd never heard the name Emily Webber before, and here she'd come up a dozen times—turning up over and over like a bad penny. It had to be because of Andy. I'd gone off and dragged him into the house with us, unlocked a box of trouble, let the past out. "You can't, like, drown someone if you…" I stopped talking for a second. "I mean…can Mom even swim? I sure as hell know Sarah-Anne can't. Never seen Mom out there either—imagine living on all this water, but you can't swim. Imagine it."

"She was wet," Freddy said enthusiastically. "When we got home."

"Okay so maybe she can swim. Lotsa things I don't know about her, I'll say."

Peter cut his eyes at me again. I knew I should be more careful. There were things stuck in our net; things I shouldn't say, things I didn't know. Peter looked at Officer March, who was staring at his thumbnail, and then back at me. I nodded smally. I figured it was us against them—that's how we were raised, and even though

Mom was taken off for murder and Dad was out on the boat, we were sticking to our principles. Principles are all people like the Whitakers have. March had perked up a little when I sounded off, but I could only assume, given the state of his uniform, that he was not a man of action. He said nothing and merely rolled his weight from one butt cheek to the other.

"Has anyone called our dad?" Freddy asked.

"We got word out," March said. He was about to say something else but stopped. I figured it had something to do with them looking for Nile Webber too. My dad was off with the man whose wife my mother was supposed to have killed. You couldn't make this shit up. What a hoot! I flushed purple at this thought—angry with myself. It was like I couldn't take anything seriously.

"What's he gonna do about it?" I said. "Dad's about as useless—"

"Kay!" Peter said.

"And there's no word on Sarah-Anne?" Freddy said.

"We're still lookin." March leaned back in his chair, signaling that we were not on his level and that he did not feel he needed to explain anything to us.

"Are they saying my mother killed Mrs. Webber a long time ago?" I said, undeterred by March's attitude. I leaned back in my chair too. Anyone can lean back in their chair, I said without speaking. "'Cause she died a long time ago," I went on. "I mean…before they went to California, so…seems like…isn't it too late?" Peter cut his eyes at me for about the tenth time that day.

"And anyway, she doesn't...I mean, Mom doesn't go anywhere or do anything, so...this is...she couldn't really...with those muscles? Have y'all even talked to Nile? He works on a boat—the man has some muscles, not Mama though. I mean...c'mon."

Officer March didn't answer while Peter and Freddy kept their gaze on the table. Freddy seemed as confused as I was. With Peter, it was something different, like disappointment. He was like a person who finds out the meaning of life and that it's not all it's cracked up to be.

"I have to go to the bathroom," I said rather abruptly, after a long wave of silence. My observations as to the absurdity of what we were being told had really put a hush over the room. My mother wasn't capable of leaving the house much less killing another grown woman; anyone who'd ever met her would have said she wasn't capable. Incapability was her single personality trait—that and being the quietest person my father knows.

"Restroom," I corrected myself even though I knew no one was paying much attention. Freddy drew his brows together, thinking deeply, but didn't say anything. I had no idea how long we'd been sitting there. There was, apparently, someone on their way to take us somewhere else where we would wait more—for who or what, we hadn't yet been told.

"Like...really gotta pee," I said. "Cryin' isn't the same as pee," I said to disinterested faces. Peter glared at me but did not respond. "I cried out all the water up here." I pointed to my head. "But...man this table must be interesting. A real thing of beauty," I said to the three of them, none of whom would give me a moment's notice.

"Kay, seriously," Freddy said.

I walked toward my parents' bedroom, turned to look over my shoulder to see that no one was watching me, before continuing on.

I walked by their bed—tidily made with a blanket folded at the end—trying not to run, trying not to scream, trying not to smash their window with my fist, trying to do nothing but go quietly away from March and my brothers. I went into the bathroom, closed the door as best I could with its uneven hinges and warped frame. I stood very still for a moment then flushed the toilet and turned on the sink at the same time. With the water running in two places, I reached for the latch on the window, turned it, and lifted. I knew this window opened because my dad could sometimes be found holding a cigarette out of it when it was cold outside, too cold for porch sitting. I came around to this side of the house on occasion. This is where the peach trees sat—they were a sight in the spring.

I pulled myself up on the sill, thanking God for my flat chest, and rolled myself out on to the ground next to the house. It had only been about a four-foot drop, but my heart was pounding and I felt I'd survived something significant. I crawled along the ground, which was somehow both damp and dry, crackling and moist, cold and bitter, until I'd reached the edge of the house. Officer March's back was to the screened porch and what lay beyond. All I had to do was run. I hoped Freddy and Peter would be able to hold it together if they saw me. I hoped they would just let me go.

I stood up and froze for a second, waiting to hear if someone had followed me—hollering my name, Officer March on his radio telling his buddies at the station that I took off, Peter yelling at me to get back in the house, or Freddy explaining how many years of hard time I'd have to serve for running away from the police. Nothing.

I started moving toward the water, behind the shed, where I saw that the door was open a couple of feet, falling off its hinge with one corner resting on the ground. I wondered—in a small place in the back of my mind where I was keeping all the things I really didn't want to wonder about—if Sarah-Anne was in there, hiding, afraid to come back to the house. That was where my dad took her sometimes when the people from the state showed up. We had somebody from the state at the house now, but no Sue-Bess. No Clay.

"Sarah-Anne!" I whispered both as forcefully and quietly as I could. "Sarah-Anne, you in there?" I tapped on the side of the shed but was in too big a hurry, and maybe too frightened, to look inside. No one responded.

I ran faster than I'd ever run, and I knew I might have to run longer than I'd ever run. I wasn't wearing shoes either—me and my mother in our dresses and no shoes. I knew the water would be cold and that I might have to swim if Andy wasn't at his house. I'd have to make it to Route 54. I ran. I didn't hear anything behind me, and I didn't turn around.

CHAPTER 16

Andy wasn't at the house when I got there. "Dammit!" I yelled at the front door. I sat down on the plank porch and decided I would wait. My best chance of staying hidden was to stay in the water.

I waited in the cold midday air, looking around for signs of life. I wasn't sure what I was going to say to Andy once he got back, or if I was somehow getting him in trouble by going to his house, but I couldn't go back home. I was surprised to find I was looking for Sarah-Anne out in the marsh; every distant movement I attributed to her, like if she would just come back, all of this would be over. It had been less than a full day since we came home from school to discover her gone. Disappeared. Lost. It was the first hit, and there's this thing about the hits that keep on coming. I'd heard that before too—like the lambs to the slaughter, my mother in her tights being taken away. Maybe there was wisdom in Bledsoe yet; I sure knew a lot of wise sayings. All I could hope for was that some of the smarts would someday rub off on me.

It was so quiet for a while that I could hear the fish moving under the water, beneath the house, circling, looking up at me—an impostor. My breath caught in my throat for a moment—this was where Emily Webber died. I bent down. It couldn't have been the same water under the house, not after this long. That water was out to Bermuda by now, wherever that was.

I got a little scared from the silence. The quiet got me thinking about the fort, or the ruins, or whatever they were from Marco Polo. Then I started thinking about the monkeys and how I could have run right into one of them when I took off for the marsh that first day. I didn't find the monkeys though; I found Andy. I swore if I closed my eyes for long enough that I heard a monkey chattering over my shoulder, not that I even knew how a monkey sounded when it chattered. I got the shivers from all of this thinking and imagining and all that lies beneath the surface in the marsh that I didn't know about. I started to think I needed to be careful or I'd end up stepping on one of the stones from the fort or scratched by some woman's monkeys in the dark. Who knew how long I'd have to sit out there waiting for Andy. I was nervously sweating under the cold water and praying I hadn't made a mistake by running off on my own. I looked at a mangrove, growing out of the brackish water about a hundred yards from where I sat, and shuddered. Something moved behind it, and I swore I saw the long, curled tail of a monkey beyond one of its branches. I shivered again.

What finally took my mind off monkey attacks and having bricks in my pockets while I drowned under an old stone fort with cuts all over my feet, was that I really had to pee and was curious how I was going to manage it. There were gaps in between the boards that made up the front deck—it was more like a platform for getting in and out of the water than any place to sit. I pulled my tights and my panties down to mid-thigh and tried my best to get my stream to go through the crack. I got a little bit of a kick out of my own smarts, and for one second, I felt like myself. While I'd been running out into the marsh, I swear to God, I'd actually paused to consider how much trouble I would get into for going in my parents' bathroom to pee. This was followed by a long spell of sadness while I pressed on. Nothing would ever be like that again. I wasn't going to get in trouble with my parents anymore. I had to assume that a family didn't just move on after the morning we'd had.

I let myself dry a little and pulled my panties and tights back up over my private parts. I scooted over a little so as not to get my dress wet—I hadn't cleared all the wood—and I waited. It was colder than a witch's titty in an iron bra. I was certainly sitting in the shade, which didn't help. The sun was on the other side of the house; if I wanted some rays, I'd have to get wet again. I shivered and swished my legs back and forth as fast as I could over the edge of the porch, hoping to dry my thick tights. I wondered if they made my mother take off her dress at the prison or if they let her leave that and her tights on. It was a lot like a prison uniform anyway.

The longer I sat, the colder I got—my sweat had now turned to prickly beads of frost on my skin. I was thinking that God had some kind of awful sense of humor about the weather in Bledsoe. It was so hot during the summer, a person had to go on suicide watch to get through August, and then just when it started to feel like a break, it was ice in your veins and all of this damned wind. I might have been angry enough to pray when I heard the sound of an air boat coming from the direction of Route 54. *Okay God, you're off the hook,* I thought and stood up.

I had no idea what time it was; it felt like afternoon, and from the look of the sun, I figured it was around three. I'd been waiting a long time. Andy saw me—I could tell—and waved, but it was a cautious sort of wave. I'd been so sure this was the right thing to do, but now, I was wondering if I should have stayed put at home. No one came after me—not March, Peter, Freddy. Once I had gotten about a mile from Hack Road, I let myself turn around to look. There was no one there. It was silence except for the lap of the water from the gentle tide, the sound of birds deciding when to leave, and then the fish giving me the hairy eyeball from the water that only serves as a grave to everything else but them. The bugs were all dead or hiding—too cold. The quiet was unsettling, and now it was gone. Just like that—whisked away by the blades of a boat engine, like the water where Emily Webber drowned. I frowned, trying not to think about so many things.

The boat slowed a little. Andy looked over his shoulder a couple of times at the open water from where he'd come. I really started to worry, thinking maybe he was going to turn around and go back, report me to the police, run off with my brothers and leave me behind, God only knows. He slowed even more, but to my pleasant surprise, it was to pull the boat up to the post to tie it up. He wasn't smiling though. There was a lack of goodwill I really couldn't ignore.

"Hey," I said. My tights were sopping wet, the bulk of the moisture at the balls of my feet. Andy didn't answer; he just looked at me closely, then away while doing the necessary work with the boat. I waited for him to finish with the rope and turn off the engine. It took some awkward minutes, but he was finally able to face me. We stared at one another, which got me thinking about Sarah-Anne and how she looked at everyone a little too long and a little too close. I wasn't sure what to say, especially because he didn't seem to want to talk to me.

"Sarah-Anne," I said, but nothing came out after.

"Yeah, I know," he said. His eyebrows jumped a little, half a step up his forehead.

"Right, but…" I paused, not sure what either of us was trying to say. "Your mom."

Andy winced. He'd never made that face before, like something broken off and sharp all around—he was suddenly all edges. He didn't speak for so long I thought no one might ever speak again. All the words were gone.

"Did you sleep okay out here on your own?" I asked after looking at my feet, and then the murky water, and then the boat, and then back to Andy's face, crooked like a puzzle piece left out of the box. I pulled my sweater around my shoulders. My hair was twisted in small ropes. It had gotten too long; it was always like ropes when it was too long.

"What are you doing here?" Andy asked.

"Just…I don't know. I ran away. There are police at my house."

"Yeah, I know," he said again. He was still standing on the boat, rocking with the water, tight body at home in the current.

"Oh," I said quietly. "What do you mean?"

He exhaled. "What do you want me to do about it?" He looked behind himself again, taking in what he'd just come through, where he'd come from. "You alone?"

"Yeah, just me. Sarah-Anne's still gone. You know what they're saying, right?" I asked.

He looked down and away; his brow furrowed deeply. "Well, I can't do anything about it now," he said like we were having two different conversations on different islands separated by a sea of other people's misunderstandings.

"Huh? I don't even know what you're talking about." I sounded like I was trying to start a fight—my words had a mind of their own and were coming out all prickly, with points on the end. Pine cone mouth had been a problem for me most of my life.

"Just," he said slowly. "Just, like, what do…" His eyes darted again.

"About your mom," I said. "You know what they're saying about your mom? And my mom?" Now I looked away, feeling suddenly very unsure of myself. "I mean, it can't be true." I swayed a little; my feet were like bowls of cold soup. I could barely feel my toes and was tired of damp.

Andy shrugged. "Don't know."

"Are you mad at me or something?"

"Don't seem like you have anything to do with it."

"I don't." I paused. "Like, why do they think that?" I asked. "About your mom?"

"Hell if I know."

"So they told you? The police?"

Andy turned away from me and bent down. The cooler and a couple of bags were laying on the floor of the boat. "They were looking for my dad," he said when he stood back up.

"Are they coming back?" I asked. "Our dads, I mean."

"I don't know."

"My dad's mostly worthless," I said, feeling suddenly ashamed. "I mean…I don't know what anyone's gonna do about it, and we can't find Sarah-Anne…" It didn't appear he was listening to me, so I stopped talking.

Andy looked over my shoulder, back at me, then over my shoulder again. I had my back to the marsh. I was looking the other way, at where Andy had come from, where the monkey lady was said to live, where the fort was falling down in the water. I got another cold drop in my stomach. Andy still had his hand resting on the throttle. "They're here," he said.

"Who's here?"

"Your brothers."

I turned around to find Peter and Freddy running knee deep in the brackish water. It was a comfort to see them, one I had not expected. It felt like days since I'd been home. It felt like I would never go home again.

Peter and Freddy were getting close. They were talking to one another in snarls, their feet slapping the water. Somebody was complaining about the cold while the other was saying shush.

"I'm sorry!" I said as loudly as I could.

"Shut up, Kay!" Andy whispered harshly. "Are you hiding out here or what?"

"I don't know." I ran my hand over my right cheek again—my skin was raw from all the rubbing, and I had a bad feeling this was only the beginning of having reasons to rub. I pressed my cheek as hard as I could and stood very still. I didn't want to cry anymore; the thought of it made me feel sick, like I had the flu—a fever from all the bad news.

Peter got to the house first. "Kay," he said, but not like he was angry. He was sucking on air for life and not at all concerned with feelings. It's a long run from Hack Road—I knew all too well.

"I'm sorry I ran," I said. "I was just so tired of sitting there, and they said Mom…and she wasn't wearing shoes, and…"

"Ain't one of you wearing shoes," Andy said. He nodded at Freddy.

"We left 'em at the bank," Peter replied, still huffing heavily.

"Not smart if we're hiding out." I nodded to Andy, who had made such a suggestion.

"I'll go back," Freddy said. "I'll go back and get them."

"No, we'll go back later," Peter answered impatiently. "We'll go back later." They were standing in the water while I was up on the deck and Andy in the boat. I felt like the queen of a real mess.

"So what happened?" I asked. No one spoke for a moment.

"It took him a while to realize you were gone," Freddy finally said. "We saw you."

"Yeah, but how'd you get outta there without him seein'?"

"He had to go somewhere," Peter said. "He told us to stay put."

"What a jackass!" I said, feeling bold while so freely using one of my favorite swear words without having to worry about a smack in the face. "So he just left y'all and drove away?"

"He said he was coming back," Freddy said, always defending authority. "He probably didn't think we'd hightail it out of there."

"Man, what a jackass." I laughed to myself even if it felt like sad laughing.

"I'm sure they'll come lookin' for us," Peter said.

The water seemed an awful place to be standing with the chill whipping around us like blades on a lawnmower. "Can y'all come up here? Please," I said. I looked at Andy. "Sorry, is it okay? They're gonna get ice feet. I already got 'em and I'm on dry land... or whatever this is." I stomped the platform in explanation.

"Where else y'all gonna go?" Andy wasn't smiling, but the edge was off his voice.

It took a few minutes for everyone to get inside and to get their wet clothes off. We were all standing around in our underwear—I was the only one with a shirt—in various awkwardly chosen spots in Andy's swaying house. We looked like checkers on a board; none of us would get too close to the other. My teeth were chattering; I'd yet to warm up since I left Hack Road. Andy didn't really seem to care that I was almost naked. It was a letdown, one of so many that day. I'd hoped to catch him at least taking a glance.

At first, it seemed like we were avoiding talking. Peter acted the strangest of anyone, and we were all acting strange to be sure. "It's like *The Goonies*," I said to break the silence.

"Chester Copperpot," Freddy added. There didn't seem to be anything else to say, so we were back to silence. Peter kept clearing his throat like he was about to say something, but nothing came out. Andy acted like ruler of a small, frightened kingdom. He had the power because we had nowhere else to go. It didn't sit well with me to be so desperate, but I'd always been wanting something from

Andy anyway. Maybe it was Peter's discomfort I was feeling, like a strong vibration coming from the floor.

"What do we do?" I asked.

"Why'd y'all come here?" Andy answered.

"We were lookin' for Kay, and she shouldn't have come here. We'll leave in the morning," Peter said. The house swayed with the tide and the fluid mood in the place. "I mean…if that's okay…"

I was about to ask him why we had to leave, but a strong gust of evening wind rattled the windows. I was colder than I'd ever been and nervous that I was about to say something that would make Peter hustle us out the door right then and there.

"They took Mama away, because…" I trailed off. "And Sarah-Anne's gone. I came out here, because…I forget." I didn't know why I had come.

"Have you seen Sarah-Anne?" Peter asked Andy.

"No," he said. "Where would I'da seen her?"

"She's lost," Peter said. "You were home—"

"I weren't. I went out in the boat." Andy looked away.

"Where?" Freddy said.

"Y'all, she's lost," I said, feeling like I had to defend Andy for some reason. "He went out fishin' like he's done every day of his life, 'cept when he was in California. Do they…I don't know if they have fishermen there, or—" I stopped talking.

"But did you see her?" Peter asked again. "Mom said she went out in the marsh."

"No." Andy folded his arms over his chest and stuck his lower lip out. We were all standing next to places to sit but wouldn't bend our legs enough to put our ass on anything. I kept swallowing; I figured if I didn't, I'd spew whatever was left in my stomach all over Andy's knotted pine floor.

"She's gone," Freddy said.

"We don't know that."

"Yes, we do," Peter said.

"No, I mean, like, she might not be gone, you know? Gone means—" I plopped on the ground and pulled my legs up under me, sitting on my knees. The knots in the wood floorboards were pressing into my shins. I was uncomfortable, but I felt better closer to the ground. "Like…what if something happened to her?"

"Maybe she ran away," Andy said.

"So how *did* your mother die?" Freddy asked abruptly. He'd been letting it build up; I could tell by the way the question erupted out of him like a powerful burp. It seemed to me we were about to cross a line.

"She drowned," Andy said.

"Do you think…" I started to say.

"I don't know." Andy shook his head. He seemed cautious and thoughtful. His mouth moved a little. He was looking mostly at Peter. "I don't know." Andy sat down next to me; Peter and Freddy followed suit.

"So you know what they're saying?" Freddy was having a rare

moment of confidence. It wasn't like him to take the reins. If he hadn't looked so vulnerable sitting in his wet underwear on the floor of the churning house I would have thought he'd changed. He was just pretending to be okay, like the rest of us. "They're saying our mother…"

"It don't matter now," Andy said. "Don't see what that matters now. I was little. I don't 'member her."

"You don't remember your mother?" I asked wide-eyed. He shook his head.

"They have new evidence then." Freddy pushed his glasses up the bridge of his nose. The lenses were slightly fogged. "This is an old case. There must be new evidence."

Peter coughed and looked at the door. It was still closed. We were all jumpy like we were waiting for someone to walk in and either fix this mess or blow the whole place to smithereens.

"What evidence?" I asked. "And anyway, Mom didn't do it… she was probably asleep when it happened. Woman's slept through half her life."

"They wouldn't just reopen a case if there wasn't some—" Freddy started to say.

"Listen, let's get some rest," Peter interrupted loudly. "We'll be out of here in the morning. Thanks for letting us stay, Andy." Peter stood up. It was dark out but didn't feel late enough to sleep. I watched Andy closely. He didn't seem to notice; he was looking at Peter. I adjusted my underwear and stood up.

"Listen," I said unable to control the urge to press on through these dangerous waters. Peter exhaled heavily and started to talk again, but I just raised my voice to get over his hump. "I just want to know what the hell happened to Sarah-Anne. It's not like I don't care about Mom, or..." I waited for a second, but no one spoke. "Or your mom, Andy, but that's like water under the bridge." I stopped talking again, because of the water part. I looked down. "I just... We can't do anything about that now, but we can find Sarah-Anne. I mean, where the hell did she go? It's like I don't even remember anything from yesterday. Where'd she go? She just...ran off? Where? And where the hell is Dad?" I slapped the floor with the bottom of my foot.

"He's with Nile," Andy said. He looked at the door again.

"That's some door," I said. "We're on our own. I don't know why ev'r'body thinks someone's about to walk through that thing. It's like we got a twitch or something." I jerked my head in imitation of Peter and Andy, who wouldn't stop anticipating visitors. "You're gonna get a serious crick in your neck."

"Kay," Peter said.

"Nile's not coming back," Andy said. "They're fishing."

"That's so weird," I said. "You should show respect and call your daddy 'dad' or 'father' or something like that. Calling him by his first name is like thinking he's your friend."

"He is," Andy said.

"Our parents are *not* our friends," I said. "Most of the time, they want nothing to do with us. They send us to school just to get rid of us. Your daddy wants you around all the time. That must be nice to be wanted around all the time. Kinda like Sarah-Anne," I said.

"Kay," Peter said again, a threat in his voice. My name was like the ticking of a clock keeping everyone awake all night. Just when you were about to drift off, there it was again. Kay. Kay. Kay.

"They let her stay home," I said.

"You hate being at home," Freddy said, rocking back and forth on his feet. He had his underwear pulled up to his belly button. It was as I'd expected—he couldn't do anything the cool way. I twisted my feet up underneath me and let my toes connect, knock-kneed and frigid. I was plain worried—I couldn't shake it. The reason I knew I was wound up too tight was that I wasn't thinking about underwear; this was a first for me while in Andy's house. I wasn't even really thinking about Freddy's frail-like body that reminded me of the kids from *The Grapes of Wrath* or from some war. I wasn't thinking about much of anything except being worried. Andy was acting a little strange for my liking—he'd been downright hostile to me when I first showed up, a woman in wet tights, and he hadn't totally cooled his touch since we all came inside and got our wet clothes off. *It had to be Peter*, I thought. The way he was storming around with his shoulders drawn up to his ears like busted shades had us all thinking something was about to pop—like maybe his head off his neck. "I'm just…worried is all,"

I said. "Real worried. I'm not, at the moment, all that prepared for a life of survival."

I caught Andy rolling his eyes at me. I had to bite my lip to keep it from trembling. This had been a difficult twenty-four hours. I wasn't sure how I would make anyone understand that without crying. Tears worked wonders on my father, but I couldn't be sure about anyone else.

"Anyway," Peter said, "I'm sure Dad's on his way back. When your kid goes missing, and your wife ends up in jail, you don't stay out fishing." Peter looked at the ceiling and rolled his eyes a little too. I wondered what it took to get an eye to roll straight back in your head forever. Lord knows we couldn't afford corrective surgery if one of these boys were to roll himself blind. I thought of sounding a warning.

"They can't leave the boat," Andy said. "They don't get their money if they leave."

"We've gone without money for so long, I can't see why that would matter, and anyway, didn't anyone ever tell you that money isn't everything?" I said.

"We really need money," Andy said.

"Yeah," Peter agreed.

"She..." Andy began to say.

"What?" I asked, but no one answered.

"I know he wants to get paid," Peter said to Andy. It was like they were having a private discussion.

"It's like you don't want him to come back," I said to Andy. I sounded mad, but I might have really been hopeful that marriage would be our only option with all legal guardians out of the way.

"Naw, I just don't expect them to is all."

"Our dad's about as useful as a busted toaster, but I'd feel better if he were here is what I'm saying." No one seemed to care that I'd spoken.

The moon was out; the sky clouded over, and the room went darker. We all noticed it at the same time. I was about to suggest that Andy light some candles or one of the weird oil lamps hanging from hooks on the wall when Freddy said he was going to sleep.

"Do you care if we stay here?" he asked Andy. I thought we'd already decided this, but Freddy seemed to need assurances.

"No. I hate being here by myself." He looked at me crossly. It was a bit of a victory considering he would only be upset with me if he was in love with me—people who are in love are always at each other's throats.

Peter and Freddy turned their backs on me and went to the couch where they lay with their heads and feet on opposite ends. It was breath-seeing cold in the house. I thought of lying there with them, just so we could all keep each other warm.

"We have blankets," Andy said. "And y'all can sleep in the beds. My dad isn't here. I mean…it doesn't matter."

"Where'll you sleep?" I asked.

"With you," he said. "You're the smallest."

I looked at Freddy and Peter, who were untangling themselves and rising from the couch. It seemed they had a decision to make about who would sleep where. Neither of them made a peep about me sleeping in Andy's bed with him—that's how tired we were. That or how unimportant I was.

"Are there a lot of blankets?" Peter asked. I felt sorry for him even though he didn't seem to care a lick about my honor. He was so grown compared to us, with his hairy armpits and his bigger body, like a man trying to break out of his boy skin, but here he was with us. He didn't have anywhere else to go either.

Andy walked over to a rubber container in the corner and removed several wool blankets in colors like shit, vomit, and gravel. I wondered how boys got through life with only this spectrum. Every boy I knew was hooked on bland colors and talking about going to the bathroom. I didn't dare suggest that I would like a more colorful selection. I walked over to Andy and grabbed the shit-colored blanket. I went to the bed on the left, hoping I'd chosen wisely. No one said a word as Andy passed out the rest of the blankets. I was near shaking with cold and anxious to get under the covers. I knew a thing or two about wool blankets—my father bought some at the military salvage store in Volmer and said there was nothing better. We didn't have heat either—other than the useless fire hazard we kept on the back porch; we could also sometimes see our breath in our house. It was a common plight in Bledsoe; I did wonder why it had to be like that.

At least there were sheets on the beds. When I lay down I smelled detergent mixed with seawater and fish guts. It would have made me sick if I thought about it too much. I knew they didn't have a shower in their house, not even running water. I decided, instead, to be comforted. This was where Andy slept, or maybe even Nile. They went to bed side by side every night, spent the day together working the sea. I didn't have that kind of closeness with anyone. I was given cause for a moment to feel sorry for myself. I looked at Freddy and Peter and decided that I was connected to them, like long nails hammered deep in wood. We could do this. We could do anything—together.

I pulled the blanket up over me tight and willed myself to warm up. Freddy went on the couch and lay down with his own puke-colored wool. Peter lay down on the other bed and turned his back to me, lying on his side. Andy climbed in next to me. His feet were freezing, like small blocks of ice on the firm mattress. He took another blanket and threw it over both of us before putting his head on the pillow next to mine. It was the first time all day that I'd really thought about Sarah-Anne. I started to cry. Andy put his hand on my shoulder.

"Don't worry, Kay," he said. "I didn't mean to...my mom's gone too. You'll get by. She wasn't a nice lady anyway." I wanted to ask him who he was talking about, but I liked the feeling of his hand on me and the silence around us in his bed. I kept my mouth shut. Maybe his mama wasn't a nice lady either—Sue-Bess sure as hell wasn't. I thought I heard him say Sarah-Anne's name right before I drifted off. I got a small twist in my side that I decided was envy. I sure was a rotten person if all I could do was be jealous of my missing, half-mute sister on a night like this. I fell asleep while the twist moved from one side of my body to the other and finally up my spine.

CHAPTER 17

The next day, I woke up to the shock of Andy's ceiling over my head. The morning air on his tin roof sounded exactly the same as at home, but I wasn't expecting such an unfamiliar sight when I opened my eyes. I'd slept too deeply for my bearings.

Andy was silent and not moving a muscle; I figured he was still unconscious. I glanced at the couch—Freddy was face down with only an arm and a foot exposed. It had to be a cold foot; the temperature had dropped a mile in the night—our thin blood struggled with such accommodations. I moved my own foot over to touch Andy's; he'd been like a Popsicle when we went to bed. He was warm. I let my foot linger a bit, worried I might lose contact forever if I lost it now. I lay very still and tried not to understand everything that had changed in a day.

I was afraid to move out from under the blanket. Peter was the first to brave the cold. He stood up in his underwear looking as big as an angry bear. He rubbed his arms with his hands over his chest and walked to where we'd laid our clothes on a small rack to dry. He began getting dressed. I watched him grab his crotch; I figured it was because he had to go to the bathroom. I, too, was struggling to keep the lid on my bladder.

"What do we do?" I asked Peter. I sat up and swung my feet over the edge of the bed. My stomach growled.

"About what?" he asked.

"I gotta pee."

"Go outside and lean off the edge."

"Yeah. I just don't want anyone to see me." I looked down. I was in my underwear just as I'd been the night before.

"We've got other things to worry about now," Peter said. "Everybody pees. Get over it."

I walked to the rack and grabbed my things. The dress had taken on a new meaning. I fingered the tights—dry as a bone. I put my dress over my head along with the sweater and went out on the small deck. The water was rough, choppy with a lot of white crests. I immediately had a layer of salty mist on my face. My legs were rattling in the morning air as I tiptoed over to the edge of the wood and stuck my rear end out. I managed to splash urine all over my legs and was grateful I hadn't put my tights on before going out to do my business. *This was going to take some getting used to*, I thought. I was trying to let my legs dry before going inside when the door swung open and Peter stepped out in his sweatshirt and jeans. He turned away from me, toward the Webbers' boat, and undid his pants.

"Boys are so lucky," I said.

He nodded but said nothing. I listened to the water—it was the only thing going on out there. The lap and pull, the birds skittering low then back up (also thinking it was too cold for such nonsense) the reeds swaying and bending under the wind, the mangroves looking furious at their plight—talk about cold feet.

"Why is it called a breeze in the summer and wind in the winter?" I asked. "Like in the summer, we think it's a good thing, but in the winter, we hate it, you know?"

"Right." Peter looked in the direction of Route 54, then at the boat, pausing slightly. The boat dipped and turned in the choppy water, tied tightly to the post with its marine stickers and American flags. I looked at the boat too, right where Andy had left it the day before. There was a blanket, damp with cold dew, lying like a bag of rubbish on one of the seats. You could see the layer of moisture clinging to it. It wasn't a wool blanket. We had the good stuff inside.

Peter looked up at me for a breath too long. I thought he was about to say something, but he must have stopped himself. He glanced back at the boat and then out at the water to our left.

The intracoastal was gray and foamy, like ink spilled on a hot griddle.

"Was he gonna sleep in the boat or something?" I wondered out loud.

"What?" Peter was distracted and in deep, hunched thought. He was only able to think really well with his shoulders drawn up to his ears like an ogre. I thought best with my lips pressed together and angry-looking eyes. Freddy was always thinking, so God knows what his best thinking face was; his sniffles were probably an indicator of serious brain work.

Peter looked at me sideways. "That cop lady told me that somebody saw Mom out in the marsh...the day Sarah-Anne disappeared."

"What?" I asked stupidly. I'd heard what he said. "Like, just walkin' around?"

"I guess," Peter said. "A coupla fishermen saw her out there. Up to her waist in it."

"No, Mom said Sarah-Anne was in the water. It was Sarah-Anne," I said. "Mom was wet when we got home, but that's 'cause she went lookin' for her. She went lookin' for Sarah-Anne." I was talking quickly, trying to halt the progress in my head when something clicked. I got a vision of Sarah-Anne wandering around the reed grass, just out of my sight, just beyond my perceptions—my mother trailing behind her, the hem of her dress skating on the surface of the water. There was someone else out there too.

Maybe it was Sarah-Anne I'd been scared of the day before—and not the monkeys or the fish or the fort. She did always scare me a little with that hair and that staring. The click happened again, but instead of trying to figure out exactly what I was thinking about, I got back to angry talking—the salve to my wounds. "So what if Mom was out there anyway? Why does that matter? The water's practically our backyard. Can't a person go for a stroll on their lands in this country anymore? I'm out here now—is somebody going to report me?"

Peter's eyes were darker than usual—he had brown eyes, light but not in the way of a sea green or a sky blue, more like the shell of a nut. "Kay," he started, but he didn't finish his thought.

"And when has Mom ever gone out in the marsh?" I continued angrily. "The fisher-people were seein' things. She doesn't go walking anywhere. And I mean…killing Andy's mama? Killing her? The woman drowned anyway—people drown around here all the time. If they don't drown in the marsh, then they drown in Lake Joduper. Can you imagine being from Bledsoe and drowning in the goddamned lake? There's, like, one lake for a hundred and fifty miles, and all this brackish, and you die in the fucking lake. I'm freezing out here. I've done my stuff, you know, so let's go inside." I danced a little between my feet trying to get the blood moving. "She called you sir, you know. Your first sir."

"Gonna be real cold today," Peter said like he wasn't listening to me at all.

"Low sky," I answered.

"Low sky. And anyway, she's gone and done it now."

"What's that supposed to mean?"

"Just means some fishermen said they saw Mom out here. She wuddn't alone. She wuddn't taken a stroll, Kay. It's not good." He opened the door to the house and walked inside. I had to reach out to catch it before it swung shut in my face.

"She wasn't alone?" I asked loudly.

"She was talkin' to somebody. Some guy…" Peter said with his back turned to me.

"Some guy?" I went in too, but not before Peter stopped in his tracks and turned around to face me. He looked at me a little too close and put his pointer finger over his lips. I nodded and put my finger over my lips too. *Shhhh.*

Freddy was still asleep, but Andy was awake and dressed. "I have more, like, warm clothes," he said mostly to me.

"Yeah, I mean, I'm not going to lie—I loved those sweatpants. These tights just aren't cutting it. Y'all saw that Mom was in her tights and no shoes, right? They took her away without shoes on."

Freddy moved on the couch, lifting his head for a moment before going flat like a pancake again. "She didn't want shoes," he said into his pillow. "She told them you could have her shoes, Kay."

"Why?" I asked. "She's not gonna die in there, is she? But yeah." I turned to Andy. "I could wear those green sweatpants again. It's just a bitch outside."

Andy handed me a different pair of green sweatpants; I tried not to act disappointed that he didn't remember which pair he'd given me before.

"You left a blanket in the boat," I told Andy. He stopped moving for a second, then pulled a sweatshirt over his head; it seemed like he was hidden in its folds for an hour and a half. Freddy looked at me and then Peter who was going bull-like out of frustration with my inability to stop talking. "You was gonna sleep outside?" I asked.

"I was gonna go look for your sister. It was cold last night."

"Oh," I said, feeling a little foolish.

"Thanks, Andy," Peter said. "We're gonna find her today." He went on like he was good at finding missing sisters and had done just that a thousand times.

"I mean, you were gonna just go off and look for her in the night? All by yourself?" I couldn't help but press. It was probably the jealousy making me sound suspicious and mad.

"I see in the dark just fine," he said.

"But the…you know…the world's a big place. I don't get how you'd think you was gonna find her just goin' around with a blanket or something. Where was you even gonna go? Where even?"

"Just…around," Andy said. The click popped again in my ear, but I wasn't quick enough on my feet to figure out where it was coming from—not while I was so preoccupied with playing second fiddle to Sarah-Anne.

"We'll take it from here, Andy," Peter said. "That was real nice of you."

"Yeah, it's nice that you're so worried about her," I said. The clicks were gone or maybe I'd just tuned them out. I was trying fiercely to convince myself that Andy wanted to be *my* hero, and that was what all this concern for my sister was really about.

"Well, I didn't go," Andy said. "Boat's too loud. Y'alls was sleepin." I looked at the door—so fascinating to everyone else the day before, like maybe I'd find the truth to his claims there. Instead it was just his wader boots sitting on one side of the frame, wet with muck around the bottom. Wader boots and jeans half-wet, half-mucked, laying on the floor in a lazy pile.

"Yeah," Freddy said. "Okay." He looked like he might say something else about evidence or math or more annoying subjects, so I charged back in. I was mostly hoping no one else noticed Andy's wet stuff by the door. He said he didn't go—the boat was too loud. I told myself it was his clothes from yesterday before we went to bed. I told myself not to think about it.

"Is Sarah-Anne…you know, like slow or something?" I asked loudly. I wanted to find her, and I did hope she was okay and all, but having everyone—especially Andy—so obsessed with her that they were willing to go out in the middle of the night to bundle her up in a blanket had me ricocheting off the walls.

"What?" Freddy asked as he started pulling his clothes off the rack. He'd sniffled his way across the room, shuffling left and right before making his way to his dry pants and shirt. His socks were mismatched with different colored stripes. Peter had removed his socks before wading out to Andy's the day before. Freddy, who was supposed to be the brains of the family, wore his in the water. They were in worse shape than my tights had been at the end of my trek. I shook my head in dismay. Freddy was always getting on my last nerve.

"I mean, what the hell is wrong with her?" I asked.

"Kay, stop using bad words to make yourself feel tough. Really." Peter ran his hand over his head. His face betrayed him, and he flinched. I could see that he was as tired of giving me a hard time as I was of getting it.

"But I mean it," I said. "You met her, Andy. What's wrong with her? We just let her go on being the way she was, didn't ask anybody what the hell was up with her. And now Mom…I mean, maybe that's…like, maybe…"

"I don't know," Peter said impatiently. "I don't know that anything was really wrong with her; she was just different and had trouble learning and all that, so she couldn't do school so well, or… she was always like that. I remember—"

"They told Mom and Dad that she had to go to the special school in Meridian. They said she couldn't go to the Bledsoe School anymore. They didn't have the right help for her there." Freddy interrupted. Everyone stopped moving, even poor Andy. He had enough on his hands without us around—we were only there because he hated to be alone. His mother was dead on account of some very bad deeds, or from not being able to swim. While he clearly had a strong passion for sharing his belongings with wayward families' children—between the three of us, we had about twelve pieces of his clothing already—that didn't mean he wanted to listen to us squabble and go on about Sarah-Anne and her afflictions all day. I'd have up and quit that game, but he had tolerance. I'll give him that—the boy could put up with a lot of bullshit.

"They told Mom and Dad she couldn't come back," Freddy said. "I mean...believe me, Mom was happy about it...but they basically kicked her out. Said they couldn't teach her in Bledsoe."

"How do you know that?" I asked.

"Welty." Freddy sniffled and adjusted one of Andy's jackets over his shirt. He looked like he had grown up overnight; even his freckles were fading. "Officer Welty."

"Boy, this guy is like a unicorn dragon or something," I said. "This Welty. He sure knows a lot about our family, even has your spit now, Freddy. Man's got stories and spit. I look forward to the day I meet the guy who knows more about my family than I do."

"She was nice," Andy said mostly to himself. His middling voice never really got around the bigger things in the room, any room. You could hear Andy, but it was like he wasn't sure he wanted you to.

"Did you know about this?" I asked Peter. "About her getting thrown out of school? Harder to get kicked out of Bledsoe School than it is to swim across the waterway, and that's damn near impossible. Damn near!" I was trying to ignore all this talk about Sarah-Anne coming from Andy. I figured if I kept shouting, I wouldn't have to notice this strange fixation. First it was dead Elizabeth who got all the attention, and now the love of my life couldn't stop talking about my missing sister. It sure didn't pay to stick around. "Did you?" I asked again. Yelling and repeating ourselves for effect was the Whitaker way—we could have written a how-to manual on getting under people's skin.

Peter shook his head, but I didn't believe him. Peter knew everything. He'd gotten in the bad habit of playing dumb.

"She was touching girls in the bathroom or something," Freddy said, slightly embarrassed as if he'd been discovered doing the same.

"I knew about that," I said. "But that wasn't, like, a real thing, just kids being weird or mean."

"I don't know," Freddy said. "But people were talking about it. Mom and Dad pulled her out after that."

"You said she got kicked out," I said.

"It doesn't matter," Freddy said. "They took her out when the school said she needed to go somewhere else. Whatever. She was supposed to go to the special school in Meridian."

"Oh, like hell," I said. "Like Sue-Bess or Clay woulda drivin' her all the way to Meridian. Tell this Welty fella not to get his hopes up that Sarah-Anne's gonna get to go to a special school anywhere."

It went quiet again but for the water in which the house was sitting. I sometimes didn't know if people went silent around me because what I said was so true it made them uncomfortable or if it was me who made them uncomfortable. I thought I was spitting truth. You couldn't get a falsehood off my lips with pliers. People need a person like that in their lives, who just gives it to them straight.

"But," Freddy said as if into the mouth of a cave, "she *was* pulling on girls' pants or something. I don't really want to talk about it." He closed his eyes and squeezed.

"Okay, so?" I said. This was just more evidence that there was something seriously wrong with her. I didn't understand the point of mentioning it if it was another sure sign the girl was right off. "That's what I'm sayin'... She's messed up or something. Who does that?" I put my hands on my hips and waited. The boys were all looking at me like they wished I'd go and disappear too, but no one said anything. I winced in expectation—nothing came.

The house rocked from the pressure of a swirl. They tell us gravity controls the tide, but I know it's God who does it. It was God pushing on the house. Wind hit one of the back windows and rattled it in its shoddy metal frame. God must have thought the lid on this secret was tighter.

"She was a weirdo," I said, because no one else was talking.

"Stop acting like she's dead," Freddy said. His voice came out flat and bitter.

"Sorry," I said automatically. "We're gonna find her."

Peter looked at Andy and then away. "Anyway, thanks for the clothes," he said after a minute. Peter must have been wearing Nile Webber's clothes, because Andy was a might smaller than him; it would have been hard for Peter to squeeze his chest into any of Andy's shirts. Lucky for Peter, he'd been wearing jeans the day before and didn't need pants like me—my brothers didn't wear homemade clothes; there were many advantages to being anyone else in our family but Kay.

"I'm starving," Peter said. Freddy and Andy agreed and suggested we go back to our house to eat.

"What if they're waiting for us there?" I asked angrily. "The police!"

"They probably are—we ran off. I'm sure somebody's out looking for us, but it's time to face the music," Peter said. He looked at Andy; there was a shock of electricity between them. I thought I saw something like a dark line; then it disappeared, and we all went back to pretending we were going to face the music.

"I don't want to get wet." I stomped my foot a little. Freddy and Peter looked exhausted of me. "I'm just tired of being cold."

"We have the boat," Andy said. "We don't have to get wet." He put his hand on my shoulder.

"The sky sure is low," I said, nodding.

There I was again, talking about the weather.

CHAPTER 18

Andy and Freddy did their best to go to the bathroom out of my sight. I wasn't trying to peek, but it was hard not to notice. I wore one of Andy's sweaters and his green sweatpants with my dress, tights, and sweater. I was warmer inside the house and afraid of what lay in wait in the boat. It would not be as romantic gliding about the marsh with my brothers by my side. Or maybe it would. I'd damn near lost everything—I supposed I should be thankful I hadn't lost them too.

It took us only about six minutes to make our way to solid ground. Andy sidled the boat like a man born with a fin and had us up on a sandbank without a hitch. I jumped over the edge and remained dry as a bone. My tights absorbed some of the morning mist on the ground, but I was far from soaked. I took Andy's hand after he'd lodged a few large branches in the sand and up against the boat to keep it put. I needed to hold on to someone. He looked at me closely and squeezed my fingers in his. I thought the ground would evaporate right there under my feet.

"Should we lift it up on the sand?" Peter asked.

"I think we'll be okay," Andy said. He'd done the dirty work while Freddy wiped his nose with the back of his hand and shivered. Peter made suggestions and pretended to move, but we left everything to Andy. I was his woman, so this was natural for me. The boys had some explaining to do as far as I was concerned. I couldn't get it through my head that we were all out there on our own because my mother was in jail. I couldn't look at Andy right in the eye because we all knew the reason for it.

"I'll be the scout," I said, taking the lead. "If I see anyone, I'll give you a thumbs-down."

"It's fine. We can all walk up there. We can see as well as you," Peter said. "Stop trying to be the boss, Kay."

I don't know if it was the fact that I hadn't eaten anything in almost a full day, or that I'd been cold all night with my head sticking out of the covers, or if it was that Sarah-Anne was so off and a pervert to boot, but I couldn't pull myself together and I began to cry.

"Stop being so mean to me!" I yelled at Peter. "All you ever do is tell me to shut up and quit talkin' and don't do this and don't say that! What am I even supposed to do? I'm trying to help. I just wanted to know why Sarah-Anne was always acting so weird. I

feel bad, like I guess I was supposed to pretend I didn't notice...
And Andy's mama... What are we even... I'da killed myself if I was
Andy! I mean, not killed myself, but killed me, like Andy should
kill all of us for making him grow up without a mother and no
education! I don't even know what I'm supposed to feel, but I don't
feel hardly anything at all, just bad that everyone is yelling at me.
It's like the goats—why'd he have to make me bury it? You're gettin'
to be like Dad." I pointed at Peter, my rail-like arm pulsing with
fury. "Mean 'cause it makes you feel powerful."

"I'm not being mean, Kay," Peter said. I could tell he was thinking about what I'd said. None of us wanted to be like Dad, least of
all Peter. Freddy looked at me like he was real sorry, while Andy
squeezed my hand a little tighter—he was made of pure understanding, even though he had no idea what we were talking about.
I thought God probably didn't have as much mercy in his own self,
master of the universe and all.

None of us would ever forget the goats. For me, that had been
my dad's lowest point, and he had a lot to choose from. Before the
drunk dog moved in next door, there was an old man and woman
who lived there with a whole bunch of goats. I was only about seven
at the time. We used to take crab apples down from the tree on the
edge of our property and feed them to the goats. It would pass an
afternoon quite nicely. The goats seemed to enjoy the apples and
always came running when they saw us. It had been Peter's idea,
originally, but I kept it going as I'm known to do.

The old man and woman—we didn't know their names or if they were married; my father speculated that they were brother and sister, gone rotten from too much time on earth, and too much time together—told us to stop feeding the goats the crab apples. They didn't really tell us kids, they told my parents—or my mother, who cannot be told anything without breaking into a million pieces, turning to shards on the floor. She told my father, who yelled at us and said if we did it again, he'd kick our butts with his boot. I think Peter said work boots ought to be good for something, and my father said he'd smack Peter's face. I listened to all the yelling and looked at all the hard faces, but it did no good—I still wanted to feed the goats. I tried to talk Freddy into joining me one last time, but he said no. I knew better than to ask Peter, who was more concerned with my daddy's work boots going so underused, so I asked Sarah-Anne to come.

The goats came running up to the chain link, as they always did, when Sarah-Anne and I made our way over; our skirts were pulled up and filled with mealy crab apples from the ground. There were piles of them under the trees. We must have had forty between us. We started pushing the fruit through the small diamond-shaped openings in the fence, feeling the tickle of the goats' papery tongues on our hands. Sarah-Anne was giggling; she'd come with us before but never given a goat an apple. There were about ten goats of varying dirty hues—some had horns, some didn't, some kicked their feet in the air while others stood very still staring at whatever was in front of them with a cheerful lack of interest, much like Sarah-Anne. They ate every last crab apple, so we ran to get some more. On our way back, I heard the old woman yelling something from the back of the house, from atop her clapboard deck. She was screeching bloody murder. I took my handful of apples and chucked them over the fence before running away. Sarah-Anne knelt down as we'd done before, not understanding the urgency. She pushed a few of the apples through the fence as the old woman on the porch kept up her painful-sounding yelling.

"Come on!" I said to Sarah-Anne. I grabbed her arm and yanked her away from the fence. I'd never seen her look happier; it was a little difficult on my emotions to tear her from something that was bringing her such joy. I had to figure she'd known so little of it as a mostly mute weirdo in Bledsoe. "She's gonna get her gun," I said to frighten Sarah-Anne. I couldn't be sure the woman had a gun, but I couldn't be sure she didn't either. Sarah-Anne gave a whimper of disappointment and followed me. I wiped my hands on my dress and instructed Sarah-Anne to do the same. We didn't want to be found out with all that juice on our hands and pulp under our fingernails.

The next day my father took me by the arm with an angry grip—I had bruises for a week after. He even tore at my hair, yanking me out of the house and down the front steps. "I told you to stay away from the fucking goats!" he said under his breath, furious and pulling. I stumbled after him, feeling bile rise in my throat. "I told you ten fucking times."

"We did stay away!"

He took a large fistful of my hair and shoved me to the ground. "And now you're lying to me." He pulled me up off the ground again only to jerk me so hard to the left, by my bicep, that I fell again.

"It was Sarah-Anne!" I said. I never blamed anything on her; no one did, because she didn't do anything—it would be hard to imagine her taking the initiative. "She likes the goats!"

"Come on," my father said, pulling on me so hard I tripped over my own feet and stumbled. My father had to drag me by my forearm for a few steps before I righted myself. "I want you to see what you've done."

We walked all the way to the edge of our land to find a dead goat lying on the property line. It was a gray goat—I remembered him. He had small knobs where horns were to come in some day. He must have been a young fella.

"What's that?" I asked, biting my lip hard.

"A dead goat! They can't eat the crab apples. It's like poison. I told you to cut it out. You didn't listen. They left the goat out here, so we'd get the idea, but it's YOU." He pushed my chest with his index finger. "It's YOU who needs to get the idea. YOU killed the goat."

I spent the better part of the afternoon burying the goat on the property line. I cried and wiped my nose on my dress. It was not a particularly warm day, but I remember sweating and smelling like sweat. I put the goat three feet in the ground even though my father said I needed to go neck deep. I think he was hoping I would dig so deep I'd end up burying myself. I cried the whole time, even when I told myself it was my idea to bury the goat. It wasn't. My father demanded it. When he came over to check my progress, he spit in the goat grave and kicked some dirt in my face. I thought I might never be able to love him again. I named the goat Billy as I was pulling his carcass down in the hole with me. I had to use his bloated belly as a step-stool to get out of the hole so I could fill his final resting place with the big chunks of red dirt I'd been tossing with a shovel all day. Billy the Goat, because as I said, imagination is hard to come by off Hack Road.

"We weren't supposed to feed the goats," Freddy said after a long pause. "One of 'em died."

"*We weren't supposed to feed the goats!*" I said in my best imitation of his nasally voice.

"No one is being mean, Kay," Peter said. "We're just frustrated. And we don't need all the extra…just…extra everything. Can't you go with the flow? For one day?"

"I wanted to be the scout," I said.

"Fine!" Peter said, pretending to be excited to do things my way. "You go first. Give us a thumbs-up if the coast is clear."

I let go of Andy's hand and took off running for the house, figuring that picking up the pace a little would warm me.

There was no one there. The place looked abandoned—I'd always thought it had that look about it anyway. A house with a strong tilt is not to be taken seriously. I ran back toward the boys a little, close enough so that they could see me. I gave an enthusiastic thumbs-up.

I could see Andy clearly even through the thick brush. His light face shone under the sun—a golden boy with white eyebrows. He looked just like his daddy. My breathing skipped a little, just a slight halt to the step of my lungs, not sure what was lurking in the back of my mind. It had to be more than Andy's dead mother. My own mother…I closed my eyes and stood very still, waiting for it—whatever it was—to go away. When I opened them again, Andy nodded at me but didn't smile. I wondered if our smiling together days were over. I had so enjoyed having someone to smile with on Hack Road.

The boys came running. Within five minutes we were in the kitchen eating a loaf of bread, some cheese that had to be trimmed of young mold, and apples. It was a day filled with thinking about apples. I had a hard time getting the first few bites down due to Billy and his shallow grave, but I was able to get it out of my head just enough to swallow.

CHAPTER 19

We stayed at our house the rest of that day and night but didn't turn on any lights. Peter asked me to keep out of my room at the front of the house—it was the easiest place to spot from far up the road. I saw it as my duty to stay glued to my brothers on the porch and to avoid the front rooms at all costs.

"I thought we were gonna face the music," Andy said with a smirk. Peter gave him a sideways glance, and I saw the line between them thicken—becoming more like a vein, one of those big veins on an old lady's leg, blue and bulging.

"If we're found here, we'll end up with the state," I told him. No one agreed or made any kind of response. I was growing tired of being the only passionate participant in the group.

"Let's just not draw any attention to ourselves," Peter said.

We'd plugged in the space heater and were all bundled up on various surfaces on the porch. It was colder than inside the real walls, but we couldn't be seen from the road like in the rest of the house. It might have been the power of suggestion, but the heater helped something serious.

"Of course we get a cold snap at the exact same time we become fugitives," I said, hoping to lighten the mood a little.

"We're not fugitives," Freddy said. "In fact, I actually think Peter has the right to be on his own. Or maybe if he were sixteen. You and me"—he pointed at me—"we're not old enough."

"Well, I don't know the proper definition of fugitive, and I don't care, but they carted Mom off to jail—like hell I was going with her!" I said.

"They wouldn't take us to jail," Freddy said, annoyed. "They're trying to take care of us. Department of Family and Child Services is chronically understaffed," he went on. "A liaison was supposed to show up to register us, but…"

"Okay, Freddy!" I shouted a little. "Stop talking like a dictionary and admit I had a great idea to get the hell outta Dodge."

"Kay—" Peter started but stopped himself, probably afraid of impending waterworks. I was real easily set off since our family started falling apart at our shoddy seams. I'd caught sight of my face in the bathroom mirror when we got to our house—bright-red cheeks with eyes like raw sausage. "Please," he held his hand up and waited.

We all went quiet for a minute. "I have to go sell at the market tomorrow," Andy said. "It's Friday."

"But what do you even have to sell?" I asked. "You didn't fish today. Don't that stuff go bad if it sits too long?"

"Some of it," Andy said.

"May not be worth it," Freddy said.

"I'm not hiding out," Andy said angrily. "I can do what I want. You're the ones on the run. I ain't…" He paused.

"You are too hiding out," Peter said, sitting up sharply. "Do you think the state would let you live in that house back there on your own? You're twelve years old!"

"Yeah!" I said. "And anyway, you told me they came looking for you on 54."

Andy's eyes flashed nervously.

"If you get caught, they'll take you in too." Peter was threatening, even from his position in a sleeping bag.

"They're just looking for my dad," Andy said. "I'm not in trouble."

"They didn't know you were on your own," Freddy said. "They do now. I'm sure Mom's told 'em."

"Why would Mom tell them anything about Andy?" I asked. Peter and Freddy looked at one another but didn't answer me. "What?" I asked again.

"I don't know," Freddy mumbled. "I'm tired."

"Is something going on?" I looked at Peter too.

"No, Kay," he said more gently than normal. "Don't worry about it. Not now." He glanced at Andy and then back at me, shaking his head ever so slightly. I got a chill up the back of my neck with all the secrets and nervousness around me.

"There's no more food here neither," I told the room in a loud hurry to clear the air. It seemed to me like the boys were ganging up on Andy, and all he'd done was help us through our worst times. "Andy might have to share his fish with us if we're going to survive. We're real lucky to have him."

Andy snorted like a mad horse and lay down, turning on his side to avoid looking at any of us. I snorted too. I didn't really know why.

That night I crawled from the porch to my bedroom and got in my bed, shivering but comforted by the familiar sights. I couldn't fall asleep on the porch with the space heater buzzing and cracking every three minutes, not to mention it was windy as hell, and debris was flying up against the screen left and right. Just when I'd be calm enough to doze off, a bunch of leaves or a sharp twig would slam against the screen or the post holding it, and I'd be back to square one. I fell asleep almost immediately once in my own room only to wake up some hours later with a jolt. I sat up in my bed and had to try four times before I could properly swallow. My heart felt like a rocket launch in my chest, and I was breathing double time. "Why?" I said to myself, not about my vital organs going rogue, but about this itch I'd had in my head all damn day. My dad drunk and mad, outside banging away at the air, at his life, at the night sky, and Elizabeth's tree the night before he said he was skipping town was like a tick in my armpit. I asked my dollhouse why, on almost exactly the same day as Sarah-Anne disappeared, they suddenly thought my mom killed Emily Webber? It did not answer. I asked my record player too; it also ignored me. I glanced out my window at the Spanish moss before I fell asleep again, uneasy and churning.

I was up early. I walked back to the porch before anyone else had stirred, just so I wouldn't get caught breaking rank. I lay down on my cot out there and waited. I must have nodded off, because I was surprised to find myself still there when Peter woke everyone up with a jolt of energy like an electrocuted frog. "I have a plan," he said. I woke suddenly and enthusiastically at the sound of a man on a mission. I hated long, empty hours. It was all life had handed me so far. I wasn't thrilled by the bad direction of things, but if we had a plan...if there was something we could *do*, then I might be able to forgive all of my oppressors for my sad circumstances.

"Please don't say we're going to bust Mom out of jail," Freddy said, rubbing his eyes and rolling around on the mattress like a bumpy potato. He was always so hard to rouse; it took hours for him to look fully awake. "I just want to go to school," he went on. "I don't care if we have to go live with somebody or...whatever."

"You hate school!" I said, sitting straight up.

"I hate this more." Freddy looked at the ceiling. "And I don't hate school, I hate the kids there. There's a difference."

I had to agree sitting around on the porch and eating moldy cheese was worse—even if only slightly—than sitting at my desk all day, trying to think of excuses to use the bathroom or the pencil sharpener, to grab a Kleenex, or visit the school nurse to discuss stomach troubles or my constantly sore throat. I didn't really mind the kids so much, but Freddy had the sniffles and couldn't run proper; it was a struggle for him. I had more options at school. The back of our house did not offer me a lot of interesting distractions—it had only been a day and a half, and my fuse was about to blow.

Andy didn't leave for the market that morning; he admitted there was little to sell and that fall and winter were slow. It was not worth it to sit there all day. This was, of course, one of the reasons his father went out on the boat—they needed money. It was not easy to argue with needing money.

Peter's great plan was that we go and find our dad. He said we could take the air boat out into the ocean and catch up with the big boat where Andy's dad and our dad were making their fortunes. Freddy laughed, and I tried not to. Peter didn't usually say such ridiculous things. He tried to persuade us a couple of times that chasing the boat was a good idea before giving up and saying that he had about forty dollars in his room and that we could send Andy to the store to get us food.

"He's the least conspicuous," Peter said.

"Maybe," Freddy said. I still felt like there was something I didn't know.

"I'm not conspicuous," I said, even though I wasn't sure of the meaning. No one responded. "Hey guys," I said as seriously as I could. "I mean, inn't it a little weird that the same damn day Sarah-Anne goes missing, Mom is suddenly arrested for an old murder?" I looked at Andy involuntarily. "Not old like...but isn't that just about the strangest timing ever? Like something out of a movie. No one's ever come here about the...murder...or...but then all of a sudden. Did anybody even think it was a murder? People drown left and right around here. Who said murder, you know?" I squeezed my toes and tried not to flinch. I kept forgetting about the rumors that Nile Webber killed his wife. "I mean, it was the next day, but a pinch less than twenty-four hours. Sarah-Anne gone, then POOF Mom's off to prison?" I was about to say something else about the weather but couldn't bring myself to comment on another passing cloud.

"Those fishermen saw Mom in the marsh," Freddy said. "Talking to somebody. That same day."

The room went quiet. I tried not to look at Andy but mostly couldn't help it. "I just wonder who she was talking to. Like, maybe he turned her in or something," I said. I thought about Peter with a finger over his mouth; my shoulders dropped in nervous discomfort.

"Let's just..." Peter said, "let's just not worry about that. We need to find Dad."

"And Sarah-Anne," I said. I thought Andy said something

under his breath, but being as I was trying not to look right at him, I couldn't swear to it.

After we'd decided not to take Andy's small, flimsy swamp boat out into the open ocean, and thought it better to wait until later to send Andy to the store on foot—when it was dark—there was nothing to do. I tried to talk about Mom's mystery man friend in the marsh again, but no one answered.

"Do we know what he looked like? Maybe we could track him down and find out what he was sayin' to her. He might know where Sarah-Anne is. He might have told the police about Emily. Like, maybe he lives back there too, and..."

Silence.

Instead of trying to figure out what to do, we watched *Hoosiers* on the porch. We'd initially thought it wasn't such a good idea to have the television going, but the day was long, and with all the free time, we were losing track of our minds. Peter kept saying we needed a plan, but we didn't make one. We walked around the cold house listening and waiting. I looked at Sarah-Anne's bed off and on throughout the morning—a morning that felt like three days. For some reason, I was convinced that if she came back, everything would be all right. We'd all realize there was a mistake about the murder. Our mom would come home and Andy would go back to his old self—kissing me and smiling all the time. I still might get to be a Webber in the end, if only Sarah-Anne would come back. I'd been thinking the whole time that she just wandered off and got lost, but she didn't wander off, and my mom didn't talk to men in the marsh, and my mom wasn't strong enough to drown someone, and Sarah-Anne never left the house, and my father had never been gone from home before, and now he was gone for a month. It all changed in a day, like flipping a grilled cheese over in the skillet a minute too late—one side black, the other one still puffy white. We were charred, and the only way to even it out was to burn the other side too.

During movie breaks, Peter continued to suggest we try to get in touch with my dad. We talked about calling the boat, but we didn't have a number—I wasn't even sure if boats had phones. I asked, but no one answered me. "I mean, where would the phone line go, right? No telephone poles." Blank stares.

Peter rifled through the papers on the counter by our phone to see if my mother had written down a name or an address for the company our dad and Nile were working for, but there was nothing there as far as we could tell. Andy said he didn't know how to call the company—they didn't have a phone in the high heel, so what was the use? He hadn't even asked his dad what it was called—the boat, or the company, or where they were going.

"What good would it do to call the company?" he said. None of us knew anything about companies either, so it was more blank faces.

"Yeah, but what if something happened," I said. "Then people would need to get off the boat." I assumed that my dad had no idea that anything had happened at home and that we wouldn't see him for a month. This was an injustice as far as I was concerned. We were left in Bledsoe doing the dirty laundry while he was pulling nets and hanging out with Nile Webber. "It's like you're just on your own when somebody leaves on a boat. They can't be held accountable, can they? You should have to check in with your family some-uh-tha time," I said bitterly. "That's where I'd go if I killed somebody..." I glanced sideways at Andy. "I mean, it's the same as running away." I thought about mentioning California and whether they had boats there, but I wasn't sure where I was going with this line of thought. I was pretty certain I was about to say something really troublesome if I hadn't already.

"I don't think that's how it works," Freddy said as if to rescue me. It was another dead end.

We toyed with the idea of going to look for Sarah-Anne ourselves, or of breaking my mother out of jail with a saw—that wasn't my suggestion. I didn't think my mother could do a damn thing to help us or anyone else. Other than having dinner prepared at six, she wasn't much use. I couldn't even count on a hug or a pat on the head most of the time with her around. I did miss her, but I couldn't figure out why.

No one could look Andy in the eye when we got going about wrongful accusations and my mother in the clink. Peter tried one more time with the following-the-shrimper suggestion, but no one even bothered to argue with him. The only thing we could all agree on was that we didn't want to get picked up by people from the state. They were bad news in our house—no matter which way you sliced it. Stay away from the state or keep them away from us was our only decision that morning.

No one was paying much attention to the movie. *Hoosiers* played for a second time at a low volume to our wide faces and blanket-covered bodies. Unable to really get into the movie, we were left with more time to sit and wonder at our fate. We were about a disinterested hour into it when we heard someone at the front door. Freddy had gone around and locked the doors the night before, so when we heard the front door open, it was a shock like the floor turning to Jell-O. We heard the click and swing at the same time. Our faces turned to one another—Dennis Hopper's great acting ignored for not the first or last time—and went a unified shade of white. I nearly lost my lunch out the seat of my pants for fright. I can't really say what I was so afraid of; all this talk of the state was turning my stomach.

"Kay?" I heard my father's voice. After recovering from my initial surprise, all I could muster was pride that he'd called out to me first. I was the first one on his mind; this had to mean something.

"Daddy?" I asked. I'd been lying on my stomach, facing away from the television. I pushed myself up onto all fours and then to my bottom.

He came around the corner of the porch before I could rise from the cot. "Where are the boys?" he said, even though everyone was right in front of him. It took some of the wind out of my sails that he cared about Peter and Freddy too. I wanted to be number one.

My father's face clouded when he looked at Andy. The boys, including Andy, all sat up with a bounce. "Dad!" Peter said.

My father stood very still, taking us in. He changed his focus to the screened walls of the room and felt the long stubble on his face as he did so. He couldn't have shaved since he left; he had almost a full beard. It smelled like dirty fish in the room—fish and sweat; he couldn't have showered either. "What happened?" he finally asked.

"I don't know." I didn't get up to hug him. I'm still not sure why—no one did. I suppose I felt we'd been left to rot at their rotten house with my parents' rotten deeds hanging over us. "They arrested Mom, and Sarah-Anne's gone." I let my eyes flash anxiously to Andy, who suddenly looked like a pickle in a bag of cucumbers.

My father exhaled heavily. No one else spoke. I thought he would offer an explanation. He didn't. I don't think he knew what he was supposed to explain.

"I don't know how Sarah-Anne got pulled into this mess," he said, mostly to himself.

"What?" Peter piped in, sounding angry.

My father collected himself and quietly said, "Never mind," like he had some good ideas that we weren't old enough to hear. "Sarah-Anne," he added even more softly. He put his hand over his face trying to stifle that guilty conscience again.

I stood up. "What's going on here, Dad?" I was irate, like a badly wired socket in rain. It must have been building for some time—maybe even my whole life, as I'd never wanted to grow up on marshland in the middle of nowhere. I'd never wanted to be the daughter of depressed people who couldn't cook food that wasn't potatoes or leave the house without feeling sorry for themselves. I didn't want to have a dead sister—maybe two of them—or even a sister who touched kids at school and got kicked out. I hadn't asked for this sentence in life. The only person I had to blame was my father. "What's going on?" I demanded.

"I don't understand how Sarah-Anne—" my father began. The boys were strangely quiet. Peter had been so hot on finding my father not an hour earlier. Now he was silent, silent and sitting on his hands.

"Yeah, what about her?" I interrupted. "And how come Mom just went off with the police—just went off with them, like she didn't care at all that they accused her of murder. I'd care! I'd care if someone said I killed you...or him." I pointed at Andy. "Or anybody. I'd care if I didn't do it! Seems to me if you...just go off with the police then you might have something to feel bad about. Like I'd at least put up a fight about my innocence. She just walked off with 'em like a dog on a leash."

"Well, that's...that's not our business anymore," my father said. "We need to focus on—"

"What the hell are you talking about?" I shouted. "It *is* my business! She's my mother! Look at my life. How can it not be my business? I'm livin' here. This is the only life I've got. Can't you understand anything about being a kid off this road? This is no place to live a happy life. People just want to off themselves here; it's so boring, and the school's like a place you go to get pregnant. And you..." I pointed at my dad. "Without a job all the time, so we have to eat potatoes. Your kids are dropping like flies," I said, shaking my head in disapproval. "You won't have any of us left if this keeps up."

He turned his body to the side with his arm outstretched. I'd been popped enough times to know what was coming. I gritted my teeth and steeled myself for the blow. It didn't come. My father was able to settle himself back down into his feet. I knew this game; I too had to get my feet back on the ground all the time.

"They said they saw Mom in the marsh," Freddy added calmly.

"Right," my father said, nodding. "I know. I talked to the police, so—"

"So what?" I said. "Lady cop came here. Called Peter 'sir.'"

"Sarah-Anne's lost, I'll bet." My dad sounded agreeable, almost naive, like me when my parents told me if I was good for long enough we could go to Disney World. I'd stopped believing them but not until after years of being extra helpful and polite around the house, thinking we were just about to pack up to go see Mickey. I must have looked like such an idiot wiping the windows in the front room with Windex and a paper towel talking about

Cinderella's castle. "I'm sure she just got lost," my dad said again, almost cheerfully.

"For a week?" I said. "Who gets lost for a week? She never goes back there anyway. Mom neither—they don't go back in the water."

"She used to." Peter looked at Andy. "Mom used to go back there all the time. She was talking to somebody. A boy..." He shook his head a little like he'd misspoken. "I mean a guy...or a man."

"Who was it?" I asked. No one answered.

CHAPTER 20

The interviews took place in a few different rooms that all looked the same. It was a little like school with all of the fluorescent lighting and tables made of plastic wood. I sat on one uncomfortable chair after another. A woman had been appointed to go with me to the "meetings." I didn't understand when they said "interviews," so one of the officers who had large thighs and a way about her that suggested she thought I was as off as I'd always thought Sarah-Anne was started to tell me I could go to my next meeting.

People were asking me a lot about my mother's character. "It's a fine character," I said the first few times. "She's no character, though. I mean, she's not funny. Not at all."

"What do you mean, not funny?"

"She doesn't have a sense of humor. She likes to read, but not funny books. Read and sleep. Now, Sarah-Anne is funny—not like a jokester or something, just plain funny, like funny acting."

"When was the last time you saw your sister?"

"Morning. When we left for school, she was there." I actually wasn't sure. I didn't want to admit that I usually didn't notice Sarah-Anne being there or not.

"What was she doing?"

"I don't really know. Just being Sarah-Anne. She was never really *doing* anything."

"What was your mother doing that morning?"

"These are the strangest questions to ask about my family. My mother doesn't *do* anything either. Like ever really. My daddy and Nile left that day, so she was up before we went to school… A miracle if you ask me. She's never up that early. Doin' nothing. Just sittin' around and staring at things."

I talked to several people; they all asked the same thing. "No one was doing anything when we left for school. Not a damn thing." I felt powerful breaking house rules in the Bledsoe Police headquarters. I said "damn" again. The woman I was talking to didn't seem to notice.

My father walked around the station in his faded blue T-shirt and torn jeans. We usually had meetings in the evening so that we could go to school during the day. It had been almost a week since they took my mother away.

Wade Welty, Freddy's spit tester, became my liaison. He was an officer with the Bledsoe Police but new in town. He'd actually come from Columbus—just a few hours up the road—which was a bigger, better place by a mile. He explained to me, like it was a requirement to tell me why he ended up in Bledsoe, that his mother was ill. Her sickness had prompted him to live his dream of deep-sea fishing—this was something he couldn't do in Columbus.

"Sounds like you came to the right place," I said. "I mean…" I exhaled with a shrug. "I don't even know… I wouldn't come here for all the money in the world, but I guess if you like to fish. Do I have to take a spit test too?"

"I hope so," he responded. To what part of what I'd said, I wasn't sure. I was not given a spit test that day, so I figured he was talking about the fishing.

Welty was portly in only his upper body, thick in the arms and rib cage area. He had dark hair that he wore gelled back. His face was like pancake batter bubbling on a hot plate. He was mushy and full with thick eyebrows and eyes that sat in a constant squint, like the sun was peeking around a shade. He pressed his nostrils together a lot—maybe he was trying to make his nose smaller. I'd pulled my lips inside my mouth for about a year, thinking them too large, and was sure that with enough effort, I could stop their spread. I didn't yet know people all over the world were paying good money to make their lips bigger. Welty had big lips too, but they were misshapen, so they looked like one large lip instead of an entryway into his head. He couldn't have been more than thirty-five, just like my dad.

Peter said Welty drank; that was the reason he looked that way. "Your face gets puffy when you drink all the time. His nose is all red like that from drinking."

"I'll be damned," I said. It seemed to me that Welty had such a commitment to physical fitness, what with all the dumbbells around his office and the pull-up bar in the doorway. I noticed his wedding ring, but he never spoke of a wife or kids. I suppose he figured that since my family was falling apart at the seams, it would be unkind to talk about his own.

Nile Webber was home now too, a day and a half behind my dad—broke as hell and stocking at the liquor store near Volmer since about an hour after he set foot on Bledsoe soil. Andy had gone home to stay with him, telling us goodbye one afternoon with a weird flick of his hand that was like a half wave, half middle-finger bird. I hadn't taken his departure well and cried more about being separated from him than Sarah-Anne—a fact that made me cry even more, because being a terrible sister is a real burden on one's soul. Before he went home to meet his dad, I was near one hundred percent ready to ask Andy to run away with me, leave all the trouble behind, forget our families, but seeing Freddy's red face and Peter's new, permanent scowl made me think I owed my presence to my family—they would be lost without my reliable bad attitude. We'd gone back to school and were otherwise living a normal life—save my mother being locked up and Sarah-Anne still gone. There was no trace of her. My mother wouldn't talk. She hadn't said a word since they brought her in. Not one. She never talked anyway. I failed to see why this was such a surprise.

In the week since my mother had been arrested, fall had set in, not a Bledsoe fall, which is like summer without as many bugs, but like we were living in Massachusetts or someplace north and dark like that. The air was wet, like soaked leaves ground up and sprayed in our faces—rotten confetti. There was the strong smell of the sea and wilted life. Night was coming on earlier and earlier and, with it, a blackness on the marsh that moonlight couldn't break. I could feel the slow, creeping decay and rot of so many things dying all around me. I was always curious how autumn could be anybody's favorite season. Everything was falling to the ground and turning the color of a leaf corpse. There was a light wind bringing the smell from the water over us; the marsh whispered in my ear. All I could feel was the damp cold and sleeping under a wool blanket at Andy's house. I wrapped my arms around myself trying to find that memory and its pleasant effects. Recollection wasn't enough to kill the bitter seed of ice that had been planted in the air. We were in for a wicked winter, and a bad winter this far down was about as unusual as losing two sisters in the same life. And your mother getting locked up for murder.

With all of my mother's silence, the cold northern weather, and the dirt I was dishing in Welty's office, my opinion of my family had deteriorated further. My father's terrible cooking—he'd made noodles with ketchup for dinner the night before and, when we complained it tasted strange, put a piece of Kraft cheese over the top of the skillet, like that was going to help—was making my bad vibes even worse. I started calling my dad Clay out of disrespect, sometimes even saying it with two syllables like Cuh-Lay to emphasize my lack of gratitude. I had a mean streak growing in me like a hot rod with a full tank of gas. I knew I could make it on my own if only the goddamned state and my goddamned father would let me be. I told Welty all the time that I was fit for life on the streets. His only response was what streets? Because obviously Bledsoe's cup didn't runneth over with paved roads.

I was so full of snake venom one evening, after a long talk with Welty about missing kids and how school as a convict's daughter was a real thorn in my side, that I decided to give it to my daddy—Clay—when I got in the car after my police meeting.

"You know you're ruinin' our lives," I said as I got into the front seat. I slapped the dashboard for effect and crossed my arms over my chest.

"I know," Clay said. It surprised me to hear him so agreeable to my complaints.

"Yeah," I went on, still itching for a fight, "I didn't think we had a real good thing going on before, and we sure as hell don't now. How you made such a bad thing worse, I'll never know." I rolled my window down and spat a wad and my feelings out onto the road. There was enough dust coming up in the cold night, it reminded me of my parched soul, desperate for a better life but stuck with what God dealt me. I was like a fucking dirt road in Bledsoe, Georgia.

"Yeah, but—"

"Mom's still not talking," Freddy said, interrupting my father, who hadn't sounded all that interested in responding to me anyway. I turned around in my seat. Peter was looking out the window at the night sky.

"That's 'cause she did it," Peter said to the one star we could see on account of the clouds and air pollution rolling in from bigger and better places.

My father took a deep breath like he was about to set us all straight but let the air out and said nothing at all.

"Hmmph." I crossed my arms tighter over my chest. "I really wish they'd find Sarah-Anne."

"I just don't understand how that happened." My father was talking to himself again. "God, if I—" He didn't finish his sentence.

"It just keeps getting colder…motherfucker!" I yelled to my bedroom window upon waking the next morning. I'd sensed I was not alone and, never able to resist performing for an audience, had found something exciting to say. Peter and Freddy stood over my bed like zombies at the dawn of the apocalypse. I'd heard the same said of the old people with the goats who used to live next door. I'd longed to have an excuse to say it. "You look like zombies of the apocalypse," I said to my brothers, "at the dawn of...anyway..."

"We found something," Freddy said.

"Is it morning?"

"Almost," Peter answered. "We found something in the shed."

"Okay. What about?"

"It's not...about anything," Freddy said.

"Sorry, I'm still asleep here," I said, sitting up completely. "Should I call Welty?" I asked, always looking for a reason to get outside my family. They were like a tight coil of snakes around my neck, pulling at me, squeezing, gripping, getting all the air out of my lungs. There were days when I would have done anything to be someone else, to be in any other family, to have woken up under a different roof. I was embarrassed to be a Whitaker—in a town filled to the brim with embarrassing, ashamed people, I was the most embarrassed and the most ashamed. I wanted out.

"Maybe," Peter said. Suddenly I was hopeful. "Come on— Dad's still sleeping." He walked out of my room in front of Freddy. I followed closely, in only a T-shirt and my underwear. I grabbed my sweater from the floor on my way out. We went to the back of the house and out the porch door. I'd slipped on a pair of my father's shoes. They were stiff with fake leather insoles. I wished I'd gone barefoot; it would have been more comfortable.

"You gotta cut your hair," I told Peter. "I know we're running from the law and all, but your hair is really gettin' to be like a cactus."

Peter ran his palm around the top of his head self-consciously. We'd made our way from the house and out of my father's direct earshot—if he was even awake and listening. We were standing under a waking sun, shooting its light at a sharp angle, that did nothing to stifle the bitter temperatures. I squinted while pressing my teeth together to stop them chattering at the same time—there had to be something queer about this. The sun did us no favors in Bledsoe. It was not a land of favors.

"Where we goin'?" I asked.

"The shed," Peter answered.

"What? Mom's got another kid buried in there? Tied to a pole? Just her style..."

It caught me off guard to be knocked upside the back of my head so hard. I didn't know it was coming and I would never have expected it from Freddy. My teeth cracked together, causing me to bite my tongue—just the right side of it. The trees shifted a little from their roots in the ground. I knew they weren't moving; it was my eyes trying to figure out what the hell just happened.

"Stop talking like that!" Freddy yelled. His excited voice was like a fork being pulled over glass—tines down. "Whose side are you on?" he said even louder. "Stop talking about Mom like you don't care about her!"

"Freddy!" Peter said.

"She is always like this!" Freddy said, pointing at me. His redness had become confusing—I couldn't tell where his hair began and his angry face ended. "She gives them such a hard time."

"Somebody has to!" I rubbed the back of my head then put my hands on my waist. "Somebody's gotta tell 'em like it is. They're supposed to be looking out for us, but they're just a goddamned mess! I mean, you do realize what's going on, right?" I felt like this was the first time anyone had spoken plain truth in a decade. "They're sayin' Mom killed Emily Webber. She's a bad person! Sewing and reading and hiding out, and here we all thought she was this little sweetie pie, and she's just...awful! She's so awful she can't even face us! She hasn't spoken to us in weeks! We're her flesh and blood! We're her kids and she can't even look us in the eye. She's made of a real bad material. Devil spawn if you ask me, and here I always thought I was the one...you know, I was the one making trouble... Freddy, they're saying she KILLED someone!"

No one said anything for a while. Maybe I'd struck a chord. It was my desired life's work—to strike as many chords as possible.

"But you're so mean about it," Freddy said. "We're a family. You'd rather be a family with Andy. Or Welty...or whoever'll take you in. Families go through bad times, but you're just mean—and you never shut up! You *never* shut up!" I thought he was going to start crying he was so upset about how much I talked.

I knew I was a motormouth, but maybe I *was* mean. It sure seemed as though my mother was a mean person. I'd always thought I was mostly like Clay, but Sue-Bess and I had more in common by the day. But I sure as hell wouldn't kill some kid's mother. I wasn't sure what I believed about Emily Webber anyway. The trouble was our father hadn't really denied that my mother did it. He looked away when the topic came up—you'd think we didn't have anything else to talk about, but the *murder* rarely came up, and when it did, it was shut down as fast as a bug under a mallet. Peter and Freddy were better at quietly pretending they weren't paying attention; I liked to take the hammer to the glass.

I knew I had some things to figure out—deeply within myself—where I hid all of my worries about my personality being so annoying, the way I couldn't sit still for more than a second-and-a-half, my desire to have so many husbands, and my obvious dislike for both of my parents. I couldn't remember missing my mother or crying for Sarah-Anne. I definitely hadn't cried for my mother, not one tear. I found it was easier to cry for Andy, out there alone with a dead mama and a father who didn't like to be called dad. I certainly cried for myself all the damned time. I started to wonder if I only cried a little about Sarah-Anne because I didn't really feel awful that she was missing—it sure seemed that way. The thoughts and feelings in my head were clashing and crashing into one another like waves up against a steep cliff. I didn't know what I thought, so I talked to try and figure it out. I would have thought the two boys who'd lived with me my whole life would know that by now. I *had* to talk.

I was breathing heavy, thinking of all of the things I could say to my brothers right there, outside the shed, in the slant of the sun, but I didn't say anything else. I choked on the unsaid words; some stuff is a real bitch to get down so early in the morning.

"I care about Mom and Dad," I said after a long while of all of us looking at one another. "I don't think saying mean things about someone means you don't love them. But I'm not blind. And I just don't know what we're supposed to do."

"Neither do I," Peter said. "I really don't. Maybe we're not supposed to do anything."

"Is Dad still asleep?" Freddy asked.

Peter nodded.

"What's in the goddamned shed?" I asked. "I can't do any more sitting around here talking, and thinking, and getting hit in the face." I pushed Freddy in the chest. "You should say you're sorry, and I shouldn't have to tell you that!" Now I was mad. It had taken me a minute, but I was as pissed off as I'd ever been. "You don't hit me!"

"Sorry," he said. Even as a victim of his violence, I had to pity him some. It was how I'd always handled my disappointment in my dad.

"So what's in the shed?" I asked again. "Come on, now." I tucked my hair behind my ears. I too needed a cut. We looked like wartime children from my social studies book. Freddy sniffled as if in agreement with my thoughts.

We followed behind Peter who bulldozed his way through the thick brush—weeds grown over vines, grown over something that was once a viable plant but now lay gnarled beneath a mound of tangled, strong fingers, gripping the life out of it. My bare legs were ashy in the harsh light. I'd gone a little knock-kneed from the cold and was shuffle-stepping to keep my dad's shoes from falling off my feet.

Peter opened the dislocated door, hanging on by only part of a rusty hinge, and presented the inside of the shed to me, like I was to be amazed by the sight of such a dumpy, small building. Inside was Peter's boat, a relic left over from our childhood. I remembered it well.

Peter had been fond of taking the boat out in the shallow water when he was younger. He used to pretend for hours, gone a whole afternoon in the marsh. We could hear him talking to himself or maybe an imaginary friend. He took the boat out with his collection of rocks and sticks and various other treasures. He never let Freddy or me go with him; he preferred to play alone. There came a time when I think it embarrassed him that he was out there, pretending to be a pirate, or a Viking, or whatever it was, but he kept at it—just becoming more secretive. Freddy went through the same thing with his comic books. He'd been proud of them for so long, carrying them everywhere, talking endlessly about the Green Lantern and Porky Pig, and then all of a sudden, they were under his bed and hushed over. If I said something about The Flash in front of Cort Hat, Freddy would tell me to shut up and then blush so bright I could have seen him from the moon. Goddamn, how a person survived with that kind of skin.

I didn't play so much as a kid; it seemed I'd always been bored. I never mastered the passing of time the way the rest of my family did. Thinking of Peter and his boat adventures, and Freddy with his secret comic book world, and all the miniature plastic figurines that went with it made me remember something else—my mother walking in the marsh; she was different then, stronger—but it went away too fast for me to take a good long look. Peter was talking about the boat being in the wrong spot, and Freddy had raised his voice, saying something about water, and I lost what I'd just been about to remember. I saw my mother with blood all over her dress, crying and yelling at my dad, and then she was smiling real big like she never did, my father sneaking in the back door of the house—through the porch. He saw me and…the memory was gone. It flew away with Peter's and Freddy's ability to pretend, to escape, to be happy where they were. I'd never known how to do that—Sarah-Anne and I were too close in age, and then Elizabeth. I got caught in their middle.

"What?" I said. I hadn't yet told anyone the door was open the day Officer March was at our house.

The boat was not lying on its side against the wall where it always was—or at least where it had been since we last saw anyone use it. The boat had been recently moved. There was no floor in the shed; the dirt was freshly plowed where the boat had been. I could see footprints in the damp soil and lines where the boat had been pulled out, then pushed back. I hardly ever went in the shed, but I knew someone else had been in there. It was clear as day—the mark of a body—feet on a body, shoes on feet. Boots. I couldn't help but close my eyes.

"The boat's wet," Peter said like he didn't know boats went in water.

Freddy peered over my shoulder and stuck his chin out. He looked like an owl—a red owl. "It's wet!" he said loudly. He was edging on shrill. I hated shrill—it reminded me of the goat people and the drunk dog. There was always some asshole next door.

When we were smaller, my dad took us out in it one at a time—sometimes me and Sarah-Anne together. It was Sarah-Anne's favorite thing to do. "You wanna go for a boat ride?" I could remember my dad asking. Next to killing the goat with too many crab apples, riding in Peter's boat had been the only thing that ever made her smile like a regular kid. She tried to take it out on her own a few times, but my parents wouldn't let her. My mother saw her dragging it through the reeds and screamed for my dad, who went and pulled Sarah-Anne and the boat back to the shed, to the house, away from the rest of the world. That was a long time ago. She was little then. I hadn't seen her near the boat in years. It was like a half-boat anyway, *light as a feather* I remember my mother saying. That was why Sarah-Anne could lift it. I shook my head to get rid of all this extra memory—it was stifling, like the smell in the shed.

"Light as a feather," Freddy said in a sing-song voice that

sounded a little like my mother's, breathy and up high, above us, where no one could get to her.

"Why's it wet?" I asked. "I mean, even if Mom… Would it still be wet?" I sounded angry. It might have been that my legs were freezing or that I was tired of making strange discoveries. "Have they even gone looking for Sarah-Anne in the marsh?" I asked. "You know? Like, are they saying she drowned? Does Bledsoe have the money to send scuba divers out into the water? Should they be out looking for her? Someone said they saw Mom out there. The fishermen…they said…but that was over a week ago."

"It's wet in here," Peter said dismissively. "Nothin' dries in the shed. What I'm saying is somebody's been in here. It's been moved. Somebody went out in it." Peter stuck his fingertips in the small layer of water in the corner of the boat; it was tipped on its rear, leaning on a tower of paint cans. I saw it was the mold paint and turned my head away in disgust—we had to be the only family around with mold paint. We were really scraping the bottom of the barrel on Hack Road.

"Door was open the other day," I said under my breath like a confession.

"It was?" Peter asked.

"When I ran from March. The door was open. I thought maybe the police went in there, or maybe…Sarah-Anne or…"

"Did they say they saw Mom in a boat?" Peter asked after fingering the old water for a while. "I thought they said she was walkin'."

"They said she was walking," Freddy said calmly.

"She couldn'ta got the boat to the water anyway," I said. "It musta been Sarah-Anne; she can pull the boat."

"She doesn't wear boots," Peter said. "Dad either."

"No." I looked away. "Could be police boots. Maybe they were searching around in here?"

"The boat's been out in the water. The police wouldn'ta done that. And anyway, I never saw 'em back here. I don't think they even knew the shed was here."

"Not much to look at." I nodded at the rotting wallboards. "Probably thought it was a trash dump."

Peter leaned over and pulled a long thread from the bottom of the one plank seat. It was a shiny metal thread, twisted like hard dental floss. It had kinks in it. I reached for my hair—all the wrong stuff reminded me of my rat's nest.

"What's that?" I asked.

"Dunno." Peter put the string down. "Prob'ly somethin' Dad found."

"Twine," I said.

"I'm just…" Freddy threw his arms up and let them flap back down on his legs like broken wings. "I thought it was dental floss."

"It ain't dental floss," I said, taking a great deal of pride in knowing more than Freddy about something. "It's silver, or metal or something. Dental floss is green." I knew full well what we'd found, but something was telling me to leave it alone.

"I'm sure there are different—"

"Okay! Quit it!" Peter put his hands on his head and squeezed his face real tight before releasing it and letting it flatten wide, pale, and bug-eyed. "Let's go. Let's get outta here. Now." Peter took a step back, stumbling over a hammer on the floor. My father could spend hours sharpening knives and organizing hammers he rarely used—he was some strange sort of busy. Now it appeared he was collecting guitar strings.

"No, I'm not going," I said. "Somebody was out in this boat. Recent. I know it's been over a week since all this went down, but the shed's like a mold factory. I haven't been in the boat, you neither." I pointed at Peter and Freddy. "And Dad just got home. Plus he'd capsize the thing, and he don't wear work boots, 'cause, you know— what's the point? I wanna know who the hell took this thing out!"

"Let's get out of here," Peter said firmly. His face was twitching with all the terrible things that could have happened.

"What about Sarah-Anne?" I asked.

"But the boat's back," Freddy said.

"So?"

"Sarah-Anne's not back." Freddy looked at the ceiling. I did too—nothing there.

"I think we gotta forget about Sarah-Anne," Peter said. He looked at the ceiling too, so it was like we were watching a rocket fly over us, but it was just the roof of the shed, gray and rotting. We all looked down at the same time, at our feet, then at the shoe prints on the floor. "I think something really bad happened."

CHAPTER 21

I gotta lay down with a compress," I said. "Like, really lay down with a compress, hot."

Neither of my brothers responded to me. I opened my mouth to again announce my intentions but was interrupted. We'd gone back inside and were staring at one another in my brother's room like we might as well end it. I figured it was as good a time as any to complain about my headache.

"There's Andy!" Freddy said. I felt a wave of relief wash over us; Andy gave us something to do. We hadn't seen him in almost a week. When Nile and my father came back from the boat—early and empty-handed—Andy went home; that was the last we saw of him. I asked a few times if we could invite him over, but my father wouldn't answer me. Clay just turned away. Sometimes I forgot to disrespect him while thinking about him, but when I remembered, it was plain Clay.

"What's he doin' here?" I asked hopefully.

"He prolly left somethin'," Peter said.

"Or maybe he ran away!" I was excited and wondered if Andy wanted to keep running, like through the house and straight out the front door with me in tow. I was optimistic, feeling like in a matter of minutes, I would be able to leave. Forever.

My father was still asleep; at least we thought he was. No one had heard a thing all morning. I thought to suggest we check for signs of life, as he was never this peaceful. He would lie around, angry and upset at the state of a world that had been so unfair to him, but he didn't sleep. He didn't remain in his bed. He didn't retreat. He and I were made of the same dough—we confronted our enemies. Being flat comatose is no confrontation—unless, of course, you're my mother. But then I guess that wasn't entirely true.

We made our way from the boys' room to the back porch so we could greet Andy. I stepped up on my toes a little, prepared for flight. Andy was hightailing it through the sticks. I shuddered a little. It didn't matter where you were in the house, it was cold and damp. I'd donned some tights and a dress, along with socks and a heavier sweater. Freddy suggested I wear a hat, being that heat escapes most rapidly from the head. I wrapped my scarf around my neck and corrected him, saying it was actually the neck. "Thinnest skin's on the neck," I said.

We walked to the edge of the porch, our faces practically pressed up against the dirty screen. I figured we were a sight, standing there looking at the marsh. Everything was at the back of the house, it seemed. Just me in front. I was the buffer between us and Hack Road. I let my face touch the screen; I pressed a little, hoping I'd get some sort of sensation back. Numb is worse than silent.

Andy came in the back door slowly, unsure of his surroundings. He'd seen us but hadn't yet spoken—we were hard to ignore, standing there like some sort of screen-worshiping cult trying to get a sign from our god.

We were all motionless for a moment, silent and still on the porch's concave middle—the boards retreating down an invisible drain. No one knew what to do or say, the blind leading the blind. I guess we all thought Andy had come to rescue us. He looked as lost as we did. No one said a word. It was the lowest I'd felt since Sarah-Anne disappeared. I didn't want to feel myself sinking in the mud anymore in Bledsoe. It was like with every passing minute, I became more like the people who couldn't leave—up to their knees in it.

"What?" Andy asked even though no one had said anything.

"Mama went out in the marsh," I said. "The day Sarah-Anne went missing. Did you see her?"

"Oh." Andy's face went from the yellowish brown I'd come to associate with him to a pink version of it. "Naw, I didn't see her." He didn't sound sure. "I left my bag here," he said.

"I didn't see no bag," I replied.

"It's…" Andy pointed at the cot lowest to the floor.

I looked—sure enough, his duffel was there. "We think Mama took out the boat," I said. "You woulda seen her. A woman in a half-boat is somethin' you don't miss."

"I didn't see your mama in the boat," Andy said.

"Well, some other fisherman types did," I said. "They said she was with somebody…"

His face twitched like he was trying to remember a helpful detail but couldn't quite get at it. "I never saw your mom in the boat," he said. He was definitely about to say something else, but Peter jumped in.

"Andy, do you *really* know how your mother died?" Peter said angrily, like he was accusing somebody of peeing on his tooth-brush. It was an out-of-the-blue question. I couldn't figure out why he asked it. Not then, when we were talking about our little boat lost out in the marsh.

The words had barely left Peter's mouth, when we heard footsteps coming from the kitchen. Our house told a million tales with its ill-fitting boards and joists. If a person was having a hard time getting their socks on in one room, the whole family knew it—what was left of us. We were three down this cold October. Bledsoe was no place for a girl, this was for certain.

"Drowned. Wuddn't nobody's fault as far as I know. Just drowned," Andy said. I thought maybe Andy got used to telling people that since he and his daddy got run out of Bledsoe after

Emily died. If it wasn't anybody's fault, then it wasn't his daddy's neither. It was good enough logic.

"Drowned what?" my dad asked as he rounded the corner. He wore the expression of a man who knows exactly what.

"Have you been in the shed?" Peter asked him. "The boat's wet. Somebody was out in the boat." Peter and my father shared a look that had my stomach in a terrible tangle. Peter seemed to be suggesting something.

"No," my dad said slowly.

"Why's the boat wet then?" Peter stood taller.

"Goddamn," I said under my breath. My dad looked almost as bad as my mother being taken away in her tights, her little head dangling over her weak neck like a sucker on a broken stick.

"Did you go out in the boat, Dad?" Peter asked again.

My father said nothing. He was dressed but limp; I wondered if he'd slept in his clothes the way he was so rumpled. His face looked pitted, hanging off his bones. He had clearly been crying. His cheeks had trails of tears down them, like his waters were made of bleach. If I had to guess, I'd have said he went about four hours with a wet face.

"You don't know?" Peter said to my father's silence.

"See, I was thinking the water was left over from when Mom took Sarah-Anne out there and drowned her ass," I said. The crack across my cheek was chilling just like an icicle in my ear—I knew all about that. We froze water one dull day during an especially dire

Christmas break and took turns putting the sticks of ice in various holes on our bodies. The hit came up against the right side of my jaw. I actually fell hard this time—crumpled on the ground like a hornets' nest after somebody knocks it with a broom handle. I lay very still; a hand went on my back, then another on my shoulder. I could hear talking, but my head was thick, like with clay between the ears.

I sat upright to see Andy's face before me. He was stricken, most likely with fear but probably a little grief. This was certainly not what he'd bargained for when he saw me running through the marsh that first day. He didn't need friends like this. Or maybe he already knew we were bad news; I was of the bloodline that took his mother.

My father grabbed my upper arm hard and yanked me to my feet. He was talking, along with another voice coming from close by. I shook my head a little and squeezed my eyes shut before opening them again to a room with a better view. I had an itch on my head and ripped my left arm out of my father's grasp in order to reach it.

"You have to stop hitting me," I said to everyone who'd ever taken a swing. Andy was the only exception; Peter had done his fair share over the years too.

"Don't say that," my father said in a hiss. "Don't say that about Sarah-Anne or…"

"Or what?" I challenged.

"We have to work together." My father clasped his hands as if desperate to demonstrate what he meant. "We've got to find Sarah-Anne." He looked like he was praying again. I'd certainly never seen the man pray before; it was a sight for sore eyes if I believed he could lower himself to ask someone for help—God or otherwise. "We can't have lost her." He was having an inner struggle of some sort—or a struggle with his hands. He kept running them through his hair and over his face. If I didn't know better, I would have thought he was trying to get out of his skin from the top down. "We can't have let this happen."

"I didn't lose her," Peter said. "I didn't let anything happen to her or anybody else. I haven't done anything wrong."

"Me neither," I said proudly. "Ever. And if we're gonna work together, you can't crack me upside the head!"

"I know!" my father said in frustration. "I know." He wouldn't look at me; that's how I knew he felt really bad about it.

"Did Mom go out in the boat?" Freddy asked my dad. "Looking for Sarah-Anne? People are saying they saw her out there. Andy says she wasn't in the boat though." Freddy pointed at Andy eagerly.

I felt my breath catch in my chest.

"Dad, did Mom take the boat out?" Peter asked again before Andy could say anything. He seemed excited to give the impression he was now in charge.

"I don't know," my dad said. "I haven't talked to your mother."

"You haven't talked to her?" Peter asked.

"She won't see me."

No one dared move. I squeezed my lips and my face like I'd eaten a ripe lemon. I turned toward Andy, who was looking away, not at anything in particular, just away.

Clay frowned deeply and put the tips of his fingers on his brow. "Anyway..." He drew his lips into his mouth and looked up. He was about to speak, but I interrupted him.

"Anyway what? Where the hell is Sarah-Anne then?" I pulled on the skin under my eyes and tried to get my head right. "This is like...out of a dream or something. I just can't..." I was trembling. "Mom musta taken the boat. I mean, that's what we're thinking, isn't it? So *did* Mom take Sarah-Anne out in the marsh and drown her ass?" I curled my fingers around my mouth and shook my head from side to side. "Is that why she won't see you? Her own husband?"

"Dad, is that what you're thinking?" Freddy asked.

My father had clocked me up the side of the head only minutes earlier for saying as much—now we were all considering it, like a fact. There's no arguing with facts. "I'm not thinking anything," my father said proudly; his empty head was now something to brag about.

"I don't believe it," Freddy said. "I don't believe a word of it!" He was going to cry; I could see it in the shade of magenta on his cheeks. His eyes were going the way of pinkish red too, welling up, filling, blinking rapidly and then straining to remain wide open.

My father looked at Andy, who was lingering around us like smoke from a burning cigarette. He hadn't said anything. I looked at him too, curious why he mattered right now. We were an oddity—the five of us standing there—like a group of people all struck by the same bolt of lightning who were just now meeting for the first time.

"Woman's sick in the head. I coulda told you that a long time ago," I said. "Looong time."

"Shut up, Kay," Peter said.

I was considering telling him right then what I thought of all the shut-ups and his stupid plan to go out in the ocean in Andy's boat. He kept looking at my father—perhaps waiting for him to evaporate. One of them was the problem here; I couldn't figure out who. They both looked at Andy.

Freddy dropped something on the ground; we were all lost and regained our footing at the same time. It was his Walkman without the headphones; they were still around his neck—the plug had come loose. "Sorry," he said.

"But she didn't kill Sarah-Anne!" My dad now raised his voice and spoke strangely, like he'd rehearsed a speech and was trying to recite it for us without weeping. His eyes were bloodshot; his voice was like a lit sparkler down to the last of its powder. He looked at Peter for a second too long. "She wouldn't do that."

Peter watched my father then lowered his eyes. I thought I heard him say something. I knew I saw him shake his head. Freddy and Andy were still as blades of grass on a scorching hot day. No one moved a muscle, except me—I had an eye twitch.

"I need to get my bag," Andy said. "Sorry." He walked toward the cot where he'd slept. "Sorry." He grabbed his things and took off through the porch door without another word. It seemed to me he was walking the wrong way—toward the shed and not back to his house on stilts. It was the second time I'd seen him in shoes. Wader boots like the day Sarah-Anne disappeared.

CHAPTER 22

C lay started driving us to and from school. I'd never had the luxury; it felt strange. My father said he would do this "from now on." He said it like he was afraid.

The temperatures had settled down a little; we were having a normal October where a person didn't know what to wear. Early in the day could be bitter, while the afternoon was sweltering.

There had been no sign of Sarah-Anne. She was missing. No body. Like Jesus in the tomb—no body. The longer she was gone, the stranger my father acted. He'd really hit a bump in the road with this business. All sorts of chinks began to show in his armor. I'd always known they were there, but I wouldn't have guessed at how helpless he really was. He didn't know how anything worked; he was afraid of the police and anyone he thought might be smarter than him. He cleared his throat every two seconds and put his hands in various pockets or right there into his armpits. He ignored people he didn't understand, finding excuses to end conversations and leave. The lawyers had far-off looks when they talked to him. They couldn't seem to figure out what to do with such a man. He had no idea how to help my mother or even what to say to school administrators who needed to know where we'd been and why we were leaving early, arriving late. In an instant, my dad's ability to seem above it all was gone.

We had near constant meetings with various authorities who didn't seem to know school hours and that our meetings were always interfering with them. Initially, they'd been accommodating, but the longer my sister was missing, and the longer my mother wouldn't talk, the more urgently they needed to see us—even if it meant I had to miss making circles with my protractor.

What bothered me even more than his fall from grace was that my dad seemed to be hiding out in our house while we were at school. I'd always thought of him as hiding, but something was different. Nothing scared my parents more than unannounced visitors; my dad was the first out the back door when someone came knocking or if we heard a car in the gravel. Cort Hat's mother was the one exception, but we knew she was coming. I tried to shake the feeling that my dad didn't want to be seen, found, discovered. My suspicion wasn't unfamiliar, but something had transformed—like a fine oak in winter. No leaves, branches bare, sitting exposed and vulnerable.

He didn't want anyone to know where we were—we were never there. Bledsoe is a place for people who were never there. Imagine being Emily Webber and drowning in a place like Bledsoe—you were hardly real, and then you were gone; almost as bad as being a weed growing in the cracks of the asphalt at the gas station. Some people get to be flowers in a parade, but not us—we're weeds coming up in the crack. Killed with poison from a spray bottle, or run over by an old shitty car, the stem cracked.

"Is Dad hiding?" I asked Peter while we were waiting for him to pick us up. My dad waited until the buses had come and gone before pulling up to the school. Sometimes we could see him, sitting in the car smoking, some hundred yards away, waiting to make his move. "Like…why'd he be hiding? They never said he did anything to Sarah-Anne or Emily Webber or…"

"I don't know." Peter stared at the ground.

"You know, I was thinkin'…just thinkin' that every time somebody comes to the house, he hightails it outta there, like a bolt of lightning, just takes off out back, gone for a spell, sorta strange like, and then the night Nile Webber shows up, he's at the door all cheerful and invitin' people to come in and all that. That's the only time. Maybe when Cort Hat's mama needs to get milk or whatever, but that's the only time I ever saw him answer the door like a normal person. Ever."

"I don't know, Kay." Peter kept his eyes on the ground. "They were talkin'. We know that."

"Who?"

"Dad and Nile. We know they were talkin' a long time before Nile showed up at our house." Peter squinted and batted his hand at a bug I didn't see.

"What do you mean?"

"I heard 'em in the car on the way to the boat. Just seemed like they'd been talkin' is all. Nile knew Sarah-Anne and—"

"What?" I was downright hostile. "How the hell did he know Sarah-Anne? I nearly got my head tore off for lookin' twice at the Webbers, but they knew Sarah-Anne?" My heart hit a trip wire; I just sat there waiting for the bomb to go off.

"You weren't the only one who wandered back there, Kay. Whaddya think Sarah-Anne does all day while we're at school? She gets out. Mom's asleep half the time."

"What are you even saying?" It sounded like we were talking about a dog digging under the fence. When we had Elkie, we didn't have a fence. She got the worm from running off and having sex with other lowlife dogs in the area.

"She got lost or something. Nile had to bring her home a couple of times, I guess. I don't know—it sounded like she was going back to their place all the time."

I squinted hard, thinking about my dad going to the market on Route 54 with Andy's clothes. He'd been talking to Nile Webber all right. "Yeah, she prolly just got lost. Or somethin'," I said coldly. If the bomb went off, it was way back in my head. I felt the pressure but there was no release. I thought about people whose eye gets a red mark from puking their guts out. I'd have to check in the mirror when I got home. I felt like I'd puked my guts out but had nothing to show for it. "She keeps getting lost, doesn't she," I said more to myself. "How long they been back in Georgia anyway?" I asked.

"I think they were back a while before you found 'em, Kay. You didn't, like, *discover* the Webbers or something." He sneered a little, always ready to be annoyed with me.

Freddy approached slowly from the school. He looked like he'd been crying, but being a redhead, this was common for him, especially now that I did think he was crying in secret some. We all were. I had even caught Peter wiping his cheeks when he came out of the bathroom the day before. It was a hard time for us. We were all looking skinny as posts and worn out like old dishrags—maybe we'd always looked that way. I was certainly more aware of it with Mom locked up for murder.

"What's wrong?" I asked. I rubbed my left eye, wondering if I would be able to feel a popped blood vessel from the outside.

"Just people talking shit," Freddy said in a way that was very unlike him. He didn't say *shit* or *talking shit*. He usually used good, tricky dictionary words, so we'd hardly understand him and feel dumb about it.

"Ignore it," Peter said. "Who cares what a bunch of hicks in this backwater place think?"

"Are we hicks in a backwater place?" Freddy asked.

"God, I hope not." Peter finally looked up, but not at either of us. He was staring into the sun. "Here comes Dad." He rolled his eyes almost imperceptibly. I thought I heard him say "Fuck 'em." Or "Fuck it."

"Yeah," I said in agreement. "Fuck it." I didn't even blink when I dropped the f-bomb anymore.

My friends at school had, of course, caught wind of my family's *situation*. Sarah-Anne was the talk of the town—a town that never had anything to talk about and mostly had no idea she existed before she disappeared. People were saying they remembered the other kid deaths, the boys who had died when they went out swimming in Lake Jackson one night, but everyone was corrected, because all three boys didn't die, only two. The other kid went deaf and blind from nearly drowning. We didn't know what became of him; there weren't accommodations for that sort of thing at the Bledsoe School. He would have already graduated anyway—graduated or dropped out. And Lake Jackson was a county over.

On top of Sarah-Anne gone in the blink of an eye, there was Sue-Bess in jail for killing Indiana Jones's mother. Thankfully, hardly anyone believed that part. Sarah-Anne was clearly gone, but this riddle of a woman who'd drowned almost ten years ago was another story.

"I didn't know she had a mother," I had heard a few people say of me.

"That skinny lady with the blond hair?"

"She wears dresses just like Kay...like they're sisters or something. Homemade clothes. They got no money, not even a dollar to their names."

"The Whitakers don't leave the house much less kill people. Everyone knows they don't leave. Don't work. Don't do nothin'."

"His daddy did it...that's why they ran off to San Diego or wherever they went."

"You know," was all I'd say in response. "Come on now." I turned away when asked direct questions about my family and pretended to wipe tears when someone mentioned their own sister.

Claude Greystone was the only one who had the nerve to say my mother belonged in jail—to my face. I'd overheard it from across a room, or in line for lunch or when we had a fire drill, but no one said it directly to me. I heard some murmurs and some grunts of disapproval, but alongside all of that was pity for me. My family had always been backwards—certainly not rare in Bledsoe, but everyone knew my daddy was lazy and my mother was a shut-in. They knew Elizabeth died and that Sarah-Anne was a few bulbs shy of a strand, and that we had a house with a tin roof. People knew our plight, and they respected us for it. It's hard to be dirt-poor around a bunch of other dirt-poor people because no one knows who to feel sorry for. The Whitakers were special though—we were a special kind of poor.

"They're sayin' your mother killed Sarah-Anne," Claude told me. "'Cause she killed that other lady."

Claude was a real jerk and had been held back twice. He would have gone to school with Sarah-Anne before she got kicked out, and he was held back to repeat his math quizzes for a third time.

"She didn't do it," I said with a flick of my hair. "We're gonna find Sarah-Anne. And she didn't kill the other lady neither. Dumbass." They were just words; I was good at spewing them. I didn't know what I believed.

We got in the car with my dad, who'd clearly had a few and smelled like a liquor store, which was his new daily routine. None of us wore a seat belt—my father cruised at low speeds. Peter said something about "all the smoking," but who cared about cigarettes when a man was drunk at three in the afternoon while picking up his kids from school.

"Dad," I said, "you gotta use something other than your finger as a spoon. It smells like you spilled the bottle on your head in this car. And everybody sees you there, brown-bagging it and all that." I clucked my tongue in dismay; no one said a word. "I don't care," I said. Still no one responded. "You could put the bag over your head to keep it secret," I suggested. "All secrets and lies in this house. Just secrets and lies." Silence. "And how the hell come you didn't tell me Sarah-Anne was running off to the Webbers' house? Just secrets and lies all around me. I damn near got killed by my own father for doing the same, but…just a buncha secrets and lies." More silence.

"Well, don't blame me. If she was followin' me, it was 'cause she was so bored stiff of being Mom's little baby and sittin' around the house all day trying to do her best Sue-Bess imitation. No, sirree—don't blame me. She's bound to go off and get lost if she's wandering back thataway. There's the monkey place and Andy's all floating around in the middle of the water. It's as good a place as any to get turned around all right. I never even knew that was there, but we got half the family out there murderin' people and gettin' lost and rescued and the whole nine yards." No one spoke. I would have checked for pulses if I could reach anyone from where I was sitting with my arms crossed over my chest in the front seat.

When we got home, my father told us we had to go back to the police station later that day. He also said that Andy would be there. "Why?" we all asked at the same time. My father didn't answer that question but said Andy was meeting us at the station.

"Why?" Peter said again, still sounding furious.

"He just has to," my father said. He walked to his bedroom and shut the door.

"Mom's home," Peter said as a joke, but we all looked at the front door anyway. "I just meant, because…" He stopped talking.

I went to my room to recover from such an eventful day of defending my family's honor and riding in the car with an alcoholic. I was closer to Freddy and Peter than I'd ever been, suddenly feeling as though I needed them, attached by the force of God. We were stuck together, like animals in a cage. I looked out my window; Elizabeth's tree had lost almost all of its leaves. It looked like a weeping willow even though I knew it was a sturdy oak. Sarah-Anne was a weeping willow. If I was a tree, then I was a pine—my head in the clouds and very few roots to speak of. I was thinking about dropping large pine cones on all of my enemies and agitators when I saw something move beyond the oak. I saw the white hair that was my mother's favorite. I looked again after closing my eyes. I was either trying to clear my head or forget what I'd seen. It was gone. *Sarah-Anne*, I thought. Maybe she went out to talk to Elizabeth and never came back. I looked again. I saw something far away. It was my memory.

"We have to go," my father said loudly to the refrigerator as he walked out of the bedroom. "They're expecting us. The police." No one had asked who he was talking to. He was more or less talking to himself most of the time anyway. It was his only advantage that our house was so small we could hear each other from every corner. I was still lying on my bed when he made his demands. I took a deep breath and a long time to move.

In all of this time, we had seen my mother only once. It had been between interviews at the station. I'd thought she was in some sort of maximum security jail where we weren't allowed. My father squashed that bug by telling us that my mother didn't want to see us, and more importantly, she didn't want us to see her. We did see her though; she wore an orange jumpsuit like in the movies, only it wasn't bright and neatly pressed—it was wrinkled and too large. She was thinner, or maybe she just looked it, because of her ill-fitting clothing. She walked by us in the company of the same lady officer who'd arrested her at the house. She didn't look up or down, just straight ahead, eyes fixed on the air in the hallway.

After we saw her at the station, I told my dad we should bring her some potatoes. All he said was, "We can't bring her anything." That was it. Maybe it was supposed to be a joke about the potatoes; I wasn't sure when I was joking anymore. Things were serious. I couldn't get a chuckle out of anyone, least of all myself. I continued to make jokes, but all I did was press my lips together in a mess of uncomfortable self-consciousness after I said them.

I was hopeful that we would see my mother again that night— maybe that's why we had to go so late, on short notice. We were going to get to talk to her. I held my hope dear and tried to ignore my father and his new, awkward, drunken personality. It wasn't that I missed my mother; I wasn't even sure why I wanted to see her.

It was finally cold in the afternoon too, although sunny and dry. The leaves were like giant dust particles—every time the wind blew them, they'd end up in your sinuses or your eyes. I prayed for rain right before we got in the car—it was coming on six o'clock and dark as an inkblot—and remembered that it had just rained. I had hardly ever prayed before. It seemed like a good day for praying, even if just for rain we didn't really need. Rain and dust. I swear, it was like the apocalypse started in Bledsoe, Georgia. I figured maybe God was calling out to me to join his forces for good the way I was going on and on in my head about the plants needing water and all the dust from the leaves. *The earth could really use a nice wash, God,* I thought then paused, trying to figure out what I really wanted to say. *Can't we please find Sarah-Anne? Please don't let my mom have done something awful.* Unfortunately, however, I knew—during that brief car ride to the police station—that I thought my mom had done something awful.

We were there in a blur. Freddy asked what we were having for dinner as my father pulled the car into a spot in front of Bledsoe Police Station. "Oh," my father answered.

"Yeah," Peter said.

"Yeah. And I'm sure Andy didn't eat dinner either," I added, pointing at Andy sitting on the steps in front of our car between us and the police station. We'd taken the best spot in the parking lot. Andy had his collar pulled up around his chin. He wore a bomber jacket over a corduroy jacket like a guy from *Top Gun,* or the guy from *Top Gun* if he lived in a house without heat.

His face was serene, unworried, beyond my reach. I felt suddenly silly for thinking he and I were meant to be together. I felt a million years younger than him and miles behind him. It was as though all my family's flaws suddenly landed on my face like a big wart that he could see from where he'd just stood on the sidewalk in front of the police station.

The car idled like it was in pain, making gurgling noises while in park and running. It preferred to move. If it sat too long, it might die—that's the message I got. My father seemed to agree and avoided traffic lights and stop signs at all costs, sometimes even going miles out of the way so we didn't have to sit. We all practically rolled out of the car at school, and then back into it at the end of the day; he barely slowed down. I blamed the car and its barely working parts; I also blamed my father's embarrassment. He was definitely embarrassed about the car, my mother, something— but I guess not too embarrassed to spend all day at the store with the boot cleaner getting a Coke for his whiskey, and then running home to cower under the bedspread. I frowned again—it was becoming automatic.

"We'll get something on the way home," my father said. There was a McDonald's near the interstate, but I couldn't think of another place where we could "get something" as my father was suggesting.

"But then we'll have to cook it," I argued.

"Jesus, Kay!" my father barked. The car stuttered to a stop. I gulped from nervousness but saw him remove the key from the ignition. There was a chance we would get home after all.

"My stomach's growling," I said. I thought I would cry, but I couldn't make the tears come out. I sat squeezing for a moment before all the car doors started to open; my face was still dry. I was of no concern.

Andy stood up and went inside as we got out of the car. He let the door shut hard behind him and didn't turn around. It was like he was waiting for us but didn't want to be seen in our company.

There were a few people waiting as we walked through the door. Up to this point, I'd thought the police station a friendly place full of good-natured folks who wanted to give me crackers and Sprite. It was different on this evening. We had a little trouble getting the front door open on account of a strong suction that must have been due to central heating inside and the wind outside. My father yanked at the door looking weak and frail. I adjusted my dress, feeling my thinness beneath it—hip bones and ribs. My stomach growled again. I took notice of Peter, who, although never puny or very light-on-his-feet-looking, suddenly had hard angles. I swore you could say it had been a month since his last good meal. It might have been. My mother had been gone for two weeks.

"Where does the time go?" I asked myself, but loudly enough to be heard by the mess of people waiting for us inside the station door. A few of the stern faces—some of them familiar, others new—gave me a glance, but no one answered. These were professional people who didn't wonder at the time going anywhere. Those concerns were for marsh girls like me who had nothing else to think about. Time's like currency if you don't have any real money.

"Andrew Webber," one of the women said. I'd seen her before, but we'd never spoken.

Andy nodded at the woman before looking at me with a weak smile. He looked down again, shoving only the fingers on his hands deep down in the pockets of his jeans. They were full length—I only ever thought of him in his jean shorts, bare chested, and sunned like a snake. He was quite handsome and grown-looking in the police lobby light. Andy stepped forward like he was going to the gallows. I took a step with him; my father tried to restrain me but was corrected.

"It's okay. We need to talk to her too," one of the other women said. There were about six people—we were outnumbered. Peter puffed out his chest and made an aggressive gesture with his shoulders. We were really losing our grip here as far as I could tell; I thought my brother would try to fight the fancy police people right there in the station. I thought maybe they wanted to talk to Andy because the fishermen had seen my mother out there in the marsh and Andy lived in the marsh. Maybe they thought he saw her too. People were seeing stuff left and right, and here I didn't know a damned thing. I puffed my chest too.

Welty walked in like he owned the place and asked me to follow him. "Kay," he said. "Come on. Room B."

I said nothing but followed him both dutifully and with pride. I liked to be known by officers of the law with bulging biceps. Even if it was a slight betrayal, I thought maybe Andy would find me more attractive with all of my law enforcement connections.

Welty had barely put his ass down in the plastic chair in Room B—my favorite on account of the red strobe light in the corner, I think meant for dire emergencies like assault of a police officer—before he said, "Can you tell me about your family's relationship with Nile Webber? I'm just going to get down to business, because it's late, and I know it's a school night."

"We don't have a relationship with him. And it is late." I looked around. No Sprites or crackers anywhere to be seen. I scratched my cheek and felt like a little girl.

"Right. But, well."

"I know his kid, Andy. He's here."

"Right. Have you met Mr. Webber?"

"I know Nile from a hole in the ground. I mean, I've been to their house and all that. He came over once. I think there's been trouble with him in the past, I mean, duh. 'Cause of Emily, but I was too small to say. I don't know a thing about it. I mean, I guess according to Peter he's friends with my dad. That's news to me though." I was talking fast, too fast, and trying to say little while talking a lot. I knew I looked nervous and was darting my eyes a bit too much. I had a tendency to look at the ceiling when I was worried about being busted for falsehoods. I wasn't lying to this fella or anyone else. I couldn't say what I didn't know. "I mean, they have a boat and some magazines." I bit my lip. "Wife's dead. Andy's mom is dead, but you know that. She drowned, under the house, with bricks in her…only in Bledsoe." I shook my head. I wasn't sure what I was supposed to say. "I'm tellin' you what you already know, you know. I don't know why he wanted anything to do with us after Sue-Bess…you know…"

"Yes," Welty said, a little uninterested. "Does Mr. Webber know your sister?"

"Who? Sarah-Anne?" I shut my eyes—maybe hoping I would disappear.

"Do you have another sister?" Welty asked a little brashly. He was a grunter who made a lot of adjustment noises on his chair; there was a terrible amount of throat clearing and what sounded like muffled burping—maybe even some gas down below escaping a time or two. I was trying to keep a good eye on him, but his line of questioning had me twitching a bit.

"No. Well, yes. Elizabeth. If you count the dead, and she died—born too early. She's still with us, though. You know. She's with us all the time. Under the tree."

"The tree?"

"Buried in the yard."

"That right?"

"It's not right," I said, throwing my hands up in consternation. "It's not right. It makes us think there's dead baby bones out there, 'cause there is, but a mother can't let her baby go."

"But does your sister know Mr. Webber? Sarah-Anne."

"I didn't think so," I said. "But I guess he did. She was gettin' lost all the time or somethin'. I don't really know. People don't tell me much in our house because I have a big mouth and bad intentions." I nodded thoughtfully, as though this news would be shocking for Welty to hear of me.

"No?" His face took on a peculiar glow, like maybe he had a secret in his pocket. "Did your mother ever talk to you about Mr. Webber?"

"No," I said. Now I was confused and worried. I thought I'd said something wrong. Welty seemed a little too grateful for the way I was rambling. He didn't seem like my friend anymore. I thought maybe I'd gotten too comfortable, which made me think of Andy for a moment. I couldn't put my finger on why.

"Did you ever see your mother with Nile Webber?"

"What? No. Never." I frowned. "I mean, that one time when he came to the house so Andy could live with us. She was there."

"The day your mother told you your sister was missing, she was not with Mr. Webber?"

"What?" I asked angrily, feeling duped. "Are you talkin' about Mom or Sarah-Anne? Where's my dad?"

"Was Mr. Webber at your house?"

"No! He was on the boat with my dad. I mean, I guess he was there that morning before they went to the boat. What is this anyway? We don't even know them. I'm the one who found their house and—" I paused. None of this was true. I knew that now. "I was a baby back then and all that," I said. I put my hands on my knees and tried not to say anything else. "I don't know what you're talking about."

"That's fine, Kay. I don't expect you to."

"I'm just—" I said, squeezing my eyes again. "I'm just really hungry. I don't even know what time it is, but we haven't had dinner or anything."

"I'm sure I can get you something. Chips?"

"Yeah, I guess," I said. I really did feel like I was going to cry. "I guess chips are okay."

Welty rose from his chair with another loud grunt and walked toward the door. He paused for a moment, looking at the floor like all the answers might be there. "Just trying to figure out why we now have an eyewitness who says he saw Nile Webber out at the marsh that day—with your mother. If he was on the fishing boat, then…how could that be?"

"What day?" I asked. "I don't really like vinegar chips," I added.

"The day your mama said she couldn't find your sister. We have two separate accounts of your mother and a male, who we think to be Nile Webber, being seen in the marsh that day. A man. That very day. Seems strange, no?"

"What do you mean?" I was trying not to make sense of what I thought he might be saying. "When was that? I mean, maybe it was Sarah-Anne. Seems like she's the one out in the marsh all the time. Why's everybody so certain it's Mom? Mom doesn't leave the house, but I guess Sarah-Anne does; goes back there all hours of the day." I lifted my hands to my shoulder, palms upturned. "I know—was news to me too."

"I'll get your chips for you." He opened the door and started to walk out of the room but stopped. I was fairly certain I'd said something I shouldn't have. "People saw both your mama and Mr. Webber out in the marsh. Just seems odd." He shrugged and let the door shut behind him. "It's these oddities that keep the investigation moving along," I heard him say through the wood.

"Andy lives out there too," I said. I was talking to the table. I think maybe I'd meant to wait until Welty left to say that.

It felt like a long time that I was in that room by myself. There were noises, unidentifiable to me. I hadn't spent a lot of time in a business building before; there weren't so many of them in Bledsoe. "Anyway," I said to myself. I tapped my foot on the floor and waited. I thought he must have his dates wrong. I thought about something my father had said, or something he didn't say. I couldn't stop thinking, and listening to beeps, and rattling, and humming, doors opening and closing, and distant voices that maybe weren't voices after all. "Anyway," I said again.

I heard the door open and looked up. It was Welty with my dad. I wasn't sure who to look at, so I looked at Welty's hands to see if he had any chips—they were empty. I was about to say something about starvation when my dad told me we were leaving.

"Now," he said. I tried not to watch him too closely; I thought I could smell booze from where I was sitting, some ten feet away. "Come on. Now," my father said. Welty frowned and stared at me; he must have thought I was going to take his side. Maybe I should have.

The drive home was rocky and quiet. We went over some debris in the road that sounded like it tore off a few parts of our car. I turned around to see if the bumper was lying in the street, but my dad didn't slow down.

I understood that no one talked to Freddy or my dad at the station at all; my father ended things before they got the chance. It was only me, Peter, and Andy who got pulled into rooms before my dad could say enough. I didn't know what happened with Andy.

Peter was in the car with us, looking mad that he didn't get to finish his conversation with the authorities.

I was sitting in the back of the car, pinched in the seat like a pearl in an unaccommodating clam. Peter was to my left—his face was drawn. He leaned his forehead against the window before closing his eyes. I closed my eyes too. There didn't seem to be anything else to do. We had cereal with orange juice instead of milk when we got home. It tasted strange but satisfying—we'd had to do this before. I went to bed with a headache and a pit in my stomach.

CHAPTER 23

We had two more weeks until Thanksgiving break. I wondered what we would do to celebrate. My father had been buying our groceries on credit. He was stocking for the store while we were at school, but said it was all he could do come three in the afternoon because of the backbreaking conditions—it was so hard for him to work like that. This came as no surprise to any of us. He left the house smelling like a brewery anyway; I was sure we weren't the only ones who noticed.

Peter had taken a leave of absence from his stocking job. He'd missed a few shifts when my mother first got picked up—all was forgiven, considering the circumstances. Marcia Bullock—who owned the store—said he could come back when he was ready, but then my dad was working there. Peter said he'd rather not. He could do without the money.

My father kept telling us he was worried about Andy. He wouldn't really say why, but he rambled on about Andy this and Andy that, always with the sternness of a warning. We needed to look out for him, watch our backs, sleep with one eye open, and so on. "Just stay away from him" was my father's only response when Andy's name came up. I could have said I heard Andy was a watermelon farmer, and my father would have told me to keep away from the watermelons. I couldn't make sense of it.

I'd told my dad that the police said they saw Nile Webber back in the water by their house. "Saw him the day Sarah-Anne went off." I swallowed. "Disappeared. Said they saw him out there."

My dad frowned. "We got on the boat that day. You know that."

"Maybe it was Andy," I said.

My dad blinked then looked away. "Just keep away from him."

"Did she go back there before?" I asked.

"Who?"

"Sarah-Anne."

"I don't know, Kay."

"How do you not know?"

"Because I'm tired."

"Tired liar," I said.

"I don't know what to tell you anymore," he said, and for a moment—brief and instantly evaporating like a Pixy Stix on your tongue—I felt sorry for him. This all seemed so out of his control.

I tried to talk to Peter and Freddy about it, but they didn't seem to understand what I was saying. "Welty said he was back there. Nile was."

"So?" Peter said.

"He and Dad were on the boat in the Panama Canal! And anyway, you yourself said that he brought Sarah-Anne home before." I turned my palms up, giving the gift of my knowledge. The boys were almost always in the kitchen on account of the cold. The porch was no longer suitable for lounging. They sat at the kitchen table, working on projects for school or pretending to. Sometimes, when lonely enough, I would join them. We were in my father's earshot in the kitchen. I knew it, and so did the boys; we were just too cold to go anywhere else. My dad had become like my mother—hiding in the bedroom, an ear pressed to the door, absorbing.

"They got their facts wrong then," Peter said.

"Maybe they saw the boat," I said, trying to agree. "Maybe they mean they saw the Webbers' boat, not Nile. Maybe that's it."

"Whatever," Peter said. He wouldn't look at me.

"You saw them get on the shrimping boat, right?"

"Yes." Peter nodded sternly.

"Both of them? 'Cause maybe Nile—"

"They both got on." Peter put his head down in his hands. For a moment, I thought he was going to cry.

"Peter, are you lying or something?" I asked. I had a hot pipe in my chest, burning its way through my vital organs at a vertical slant, like a fire slide. Freddy had been sitting there the whole time but hadn't said a word. I couldn't even hear him breathe.

Peter trailed off. "Just stop talking about it. Boat was leavin'. I saw."

"But did you see them get on the boat?" I asked.

"Yes!" Peter said. Freddy and I looked at one another, then went back to pretending we were studying—at least I had to pretend. Freddy liked the calming waters of biology.

"Secrets and lies," I said to myself. It was true.

Sometimes I went to the boys' room at night. I was having a lot of trouble sleeping. I'd fall asleep for a second, then wake up in a fright, my body shaking and my throat closing up. I was tired all day, but I couldn't make myself calm down when I was alone in my room. I had a weird sort of headache that made me blurry but alert.

"Hey y'all," I said, shuffling into their room later that night. "I was thinkin' about Mom always telling Sarah-Anne about Emily, so maybe she went out there lookin' for her. You know how Sarah-Anne's real stupid and probably doesn't even know that if somebody dies, they, like, disappear. So it wasn't like she was following me; it was probably all that talk about Emily." I stood in the muted moonlight leaking in from the front window and down the narrow hallway that led to the boys' room. Sarah-Anne's bed was just beyond me, at the tip of the moon's reach.

"I'm sleeping, Kay," Peter said. I'd sat on the end of his bed. He rolled over and pulled the blanket up to his chin. Freddy hadn't stirred. It took a lot more than hushed conversation to wake him up—a heavier sleeper I'd never known.

"Yeah, but she didn't follow me back there. That's not why she got lost. She was trying to find Emily, 'cause you know, you said Mom was talking about her all the time, so—" I guess I thought it was guilt waking me up at night. Guilt that I was to blame for Sarah-Anne getting lost all the damn time. And then lost for good.

"Kay, no one is blaming you, and anyway, Sarah-Anne was going back there before you were. But I don't care. I'm asleep. Go back to bed."

"I'm gonna tell Dad," I said boldly.

"No, you're not. Go to bed."

"I can't sleep." No one answered. I walked by the kitchen and back to my room, noticing the light on under my parents' door. I figured my dad couldn't sleep either, but I didn't want to talk to him. All he did was lie anyway. Getting the truth from that guy was like getting blood from a turnip—whatever that means.

The next morning, on the way to school, my father again said that we shouldn't talk to Andy if we saw him. "You know...he might be mad about his mama."

"Doubt it," I said. "He doesn't remember her." I went quiet realizing that I would probably have a better impression of my own mother if she'd died before I could remember her. She would be like Elizabeth—perfect—because she never got the chance to let any of us down. That was probably what Andy thought of Emily. Perfect. Perfect but drowned, and it was all Sue-Bess's fault.

I'd eaten almost nothing for breakfast and was twitchy with fatigue and nervousness. For some reason, I felt like the car was lurching all over the road; I had a wave of nausea come over me that could have taken out a small village.

Instead of saying anything more about Andy or his poor, dead mother, I told my dad, "You sound dog-tired." His eyes were blue on the inside and around the edges. "Look it too. Your face looks like a bruise." I was just trying to keep from throwing up—sometimes giving people a hard time helped calm my nerves, and my stomach.

My dad wasn't going to be able to pick us up from school that day. He was working the later shift at Marcia Bullock's store. Ralph Watson was sick, so my dad was doing a double.

"There's a first time for everything," I said to the proud announcement of his long day.

"Just look out for Andy on your way home," he said yet again. I could have told him I put shit in his morning coffee—same response. He moved the gear shift back and forth—a trick to keep the transmission in working order while the car was stopped—and we hunkered down. There were only a few brown leaves left on the trees. It was dry and silent enough to hear a twig crack from a mile away.

"Why?" Freddy asked a little too long after my father warned us. "What's Andy got to do with any of it?"

"Yeah," I said loudly. "What's he gonna do? Run us over with his air boat? On the road?"

"Just be careful."

"Why?" I threw my hands up.

"Because I said so." My dad adjusted his glasses on the bridge of his nose.

"Your sight go bad?" I asked.

"'S'always been bad, but I'm getting headaches."

"I doubt that's from the glasses," I said.

My father didn't look at us when he pulled up at the school. We got out of the car in a single file line and walked to the front of the building like we were dragging the weight of the world in our backpacks.

Things were really slipping for me in class; I couldn't concentrate to save my life. I wasn't getting in trouble for talking anymore; mostly I was in trouble for falling asleep at my desk or failing to follow along. I didn't know what subject we were in half the time; I'd answer in numbers when I was supposed to be talking apostrophes. My teacher said I was excused from being left behind if I wanted to be. I didn't know what that was supposed to mean—it seemed like a lot of people were giving me a break, or at least trying to.

I spent a lot of my days at school thinking that my dad was a changed man without my mother around. He'd gone soft and idiotic. We could talk about him right in front of his face without him seeming to notice. He'd started humming a good bit and mumbling to himself. One of the hinges on his glasses was twisted after he put them in his back pocket and sat down real hard. They looked like they were hanging off his ear, and then he went and singed an eyebrow with his cigarette lighter, taking off half the hair there in an instant. I could hardly stand the sight of such a busted person—even if I'd begun to lose all respect for him long before his hinge broke. It took me a lot of thinking—when I should have been listening to my teacher talk about the Battle of the Bulge—to figure out that all my father had really lost was his confidence. It did strike me as an awful kind of funny that he felt so much better about himself when he had my mother around to make everything strained and uncomfortable. These were such strange but powerful revelations, like drinking Coke for the first time or discovering that because you were born means your parents had sex. I didn't like to think about it, but it was on my brain—a tick that got under the skin, only I couldn't burn this bitch out with a match.

That afternoon while we were walking home from school, Peter became kicking-dirt angry and said he wasn't going back. "I'm not going back there," he said of 1234 Hack Road—there was no question as to what he was referring.

"Dad's a goddamned liar," I said to bolster our enthusiasm.

"What?" Freddy always played dumb when he was uncomfortable.

"I want to get out of here," Peter said, only slightly more reasonably.

"Where'd we go?" I asked.

"God, just anywhere."

"What about school?" Freddy inhaled a great quantity of loose snot.

"Can you blow your fucking nose?" I said. "You're just sucking it in all the time. Can't be healthy…"

"Kay," Peter said, "can we…"

"We could go to Andy's," Freddy said.

"Dad keeps telling us to stay away from him," I said.

"Who gives a shit what Dad says?" Peter went back to kicking dirt.

"Okay," I said. I dropped my book bag right there in the middle of the road. "Let's go."

I was smart enough to take my clothes off before I got in the water. I crashed into the marsh with my arms over my head in a diving position. I didn't care that I was almost butt naked in front of my brothers. We were way past good manners, and anyway only a week before, I'd been sitting around in my skivvies by moonlight. There was no time to worry about my ass cheeks.

Andy's fading tan and long face were still enough to get my panties in a twist, but really I had a mind to steal that boat. No matter how burning my desires, I had to be more practical. My intentions were clear: we needed to find Sarah-Anne and get the hell out of Bledsoe. If I could get Andy to come along with me, then the next phase of my plan (made during the short sprint through the marsh) would be in motion too. If he wouldn't come with us, then we were going to go without him—in his boat.

"Go!" Peter yelled like a football coach during a scorching summer practice. He didn't have to tell me twice; I was swimming about five feet ahead of them. We didn't need to swim; the water was shallow enough to walk, but we were in a hell of a hurry. I pushed on the bottom of the marsh with my hands and let my feet drop down to get a good kick a few times. The water was like ice needles all up and down my stomach, but I was as determined as I'd ever been to not go back to Hack Road and sit in that house with all the demons.

Freddy, usually protective of his possessions, hadn't really wanted to drop his things on the road when we took off, but after a few minutes of running with a bag slamming his back and his Walkman flopping on his belt loop, he left everything.

The boat was at the house, tied to the deck good and proper. I was relieved; we hadn't discussed what we would do if Andy wasn't home. We hadn't discussed anything. All we did was run.

"He's here!" I called out. We floated up to the house simultaneously, our breath in clouds above the freezing water. Thank God for the mid-afternoon sun and the proper deep-south November. I was begging to be warm and dry as quick as possible.

I pulled myself up on the small deck and crouched like a frog about to take a giant hop. I banged on Andy's door with a tight fist. Peter and Freddy made it up the ladder and stood next to me. I had to wonder why it was so much less of a shock to see a boy in his underwear. They were wet and rippling—their muscles taut and like half-cooked spaghetti under their skin. None of us were eating right. Nobody slept. We were like unwatered plants, or plants that aren't getting enough sun to grow. For a second, I thought we were looking an awful lot like our parents. I had to put the thought out of my mind, because I got a weird vision of my mom with the blood again, and my father taking off into the marsh like a squirrel after a fat acorn.

No one answered the door. It was silence all around us, except for the water and the wind. "What's he playing at?" I asked. "We know he can't go nowhere without the boat."

"He can swim too," Freddy said.

"Says who? I've never seen him do it." I pounded on the door again.

"Nobody here," Peter said.

"I keep thinking about Mom with all that blood on her dress," I said suddenly.

"What?" Freddy asked, clearly frustrated by every new detail. I couldn't blame him. He took another fist to the door. No one came.

I looked at Peter, who hadn't yet acknowledged what I said. He was looking at me too. "When was that?" I asked. Peter kept on looking at me with his mouth in a flat line. "What?" I said.

"That's…what happened when Elizabeth came too early." Peter reached for the door but let his hand fall down to his wet thigh.

I was just about to say something when the door flew open. Andy stood in front of us, his eyes open wide. "Whaddy'all want? Can't y'all quit coming around here?" I thought maybe he would slam the door in our faces, but he just stood there, very still and angry. If he was anything like me, no matter how mad he was, he still couldn't stand to be alone. It was like all the people in Bledsoe were living the same lives.

"We got nowhere else to go!" I said. I looked over Andy's shoulder into the house. "Where's your dad?"

"He...he's out. He'll be back in the morning."

"You're here on your own all night?" I asked, near hysterics.

"I guess not anymore." Andy backed up, angry but willing. We walked inside the house, naked, shivering, grateful.

It would be a dozen years later before I realized it, but there was something about us all being kids that made us want to help each other. Backwater kids can be as mean as any other, but if the circumstances get bleak enough, we can't stand to see somebody alone and afraid. Maybe it was a good thing I grew up the way I did and that all this happened when I was still a young girl. Andy too. We'd open the door for each other a long time after anyone else would.

We spent a long afternoon wobbling around the high-heel house, bouncing off the walls and one another, trying not to talk or make noise. We had to hide when we peed and do our best not to think about food—there was only uncooked macaroni and a can of peas to eat. When the afternoon finally rolled into the evening, we brushed our teeth with our fingers, some of Andy's toothpaste, and a small, shared bottle of water we took from a pack on the "kitchen" floor. It was barely dark out when we said to one another in unified angst that we were going to sleep. That was when we heard the sirens wailing and ran to the door to look over the tops of the lazy marsh trees. There was no question where the noise was coming from. The official wail of a police car, and then another, made its way from Hack Road, not Route 54. You couldn't even pretend otherwise. We stood on the porch—in Andy's clothes again—smelling of strong detergent and the teenage sweat it was meant to eliminate. I could see the distant blue lights pulsing in the muted sky above my family's tilted house. The lights and the sounds were far away from me—like a balloon floating on a swift wind. I could chase with my arm outstretched all I wanted—the wind wasn't going to slow down for me; I wasn't going to get that string. I saw sparse branches, dusky clouds that were a deep gray over a fading blue, and police lights that bounced off the early night sky like bad faces in a mirror. There were some voices on an intercom and some beeping, then some more voices—no shouting, just stern talking. The marsh is so quiet, a person can hear the fish having dinner conversation if they want to. If people are yelling, then it's everybody's business. This was somewhere in between. I wanted to hear. It was my business.

"Are they lookin' for us?" I asked.

"We didn't do anything wrong," Freddy said.

"Yeah, but we're as good as missing now."

We stood silently, close to one another, waiting.

"Them's comin' for Dad?" I said after the loud talking over intercoms calmed and one of the police cars turned off its lights and drove away from the house. We all stood next to one another with our breath pulled in and down to our empty stomachs.

"What'd he do?" Freddy asked Peter.

Peter looked at Andy and turned his back on all of us, going inside the house, away from the door.

"Where's your dad?" I asked Andy again.

"Go to bed, Kay!" Peter called from inside. He went and lay down in Nile's bed and rolled to his side, away from us. Andy didn't answer me.

I woke up early to the sound of waders on wood. Andy must have already been awake; as soon as I heard footsteps on the rickety front stairs, he jumped out of the bed and bolted to the door. Our sleeping arrangements were the same as the time before; I wondered if Andy was worried his father would find him in bed with me, think we'd married in secret, and disapprove. It was comforting to hope for this kind of scandal in the middle of such a shit storm.

Andy went out on the porch; I heard whispering voices and saw urgent gesturing from where I was lying. I figured Andy was telling Nile about my dad getting picked up. We still didn't know what happened back at Hack Road, but the way Nile and Andy were talking, I had to wonder if Nile knew. They looked so much alike, standing there in dawn's light, moving their mush mouths around tricky words, said in a quiet passion. I looked over at Nile's bed where Peter was lying; he too was awake and watching the Webbers. He saw me and closed his eyes, pretending to go back to sleep.

CHAPTER 24

Two months later

Welty was the one who explained to me that Sarah-Anne wasn't my sister. They didn't know whose sister she was, if anyone's, but she wasn't a Whitaker; Freddy's spit test made sure of that. The lady officer who'd come to the house to arrest my mother came back to Hack Road with the team that took my father away. She went through Sarah-Anne's things—her hairbrush, and even the sheets on her bed, to find some strands for analysis. Turns out that blond hair had nothing to do with Sue-Bess, or Clay for that matter—they gave their spit too, but over at the jail on account of their arrests.

These were the reasons my father got picked up: kidnapping,

abduction, lying to the people from the state, subverting the course of justice, impeding an investigation, and other fairy-tale-sounding stuff that was far above Clay's pay grade. Stuff that usually had to be repeated, because I couldn't understand a word of it. I was pretty sure Clay didn't either. I could have told everyone who asked that the guy didn't mean to.

"Didn't mean to what?" they might have said.

"Didn't mean to anything. Not a damn thing."

All that running to the back of the house was my father taking Sarah-Anne out into the marsh when people showed up at our door to inquire. There'd been anonymous reports that something didn't add up with the Whitaker kids. It happened more than once; there were suspicions—widely shared. The school filed something, so did a woman who lived about two miles up Gerard Road, and even my mother's cousin, Franklin. He said it couldn't have been. I guess Franklin meant all of us—together. People noticed Sarah-Anne and then they noticed she was being kept a secret. My parents let the cat out of the bag, then tried to put it back in. Rocks in a blender—I've said it before. We got rocks in a blender in our heads in Bledsoe.

At first, it was like Welty was confiding dark secrets to me—and me to him—his willing partner in the ruin of my family. I told him about the dead goats, assured from the beginning that he was not going to arrest me for killing a goat a few years back. "Yeah," I'd said. "I figured the statute of limitations had run."

"Yes," he said. "Statute."

I also told him about kissing Andy, and how Andy didn't go to school anymore after his mama died, and how Andy lived without electricity and peed in the water, and about how Andy always acted like he didn't know what we were talking about when someone brought up my mother killing his mother. "Even though we don't talk to him about it. It's like having a drunk in the family— everybody knows it's there, but you just don't say the guy's name... or the lady's. Girls can be drunks too, you know. We just don't say. She's dead, I mean...you know?"

"Right." Welty nodded. "The elephant in the room."

"No, no elephants, just a dead mom and suspicions," I said. I talked about a mile a minute when I was with Welty. He had such an inviting demeanor and a swollen face. It was like I was compelled to confess out of pity for his jowl situation, and it was a situation to be sure. I felt bad for mentioning drunks since Peter said Welty had a problem with the bottle, but he didn't flinch. I'd been given cause too many times recently to question something Peter said that I was starting to wonder if he ever really knew what he was talking about.

Most of the time, Welty talked to me and me alone, but occasionally our meetings took on a group form and included my brothers too. We'd been in every interview room in the station at least twelve times. There were three rooms, which came as a bit of a shock being that Bledsoe was such a poor place without three of anything—not even mailmen; we only had two.

"So how do you know she was abducted?" Freddy asked. It was a smart question. We were in Welty's office, where he sometimes liked to gather us around his metal desk with framed photos of big fish all around it.

"No birth records," Welty told us like he was just the man for the job of telling people about birth records. "No records of any kind."

"Doesn't seem like Bledsoe's the kind of place that has a lot of records," I said. "I mean…I'm not sure anyone knows I was born." I lifted my chin—this was explanation enough. "Maybe they didn't want the state to know she was born and all."

Welty shook his head in apology. "No records. Well—" He stopped himself. "There are records, but now we know they're fakes. The documents your parents gave to the school were forged. We've examined them now. The doctor said he was given a few different birth dates, and—"

"Oh, yeah," I interrupted. "The geniuses at the Bledsoe School. They couldn't win at Uno. And Sarah-Anne never went to the doctor. Just Freddy." I pointed. "He's the only one of us."

"She did go to the doctor," Welty said. "Doctor Earl said he thought something was strange but never reported it. He saw her a few times. Years ago. Things didn't add up."

I laughed a little, in a mocking way. "He definitely thought something was off. Dr. Earl's the one who called the police on my mama about Freddy and the syndrome."

"Okay, Kay," Welty said. He didn't say it the way that Peter said *Okay, Kay*. He said it like he really thought it was okay that I was saying the staff at Bledsoe School wasn't genius material and that my mother almost went to jail before because she was making Freddy sick with all of her problems. He thought that was okay. It did make me feel better to be understood for once in my life.

"So what's her name anyway?" I asked. "Sarah-Anne."

"We're not sure." Welty looked away.

I started to protest, but Freddy took my hand. We didn't really hug or cling to one another. I was caught off guard, but I held him tightly and didn't say anything else. He needed it.

"And anyway, she tried it before—your mom, taking a kid," Welty said.

"No way," I said.

Susan Elizabeth Taft Whitaker was arrested when I was about two years old for trying to take a little girl from a gas station in Morganton, some fifty miles west. My father said—at the time— that it was him. He told the police he did it; it was his idea; my mother was in the car the whole time and didn't know. The police took both of them in and gave the little girl, Shelton Waggoner, back to her parents. It was shortly after Elizabeth died. Shelton was six months old and in a baby carrier.

"I'll be damned," I said. "Morganton's even more of a shithole than Bledsoe, and they have police records on the computer?" Morganton was known for having a mayor who had sex with his teenage stepdaughter who he later married; they both went to jail for exploding a meth lab in the basement of her father's house. Other than that, I couldn't tell you a damned thing about the place.

We spent our afternoons in the school library. Freddy found our mom's arrest record online.

There was an after-hours program that meant we could stay on campus until six thirty. I didn't know of it before; it was meant for working parents, we were told.

"Oh, so that's why," Peter said. The program was not for eleventh and twelfth graders, but Peter was given an exception. We did not go home after school—there was no one there to go home to.

"There she is," Freddy said. I stared at the screen. It was my mother all right. We found my dad's photo too. He looked like a child with light eyes and a twisted smirk. He had a blue T-shirt on in his mug shot; I'd seen him in it a hundred and fifty times. None of us commented on my father at all. He had become irrelevant overnight.

"She looks so young," Peter said after we'd stared. We were piled on wooden, ladder-back chairs and tucked in tight around Freddy, who managed the keys on the computer like a kid who really should be in a special science school.

"Are there more?" I asked. More dates and offenses were listed under my mother's name, but I didn't have control of the mouse, so I couldn't do the required clicking.

"I don't know." Freddy pulled his hands away from the keyboard. "Anyway," he said, "I'm kinda done."

"That's fine, Freddy." Peter patted his shoulder.

The next day, I went to the library during study break. I said I needed to research Marco Polo. My teacher was confused but said okay. I was some kind of irritation, like a fungus on your feet, the way all the horrible stuff had happened with my family. There I was, still at school over and over again, breathing, speaking, existing. I was everyone's reminder that even if a bunch of bad shit happens to you, you still have to exist.

I'd watched Freddy closely the day before and knew how to get to the website where you looked up information on people. I typed Emily Webber's name and Bledsoe on the line, taking my time with the tapping and clicking. We had typing classes sometimes, but I wasn't so savvy. I used my pointers and pressed on.

Up came a bunch of things I could click on with long stories about her death, finding her under the Webbers' house with bricks in her pockets like Virginia Woolf, whoever that was. There were a few pictures of Andy's mother with her long, dark hair and doe eyes. She was young when she died, young and little, not much more than a teenager. The photos were from some school where she'd apparently gone until she was fifteen then dropped out. It was like I was reading about my own mother. Nile Webber found her under the house, face down, and dead. Andy (Andrew Kyle Webber) was inside the house, only about eighteen months old at the time, in his crib in a filthy diaper—hungry and crying. The county coroner said she must have been dead several hours by the time Mr. Webber returned home to find her. I clicked on a few more pages that had stories about her death—called *accidental, mysterious, suicide, murder,* but always *unsolved.* "We may never know what happened to Emily Reins Webber," one writer offered, like this was some sort of gift. *We know now,* I thought.

The last picture I saw of her, there were other people on the edges of her face; they'd been partially cut out of the photo, unlike her school pictures, which were of her wide smile and young eyes and no one else. I looked closely at the faces on the sides of hers— Nile and my daddy. Young man's eyes in a young man's squint— near identical in their hopeful grins. I looked closely then had to look away. Like Freddy, I figured I was kind of done. Andy looked a lot like Nile when Nile was a younger man; he looked like his mama too, but only in the eyes. *Poor kid,* I thought. Sad eyes. Dead under the house. Floating. I shuddered, channeling Sue-Bess, who was already there. She's the one who did it.

"They knew them well," I said to the computer screen. I was talking about my parents and the Webbers. "Knew 'em well." I didn't think my parents knew anyone well. I guess things had once been different—before Sarah-Anne, before Emily. Such a sad lot, really. I couldn't shake the thought of us all as weeds in a parking lot, living and dying in a crack. I left the library and went to the bathroom where I waited for study hall to end, so I could go back to my classroom and sit like an empty cup for the rest of the day. The only people my parents ever knew so well they killed off with their bad omens. I was lucky to be alive at all is what I really thought—unwanted weed or not.

As soon as my father was arrested for kidnapping, Aunt Christy came to Bledsoe without her kids and with the somewhat vague purpose of "figuring out what to do about this." The "this" was us. She drove a white van that looked like a rolling pearl. The first time I was to ride in it, she asked me if I needed a booster seat. All I could do was look confused, because I was almost thirteen and we'd never had car seats anyway.

"Sorry," she said. "I'm not thinking…"

She was going to our meetings with us, because there was no one else to go, what with both of our parents in jail. They added the kidnapping charge to my mother's rap sheet too; it was a busy day. Sarah-Anne was a bit of a Jane Doe. No one knew her real name; no one had come forward to claim her.

It wouldn't have done any good anyway; she was still missing. There were to be no reunions—records or not. Mr. Webber said he would stand in for our parents, but given we weren't blood relations, and the thing with his wife, the people from the state said no. Aunt Christy was the last resort. My grandmother was too feeble and didn't believe a word of the story the police were telling her about my mother anyway. She wouldn't have been any help at all. None of our other relations stepped in. My father's parents never even called the house.

Aunt Christy didn't want to stay with us full-time. She was

going back and forth between Bledsoe and near Savannah, where she lived. She spent the night with us and complained about it all the time. Her kids never came with her. The trip was over an hour each way, but that didn't stop her from coming and going each day. She didn't show up at the school to pick us up a second before six thirty at night, and she was out the door, lickety-split, at seven in the morning—never spending one second more with us than was absolutely necessary.

"Hmmm?" Aunt Christy said every time someone mentioned us leaving Bledsoe with her. "What was that? I didn't quite hear."

All anybody seemed to care about was us going to school. I argued some, citing the many reasons that the Bledsoe School served little to no purpose in our lives. Freddy asked if he could go to the science school in Richmond Hill, but it didn't seem like anyone heard him—the seven times he asked in my presence alone. Peter had so little time left I don't think he cared. He was waiting for his chance at emancipation—it now had a name—Peter's ultimate goal. We'd heard the word *emancipation* used several times. Even Aunt Christy joined in, asking when it would be possible. I think she meant for all of us.

Freddy made the mistake of mentioning that Richmond Hill was near Savannah, which would allow him to go to the special school. Aunt Christy's face flushed nervously as she detailed the vast distances between the two places. "And the girls, my girls, you see..." The girls were Aunt Christy's reason for not doing much.

I heard her talking of the girls all the time, especially when the people from the state were trying to make arrangements. I was not one of Aunt Christy's girls; this was made clear by the constant clarification. "No, *my* girls." "Kay." "Sue-Bess's girl." "*My* girls are at home. Near Savannah." Aunt Christy rubbed her hands together anxiously any time we met with local officials who wanted to know what was to be done. She'd made the mistake of saying she thought we should stay in Bledsoe until Sarah-Anne came back. If there was one thing that could quiet a room of Whitakers, that was it. *When Sarah-Anne came back* meant never.

"She doesn't want them. The aunt…she doesn't want 'em." Welty was talking to the woman at the station with the penny-colored hair—I'd been told her name, but I couldn't remember. There were too many names, rotating faces, accents, and funny words with meanings I didn't know floating around my head. It was like the locusts had come, and I was outside, standing there, like an idiot with giant bugs crashing into my face. I stopped caring who was who after they took my father away. Welty and one black-haired gal were the only mainstays; penny hair came and went. Welty felt sorry for us. I'd seen that look on a man's face too many times. The shame of it all—being pitied becomes like an itch you can't scratch. You're someone's reason for losing faith.

I tried to talk to Aunt Christy about my mother. "Like, how does someone end up a raving lunatic?" I asked. Aunt Christy pretended she didn't hear me the first few times, but eventually she gave in. We were sitting in her car, about to leave for school one morning near the end of her stay. Aunt Christy's van was running while we waited for Peter and Freddy. The zipper had broken on Peter's pants, so he had to go inside to find something else to wear, while Freddy was always late getting out the door. He took forever to brush his teeth and had to apply zit cream to his chin each morning before leaving the house. The zit cream was a new thing, and he really had no use for it. I guess it made him feel grown-up. Aunt Christy got it for him from the drugstore after he complained that his chin was getting red. If you asked me, I thought he was enjoying the Oxy a little too much. Some parades a girl can't bring herself to rain on though; such was our desperation that even zit cream was giving us thrills.

"Kay," she said, pausing like she was making sure she had my name right. "Kay, listen. People can be sick, and then they can be sick in the head. Sue-Bess was... This wasn't good for her." She pointed at our house. "We didn't really grow up like this." Aunt Christy pointed at 1234 Hack Road. I wanted to tell her I got the picture—our place was a dump; no one was arguing with that— but she went on. It sounded a lot like she had planned what she was going to say and was finally now being made to say it. "When Elizabeth died, she should have had some help, but your dad didn't want to ask. He never wanted to ask anyone for anything, and she just went along with it. I mean..." Christy paused. "You can't just have something like that happen and then go sit in your trailer without talking to a doctor or… You don't bury babies in the yard." Aunt Christy shook her head. "She knew better than this. I don't know why he wouldn't let her get any help."

"But what happened to Elizabeth?" I asked. It was still dark outside—pitch-black dark, like the middle of the night even though it was nearly seven in the morning. Aunt Christy's headlights were making large cones in front of the car, shining on Elizabeth's tree as if God intended our angle during this conversation.

Aunt Christy closed her eyes. "Elizabeth died," she said. "I mean, you know that."

"Came too early." I nodded.

"Not too early if they'd gone to the hospital. You were born in the hospital. Your brothers too. I don't know why he wouldn't take her in. I really don't know."

"I don't understand," I said. I didn't.

Christy shook her head. "It wasn't that early. Your dad… He didn't want them to go to the hospital. Said the baby would be fine. Said your mom would be fine. He wouldn't call an ambulance. Baby died right there in their bedroom."

"Oh." My heart and lungs turned up the temperature and flooded my face and neck red with hot blood—near boiling. "I thought…"

"I know," Christy said. "I know what they told you. But if you want to know what happened to your mother, that's what happened. She's got a baby buried in the front yard of her house. That baby came out breathing. She should have gone to the hospital. And then, when things started to get really weird, your mother should have gone to the hospital. Or seen a psychiatrist or something… *Something* should have been done."

"Did you know about Sarah-Anne?"

I heard the front door slam and looked up to see Peter and Freddy trotting down the stairs like two drunk horses. Aunt Christy looked at me; her mouth was a line on her face—flat and sorry. "I wondered. We all did. They were always quiet, but they got *real* quiet then. Living over here…away from everybody, not talking to anyone. We never saw them. We never saw you. I don't feel like I even know you kids. I didn't know Sarah-Anne. I never saw you, never spent time with you. That was how they wanted it. I wondered a lot of things, and now I have a lot of regrets, but I'm not going to uproot you and take you away from everything you know." Peter and Freddy were in the car now. They were listening but didn't say a word. "I'm not going to move you away. And I need to get home, Kay." She sounded sad; I couldn't tell if it was sad for herself, or for us, or for Sue-Bess.

Turned out, it was just sad for herself. This—not wanting to tear us away from our Bledsoe roots—was the reason Aunt Christy gave for dumping us into foster care instead of taking us into her fancy house. I wasn't mad about it at first; it was when I got to really thinking about how easy it would have been for her to help us that I got fired up. I called her all sorts of names in my head—spoiled, selfish, snobby, bitch. I swear she hardly lasted a week in Bledsoe without all of her special things. She made sure we knew where we were most lacking in our accommodations. Aunt Christy's house had a Jacuzzi tub and a lanai, whatever that was, and she had someone come get her clothes to go to the cleaners.

"I don't think you can pay people to wash your clothes here," I'd told her.

"No. I mean, no, they're not washed like in a bucket. It's dry—never mind." It seemed we were giving the impression that we washed our clothes in a bucket.

After Aunt Christy told me she had a lot of regrets but no intention of taking us in or moving to Bledsoe to care for us, we lived with a family from Volmer—the Branskis. The Branskis had, for some reason, given up their close proximity to Walmart and the freeway and moved to Bledsoe, where they were looking after wards of the state out of the kindness of their Polish hearts. I had trouble deciphering the mother; her accent was thick as cement, even though Peter and Freddy claimed she spoke clear as a bell. The father rarely spoke except to remind us to take our shoes off when we came in the house. He was perfectly understandable. His name was Ford, which didn't sound a bit foreign to me. I called him Mr. Branski when I said anything to him at all.

We had some daily chores in the Branski home and ate a lot of casseroles with cheese on top. I thought I'd died and gone to heaven given the bounty on our plates every night. The Branskis had three children of their own and had taken in strays for years. Mrs. Branski said her heart hurt to hear of our plight.

The Branskis' kids were nice to us. They were older and out on their own, even though they came to their parents' place to eat all the time. They said they'd had a lot of tough cases in their house growing up, many from worse situations than ours. Peter was offended by talk like this. I rather liked it. I'd been well trained in the art of feeling sorry for myself—it was nice to hear that others agreed I'd been dealt a bad hand.

It seemed like a constant stream of people were coming and going in our lives. I began to put my parents in that same category— water people who flowed in and out, over and under, through and then down. I thought of them as folks who'd come then gone. Aunt Christy had been a brief fixture with her rigid schedule of driving back and forth from near Savannah. Then came the Branskis, who let us live with them—something so kind I could hardly wrap my head around it. But everything was to end. Everything was "for a time." Not a long time. I had a feeling, deep in the crevices of my small intestine—twenty feet long, according to Freddy—that my parents would not come home. They were water that had already run through our river, and water doesn't travel the same riverbed twice—life is not a circle; idiots who say stupid shit like that have never been in foster care.

We were at the Branskis' when the holidays rolled around but hadn't been there for long enough for them to have gotten us any

Christmas presents. My parents didn't give us presents any other year, but I swear we were all praying on the same Bible that the Branskis would be the kind of family with a tree and Santa and all of that. We were all too old for Santa, even though I didn't want to be. My mom had never let us believe in anything fun, so we didn't. It was like so many other decisions that were made for us. No Santa, no waking up early to run to the Christmas tree, no stockings, no writing letters to be sent to the North Pole. At 1234 Hack Road, we decorated a tree in the yard with a handful of busted ornaments and no lights and then did chores on Christmas. It was any other day of the year—except we had more chores, because my mother got even more resentful when good times were supposed to be had. Chores, busted ornaments, and maybe a candle on the dinner table.

"I hate it for you, but it's damn near Christmas now, and I just haven't had the time," Mrs. Branski—Ellen—told us in her thick, twisted way of speaking southern with a Polish accent. "We can hit the sales after. That's always fun." Their house was decorated like a fancy store with glass Santa Clauses on every surface. She even had red and green napkins for dinner and mugs that looked like snowmen with stick brooms as handles. Mrs. Branski wore a special robe for the season—flannel with wreaths and sprigs of holly embroidered around the hem. I smiled when I saw these touches. "We'll go to the big sales," she said again. "That will be fun."

I had no idea what she was talking about. We found out, though, when we went to Kohl's for their after-Christmas extravaganza, and for the first time in my life, I had a pair of jeans. It was strange to have something pressing on my privates and digging into my stomach, but I felt so good wearing them that I swore I'd never take them off. I got the jeans and a sweatshirt with Minnie Mouse on it. Peter said it looked like it was for a little girl.

"I didn't get to have one when I was a little girl," I said. I found I felt this way about a lot of things while staying with the Branskis.

We all got bikes—hand-me-downs from Ellen and Ford's grown children. We didn't know how to ride bikes; this made Mrs. Branski cry. Peter didn't want to be anyone's reason for crying and refused to ride the trick bike with pegs on the rear wheels anymore. He complained of back pain and said he didn't like rolling. Freddy and I were smitten and wondered why our parents had thought to rob us of such a childhood pleasure as this. All I could think was how much easier it would have been to get to school on a bike.

I began to see things as choices rather than situations. I heard Wade Welty tell one of the women who met with us at the police station that our parents had made a lot of bad choices. It was such a strange thing to say about them, like people accusing my mother of killing Emily Webber, of stealing Sarah-Anne from some poor family who wasn't watching their baby closely enough. I'd wanted to laugh then, now, forever. My mother didn't have the strength. But then I guess she did; there was that picture on the internet with her arrest record. There were more stories, more accusations, more things we didn't know. She'd been busier than we could have expected. It all happened after Elizabeth—she took the wind out of my mother's sails. I was too small to remember it, although it was lurking, like my father out behind the house when a car drove up. I didn't think my mother made choices, but there she was—in jail, choosing not to talk. Not one word.

We had to do a few finger pricks to prove we were Whitaker kids. There was some question after my results were tainted. Could I have been snatched up too? No. We did another test; this time the technician wore gloves. I was kin to Sue-Bess and Clay—these were the facts. They already knew Freddy was in the right house. His spit test came back conclusively Whitaker.

Welty said it was the sadness from Elizabeth, not uncommon, that made my mother pine for other people's children so much. He told me this like we were old friends who shared our pity for my mother like we shared our pity for starving children in Africa—old friends on the porch, rocking away our sorrows for other people. Ain't it sad. We became old friends in a short time.

"She was plain sad when she lost that baby," Welty said. "Hard for you to understand." He had a whole lot of sympathy for my mother. His cup runneth over.

"I do," I said. It was as though he'd asked me to marry him. I added Wade Welty and his large biceps to the list of people I wanted to marry—potentially.

Welty went above and beyond his duties as investigating officer in a dumpy town. He kept a close eye on me, us, taking note of our circumstances—ever changing—sending this person over to the house, then this other person to the Branskis', then sending a car to take us to the station, then having someone else come to check on us at school. He was like queen bee to our hive. I figured he was worried for our safety and well-being, but maybe more than that, he hoped one of us would finally crack and spill the beans about what had happened to Sarah-Anne, my mother, my father. There were no beans to spill. I had no idea what happened. We kept telling people that.

"I don't know," I said. "I really don't know." I was starting to get an idea for sure, but I couldn't explain what I was thinking. It was like something I was deeply ashamed of that kept showing up in the toilet after I peed. I could flush and flush, but I'd have to pee again, and there it would be. A vow of thirst was a shitty option. I'd begin to think I knew where Sarah-Anne went, and then a crow would squawk, or a damned acorn would come crashing down on the roof, or I'd catch Charlotte Harper picking food out of her braces out of the corner of my eye, and I wouldn't be able to face the bad ideas in my brain.

I took Welty's shining to me like getting a medal for the pole vault. I was proud of his attention and thought it the only natural reaction to my fascinating personality. I must have been a curious kind of lonely. I stuck to him like white on rice but assured him that no matter how hard he tried, I wouldn't be able to tell him anything important. I didn't know a goddamned thing. This was

God's honest truth. Goddammit. I wasn't lying—I didn't know. I only thought, but then the thoughts went away like twigs on the ass end of a leaf blower going full throttle.

The house on Hack Road sat empty for a spell. I felt sorry for it there, alone. Elizabeth kept watch over it, but maybe she was more like a curse on the place being that she'd fallen out of my mother on the wrong day and died before anyone bothered to help her.

Peter told me he had asked Aunt Christy about Elizabeth, but she said she didn't really remember. "Seems a funny thing to forget," I said, feeling strangely special. Aunt Christy had chosen me to confide in. I'd never played this role. It immediately made me like Aunt Christy and feel very forgiving toward her for abandoning us so she could have dry cleaning and a Jacuzzi.

I was too little to have seen it—I kept telling myself—to have remembered when Elizabeth died. But then why was it there, in my head, like a knot in a vine? There were vines by the road; they crept up the trees, strangling them, like hard veins on an old woman's leg—things had the habit of reminding me of veins when I wasn't careful. My granny, Sue-Bess's mother, had big knots on the backs of her legs. She could barely walk; she was always holding on to my mother, reaching for her arm, stumbling around with a firm grip. I figured out later that she wasn't just trying to stay upright; she was trying to keep a hold on Sue-Bess before she disappeared further into the trap she set for herself—the Clay trap. Suddenly, I was seeing veins everywhere. Veins, and Sue-Bess, and traps. It was all the same to me. Sometimes when I was asleep at the Branskis', in my bed with the purple sheets, I'd put my fingers on my neck to feel my pulse. I had veins too, but mine were on the inside where they belonged. The traps were in my head.

I saw a missing persons poster for Sarah-Anne on a power line pole by Shane's Auto Repair. I never went over to Shane's, and I had no good reason for being there the day I saw the flyer. But there it was and there I was, like a confrontation waiting to happen. I wondered why I'd walked all that way, what I was doing there, but I had no answers. Just the flyer. It was stapled to the pole right outside the shop. I wanted to tear it down. "Who the hell put this here?" I asked no one in particular.

Shane from the repair shop caught me staring at it and must have wondered who I was talking to. He stood by the front window watching me real close. He opened the door to his shop and asked what I was doing in his parking lot. He said it in a nice but suspicious way, like maybe I was the reason for all of this—me and my dresses. I scowled at him. "Goin' for a walk," I said. I pointed at the missing persons sign but said nothing. It was one of Sarah-Anne's school pictures from two or three years before. She didn't look any different from the day she left. Her eyes were shiny and wide set. All I could think was that she had no idea where she was. They kept saying that she was too little to know she'd been abducted, but that didn't make sense to me. She knew she didn't belong. That was her whole identity—the one who didn't fit in the shit box we called home.

Shane stared at me for a while before saying that his wife was "real tore up about your sister. That kind of stuff don't happen around here."

"Yes, it does," I said. "She was kidnapped in the first place." I was about to tell him that her bed was in the fucking hallway, but I didn't think he would understand.

I walked back to the Branskis' house, some two miles away. Shane's Auto Repair was the only thing within walking distance of the Branskis'. It made Hack Road seem like the place to be. The next time I walked over that way, the poster was gone. Word spread that Sarah-Anne wasn't even really my sister at all. I don't know if that made people feel more or less sorry for me.

The Branskis said they wanted us, but Nile Webber spoke up and said he could step in. Ellen Branski was disappointed—or pretended to be. She said her face couldn't hide her heart, so she went around frowning while making us Duncan Hines brownies and filling the bike tires with air; she was good with a pump.

Freddy said he didn't want to live with the Webbers. "I want to go to school in Richmond Hill," he told our case worker—one of the many women in a wine-colored suit. I think her name was Cathy. There were two Cathys, two Lindsays, and dozens of wine-colored suits. I couldn't keep anyone straight—only Wade and my brothers, who didn't know Wade's name from Adam.

"Wade?" Peter said when I told him Wade didn't like Dad.

"Officer Welty," I said.

"That guy's weird."

I shrugged. There wasn't any use in arguing. We'd been through a lot. "I guess," I said. "Isn't everyone?"

"It's all we know," Freddy said. "That's all we knew." He was talking about Mom and Dad.

"No," I shook my head. "We didn't have anywhere else to go. I knew better, and so did you."

The Branskis gave us up. Ellen said it was a mistake to go live out in the water with a man who didn't send his own kid to school. "See, I think that's working in his favor," I told her. She said I didn't know my boot from my lace.

"I've never had boots," I explained.

"Jesus Lord in heaven," she answered.

Welty looked at the floor at any mention of Nile or Andy.

"Does seem kinda odd that we're gonna live with them…on account of what happened and all," I said. We'd been talking about our *arrangement*.

"It's like something you read in the newspaper about a backwater place," Welty said. "I can't make sense of it myself."

"This is backwater," I said. I didn't know backwater had a few different meanings until I got older—I was right on several accounts. I'd been standing in backwater my whole life. "So if the shoe fits…not that we're wearin' shoes much of the time." I stopped talking. Welty exhaled in defeat. It seemed we'd gone and defined the problems of our time.

"He's feeling bad," Welty said.

"Who? Nile?"

"Yes, but I'm not sure about what."

"Yeah," I said. I enjoyed agreeing with Welty. "What's he got to feel bad about anyway?"

"Not a damn thing, I hope."

We didn't see my parents at all. It was my understanding that they didn't want to see us. This was expected of my mother, but I had a hard time believing my father couldn't face his offspring in an orange jumpsuit. This was the same guy who taped his glasses to his face and nearly set his head on fire with a Camel. None of that slowed him down, not even the Jack and Cokes at nine in the morning.

"It's the shame of it all," Wade told me. "Your dad's ashamed."

"Think so?" I asked. I wasn't buying it.

Welty didn't really talk to my brothers, just me. Peter said he was sure he could pull a fast one on me, that was why.

"What do you mean, 'pull a fast one'?" I asked Peter.

"He thinks you're an easy target."

"I don't get it. He's just sorry for us is all. Feeling bad about our wayward family."

"That's what I'm saying," Peter said. "I'm sayin' that exactly."

We had so many meetings at the police station and an office for family affairs that a day felt strange when I wasn't talking to someone about my unfortunate circumstances. Everyone wanted to know how people were treating us. I always felt like they were hoping I would say Mrs. Branski was sticking animal crackers up our assholes, but she wasn't. I didn't even have that kind of thing to say about my parents. They didn't really do anything to us. They might have taken Sarah-Anne, but to us, it was business as usual—a strange business, but that was all I really had to say about it. It was strange. And Sarah-Anne was still gone. That was the strangest thing of all, like forgetting to wear underwear. Gone. I found it was getting harder to remember her. Maybe she'd never been there at all, but she was. My parents were in jail for snatching her up. She was as real as hard time.

Peter was the most embarrassed of the three of us—a grown-up in a kid trap. He was too old to be shuttled around like a trinket in a pocket. Freddy and I had to be in someone's charge—we couldn't drive, didn't have money of our own, weren't old enough to get emancipated or whatever it was that Peter was trying to do. He also didn't even have to go to school anymore. Sixteen was the drop-dead date; after that, he could turn in his papers and take a long walk. This was all news to me. He was mostly grown, almost a sir, and I'd missed it. Freddy said Peter would stick with us. I wasn't so sure. Maybe that was why I sidled up to Welty like a foal to a mare. I was afraid of getting left again. People weren't saying *emancipation* as much, but I didn't forget about it. I know Peter didn't either. He started acting like he was doing everyone a favor by not dropping out of school full stop. It made me sick to think of

Peter gone too. It gave me a knot in my stomach that left my skin cold. He kept promising he wouldn't go, but if I were him…that was what was bothering me. If I were him.

Time periods were brief but felt long and wide, like a Fruit Roll-Up laid flat. There were details to sort. "I think I'll kind of like living in the Webbers' house," I told a few people at the police station. Lots of women were interested in my situation. I enjoyed an audience and told them of my newest arrangement. "I've always wanted a romantic life on the water. It suits me better than the dry sands of—"

"Shut up, Kay," one of my brothers would inevitably say if they were in the room. "Shut up."

It was our last night with Ellen and Ford. We'd been told several times that this was our last night only to find we were staying another week. We had separate bedrooms at the Branskis' but chose to sleep together in the bonus room. Ellen said it was no problem and let us pull our mattresses down the hall. The room was stuffy, even though it was cold outside. It had a funny smell that Freddy said was mold. His sinuses were extra aggravated. I was lying on top of my purple bedspread. I thought to suggest opening a window, but I knew it was close to thirty degrees outside. There didn't seem to be a happy medium. I put my hand on my forehead—damp with sweat.

"Is the heater *in* this room?" I asked. "Like, under it or something?" It was our first experience with central heating other than at school.

We lay still and silent, staring at the ceiling. "You guys are all I've got," Freddy said.

I heard my heartbeat, and then Peter's, and then Freddy's. "I know, Freddy," Peter said. "I know."

When things finally did wrap up with the Branskis, I learned they had been paid to take care of us. This was protocol according to Freddy, but it melted away the layer of comfort I'd felt by believing there were good people in the world who cared about kids with psychos for parents.

"Yeah, they got money," Peter said matter-of-factly. "Who cares."

I do, I thought. Now I was like Freddy and Cort Hat. People were getting paid to pretend to like me.

Another hit came when I learned we would not be moving to the high heel but staying put on Hack Road. "The Webbers will be coming to live in your house," one of the women from the state said while we were filling out more paperwork in her office.

"They're moving in with us?" I asked, my dreams of a life on stilts so quickly dashed.

"Yes, he gets something too. Mr. Webber. He gets your house. For the time being. Your house and an allowance—from the state." The woman who was completing my forms looked at the papers on her desk, arranged them even though they were already in a perfect stack, and picked up her pen, though she didn't write anything. Now Nile Webber would be the third person in our lives who got money for spending time with us.

"The state," I said.

"Yes," she replied. "Not what I would have done if... Well, no one's listening to me, right?"

"Me neither. I wanted to live out in the water."

"Hmmmph." She arranged her tidy stack again.

It was almost three months after my father's arrest before we saw my parents. We had to have a hearing about our living arrangements; they were made to attend and sign the papers allowing Nile Webber to be our guardian, in our house, with Andy, for money. It was only the three of us. Sarah-Anne was still gone. Still disappeared.

Sue-Bess and Clay did not sit together but on separate benches in the small courtroom that did not have a place for a jury. I repeatedly asked all of the adults around us if it was really a courtroom, "because of the jury thing." No one answered me. Instead, there were a lot of knowing smiles and quiet nods. "What about the jury?" I asked again. No one answered. All I could think was that Freddy's face was redder than usual and that Peter looked awfully grown-up. We all wore the best clothes we had. I was in one of my mother's dresses. The liaison had said no jeans; I didn't have much of a choice. The boys were wearing button-up shirts and brown pants, every item a little too small.

Nile and Andy showed up wearing jeans. I tried to get the woman's attention—I think her name was Amy—to show her that other people were wearing jeans. She remained focused on the judge and either didn't hear my calls or pretended not to.

I found out later—because I was eavesdropping on Welty's conversation with a plump woman who laughed like she was trying not to scream, eyes real wide and mouth constantly trying to shut itself—that my parents were on opposite sides of the bench because my dad had turned my mom in. If they'd hated each other before, then it was double now. My dad dropped the bomb on Sue-Bess right before he left the mainland. Too bad he had to come right back.

"He's the one who called it in," Welty told the woman, making his face as big as possible by filling it with air and fake concern. No matter the seriousness of matters, I couldn't stop thinking about Welty's batter face and its ability to stretch, bubble, and spread. His expressions were of endless fascination to me. "He called us. Said he knew what happened to the Webber lady."

I listened as best I could even though I knew I wasn't supposed to hear. I was good at looking like I wasn't paying attention. I pretended to be interested in the dirt under my fingernails but was really picking up Welty's scent.

"Yeah, I guess he thought he'd throw her under the bus and skip town," the lady said. She still sounded like she thought all of this was awfully funny. "She made sure he had to come right back though, didn't she? Losing the sister at just the right time."

"Whole thing has a funny stink to it." Welty looked over at me and caught me listening. I thought maybe he was trying to smile politely or make a feeling-sorry-for-me face, but he couldn't get his pancake batter to move in the right directions.

"Doesn't seem like anybody cared about those kids at all," the laughing lady said. "Not one bit."

"No." Welty shook his head. "What a mess."

"I couldn't believe they were letting them stay with the fella with the dead wife, but I s'pose that's better than with their own parents at this point. And the aunt don't even want 'em."

"What a mess," Welty said again. He glanced at me and scratched his head. He knew I was listening. Welty and I had a bond. He could tell when I was playing dumb.

Before the proceedings began, we were shuffled off to a holding area so we wouldn't hear what the adults were saying in the big room. I quietly tried to ask Welty what my dad said to the police to get my mom arrested.

He turned away and pretended to smell something funny. "That gas?"

"Wuddn't me," I said. "But about my dad. He—"

"No, I mean…maybe we should call the fire department."

"So my dad called 911 and said Mom drowned Emily Webber? Or did he come into the station with a bloody skirt or something? If he called before he got on the boat, y'all didn't come right away. Why'd you wait 'til the next day?" He looked at me hard but didn't answer. I know he wanted to.

"I think somebody's making popcorn," he finally said.

There was no use. Some things are too hard to say to a twelve-year-old, even for Welty.

No one asked my parents a single question at the hearing. I was worried about what they might say, but I didn't have to worry long. The proceedings were over in a matter of minutes. Nile Webber signed some papers after giving a short speech about taking care of us that I could barely hear—he mumbled even in official settings. Andy was sulking and looking sideways at my parents every couple of seconds. I didn't look sideways at them—I stared hard and long.

My mother's feather-like hair was tied back with a rubber band, but not the kind for hair, the kind a person uses to secure pencils or an old newspaper. She looked at us—Peter, Freddy, and me—when she first came in the room, but her face was like a frozen lake. I would have cracked it with a spike if I could have. My father was jumpy and sneering, like this was all someone else's fault— someone he was just about to confront after he finished his lunch. He looked at me the most. I knew I'd let him down somehow, like we were supposed to be in this together.

Nile and Andy would move into our house on Hack Road, where Nile would become our legal guardian—for the time being. There was still a lot of talk of my parents' innocence, their chances at release, something they'd said that might get them off. There was to be a trial, but it was a long way off. They had lawyers from the county, because they were indigent defendants, whatever that meant. My mother was on suicide watch and taking medications to keep her calm. I laughed a little, in the quiet stillness of the room. No one in the world was calmer than my mother. If they calmed her even more, she'd disappear. I thought about Sarah-Anne. I couldn't think about missing things without thinking of her.

We left the courtroom and were shuttled into another large room where they had soft drinks, water bottles, and small packages of crackers and snacks. Out of habit, I went straight for the cheese and peanut butter. Peter took a Dr. Pepper. Freddy said no thank you. Andy—who came with us this time; he'd been allowed to stay in the room with the adults before—didn't talk to us but took a pack of Fritos from the table. He seemed angry, which was understandable given his situation. I was angry too. We all had a situation.

People were talking all around us—tall people who carried folders. Surely we weren't the first case of children taken from their parents in Bledsoe. "It was an unusual circumstance," someone said to enthusiastic nodding. We were common yet unusual. When my parents finally had their trial, then we would really know our fate, someone else said. It was a woman—she pointed at me when she said *fate*. I felt like a very young child in my dress with my hair in a long braid down my back. Mrs. Branski, who took us to the courthouse that day—probably for a twenty—had tried to convince us to get our hair cut. We agreed until we learned that it was her husband whose services she was offering. Ford was a nice man, but he had noticeably unsteady hands. I politely declined, as did Peter and Freddy. We looked like a bunch of ragamuffins. It was probably what we'd always looked like.

When we left the Reed County Courthouse that day, we got to

go home—to the house on Hack Road. We'd been there, back and forth with Aunt Christy, but we'd always known we were leaving. This time, we had all of our things with us. We were staying. I didn't really thank the Branskis when we left their house that morning with our stuffed bags and our long faces. They didn't seem all that sad to see us go. It felt like something had run its course and now we were being asked to leave—kindly.

"I don't want to talk about Mom and Dad," Freddy said almost as soon as we were all in the house together.

"Okay," Nile said.

"I don't want to talk about 'em either," Andy told us. He'd plopped down on the couch in the living room and put his feet on the coffee table. I was instantly mad at him for thinking he could make himself so comfortable without my personal invitation. I gritted my teeth, about to tell him so, but Peter spoke up before I could.

"This is Andy's house now too," Peter said. He stood very tall and sturdy like he'd planned what he was about to say a dozen times. "The Webbers are looking out for us, so we don't have to be foster kids or whatever it is they'd do with us. You don't know if the Branskis would have kept us, and Aunt Christy sure didn't want the trouble. I feel like everybody's mad, but we should be feeling kindly toward Andy and his dad. I don't know what we would have done without them." Peter dipped his head respectfully at Nile. Andy grunted loudly but didn't speak; his feet were still on the table. He spread his legs a little—taking up even more space.

The room was quiet. It was in this stillness that I looked over at Sarah-Anne's bed in the hallway. No one could find her. Dead or not, she was plain gone. "Is Andy going to sleep on Sarah-Anne's bed?" I asked, still sounding like a train off the rails.

"We can fig'r' it out," Nile said.

"No one sleeps on her bed," Freddy said sternly. He had a nervous way about him when he was trying to lay down the law. "There are more rooms now that Mom and Dad aren't here. No one sleeps there. She may come back, and then we'll look like we didn't want her to, or we'll... She might come back."

Sarah-Anne never came back.

CHAPTER 25

With both of my parents gone and the Webbers living in our house—but not the way I wanted them to live with us, or me with them, because there was nothing romantic about any of it—I went very quickly from feeling out of control to helpless to a confused kind of angry. I wasn't used to having this many different thoughts about my state of mind. I had been like a child for so long—itching for adventure, not minding a little trouble or scolding, or even a swat now and then. I wasn't much older than I'd been the day they arrested my mother, the day after Sarah-Anne left us, but I felt a long decade more grown. I could tell the way people were looking at us was changing. We'd been so pitiful and indigent—it meant poor and unable to pay for our own stuff (Freddy looked it up)—but now it seemed like we were being asked to take responsibility for our parents' bad deeds, a list that kept growing.

"We're looking for a body now. The feds don't think she's alive." Welty said the feds thought my parents killed Sarah-Anne. "It's a shame for me to tell you this," he said like he enjoyed telling me shameful things in his spare time—but just a little.

"Who's the feds?" I asked. We had lunch once a week. I went to the police station, so it was all on the up and up. Welty got me a burger from McDonald's and we talked about how things were going. Usually, we discussed my living arrangements and his fishing, but after a few weeks under one roof with Nile and Andy, Welty changed his tone.

"There was a report of an abduction in Halleran, Florida. That's where we think Sarah-Anne came from. The dates line up almost perfectly. So it's state to state now. Not just a Georgia case anymore. Federal jurisdiction."

"Right," I said, having no idea what he was talking about. "What's her name?" I'd put my burger down on the greasy paper. "Is Halleran nice? I think living in Florida would be just about the best thing ever. I never been there."

"Someday, Kay."

"What's her name?" I asked.

"Who?"

"Sarah-Anne. I know it sure as hell wasn't Sarah-Anne, because that's a name straight outta Sue-Bess's playbook. She likes that kinda name. Not for me, but for, like, other kids."

"We can't find the people who reported her missing. They aren't at that address anymore, and nobody seems to know where they went. No records." He didn't answer me about her name.

"Okay... They didn't tell you her name when—" My stomach dropped a little. I was tired of people who barely existed. Tired of no records. "Sure didn't improve her situation by gettin' kidnapped, did she? I'da hoped maybe some rich family woulda snatched me from the gas station. Poor kid—born under a bad sign."

"It's those fishermen," Welty interrupted.

"Right," I said. "You're a fisherman." I nodded at his Big Mac and super-size fries—fisherman food.

"Yes." He nodded back. I left my burger alone. I felt something coming, like vomit up my windpipe, or very disturbing news. "So, these fishermen...the one, especially," Welty said. "He keeps insisting that he saw your mother out there. He's called every day, wondering why we aren't pressing charges against your mom." He tilted his head toward his lamp as if to suggest my mother was in the room with us, sitting right behind the lamp. "She was talkin' to a fella."

"I thought you were saying it was Nile Webber." I shook my head in disapproval. "But then y'all let us live with him, so you must notta thought too much'a that."

"Yeah." Welty looked at me, then down, then away. "That

wasn't my decision. Limited resources," he explained like he didn't know what he was talking about. "Anyway…now we got another person saying they saw Sarah-Anne."

"What?" My whole body changed consistency and got flipped inside out. My skin was hot and my blood ice cold.

"Yes. There's a witness. Lives back there too. Farther out." He pointed at his lamp again.

"Farther? There is no farther."

"Oh, there's farther," Welty said. "This is Bledsoe." I had to stop myself from rolling my eyes—like I didn't know it. Please. "Said they saw Sarah-Anne with a man. The state…or the feds…every-body… She was with someone."

"What'd they see 'em doin'?"

"We've now got multiple witnesses who saw a man and a woman…and now someone who says they saw Sarah-Anne with a man. They saw her picture on one of the flyers we put out. Said it was her—young girl, not your mother."

"Okay," I said. "But Sarah-Anne don't know any men. 'Cept Daddy…Clay."

"I just want you to know what's coming." Welty put a few fries on the top patty of his burger and replaced the bun. It was a good move. I took a few of my own fries and did the same but didn't take a bite. My mouth was near frozen shut. "Thought you should know."

"Was it my dad or something?"

"What?"

"This man she was talking to."

"Lotta men look alike" was all Welty said. Then he asked me if I wanted more fries.

"No," I said. "Is it the lady with the monkeys?" I didn't wait for him to answer before saying, "A lotta girls look alike too, you know."

"What monkeys?" He put a fry in his mouth. "Who has monkeys?" Welty was sure good at ignoring part of what I said.

"Oh, I don't know… I never seen 'em," I said. "Did they see a little boat out there?"

"A little boat?"

"Like a half boat, skinny and short. Light as a feather. We think my mama was out there in it. Had to be her, 'cause it was wet and back at the house. Somebody brought it back. Sarah-Anne didn't come back to the house, wet or not. Mom was wet too, but she never wore boots; she also never killed a lady—or so we thought. So, I mean, there ya have it."

Welty tilted his head to the side. "Boots?"

"Yeah, in the shed." I nodded. "My mom and Sarah-Anne look just alike anyway. I could never tell 'em apart. Not even blood relations—imagine that."

"Imagine that."

$\sim$

Clay and Sue-Bess's trial for kidnapping was set for August, while my mother's trial for Emily Webber's murder would not be until October. It seemed a long time to wait. We were in a holding pattern until then; the arrangement with Nile and Andy was only meant to get us through until the final verdict. I was told over and over again—by Peter and Welty—that this could be permanent. Mom and Dad would likely be convicted. Sarah-Anne was not their kid. There was a missing persons report filed though never followed up on. We didn't know who Sarah-Anne's family was, but they seemed an awful lot like ours—absent-type people, living on the edge of awareness, powerless, their secrets their only "currency"—I got that part from Welty, who said my parents had enough skeletons in their closet to buy a new house, with a bigger closet. Secrets could be like money if you had enough of them.

We finally saw my dad, but not my mother—yet. Clay was talking to the police and being *helpful*. He'd had some sort of change of heart that we were supposed to automatically understand. He asked us how school was going and gave us directions about how to do things at the house. I told him I had to throw his special blue towel away. "Got oil on it," I said. "In the trash now."

"That's okay, Kay," he said, smiling distantly. There was no oil on the towel. It was folded up and in the cupboard under the sink where it always was. I just said I threw it away to be ugly.

None of us liked going to the jail to see Dad, but we did it out of duty, and also because Welty told us to. I guess he was still holding out hope that my dad would tell us what happened to Sarah-Anne. Welty could never believe that we didn't know—none of us.

My dad did say he would never forgive himself for losing her. "But you took her," I said, right after the bit about the blue towel.

"I know," he said. "I shouldn't have." I believed him—on both things.

I didn't know what my mother thought about it, and I didn't plan to ask. They were both liars, but for some reason I thought my mother was more far gone. Really they both killed somebody: my mother when she put bricks in Emily Webber's pockets and my dad when he wouldn't take baby Elizabeth to the hospital. That second bit might have been the reason for the first, so it was probably all my dad's fault. I could still give him a break, though. He had this pleading, hurt way about him that my mother did not share. She was ice, and he was a puddle—at least that's the way it was in the end. I guess she'd finally gone and done it when she snatched Sarah-Anne up. That broke my dad. Horse-whipped-broke. And I didn't have to ask—I knew it was my mother who took her. Sue-Bess got hers too.

One afternoon, we got a call at the house. Welty rang to tell Nile that our mother wanted to see us. "Alls'a ya," Nile said.

"All of us?" Freddy said, in his weird way of correcting people. We'd run into the kitchen at the sound of the phone ringing— except Andy of course, who didn't care about the phone. It was a late spring day—heavy air, lingering sun, and birds and squirrels out of the corner of your eye every time you looked out a window. They were busy. We were not. We'd been home from school for only about an hour when Welty called.

"Tomorrow," Nile said.

"I wonder if she'll confess to killing your wife," I said right to his face like an accusation.

"Kay!" Peter said.

"Dunno," Nile said before walking away. He went into my parents' room, where he now slept, and shut the door.

"Mom's home," I said.

No one told me to shut up.

CHAPTER 26

I wouldn't go by myself to talk to my mother. Peter wanted to be alone with her, while Freddy was uncommitted. He went on and on about the school in Richmond Hill again. All I could think was that I didn't blame him for wanting out. I didn't know what I wanted. It wasn't even fun to think about marrying a lot of husbands or having my own air boat anymore. My well was empty; I wasn't even thirteen without a drop left to drink.

It was quite a process to both get to the Reed County Jail and then inside it. We had to have our pictures taken and our clothes searched. Guards who seemed tired and embarrassed to be talking to kids at their job asked us a bunch of questions and led us through a long maze of doors that all made beeps when opened. I thought I recognized one of the jailers—Lucy Donovan's dad. He'd come to the school for career day once. He had showed us his gun. He smiled at me as we went through the second set of doors. I didn't smile back. There is nothing to smile about when you go see your mom in jail.

After another maze of doors, beeps, and clicks we finally saw Sue-Bess. She sat quietly at a table in a crowded room full of other inmates, all wearing matching clothes. I'd thought we'd have to go through the glass, touching plastic to feel each other's pain, but she wasn't even in maximum security lockdown. Reed County Jail was the local joint. Maximum security, where she'd have to go if she got the chair, was over an hour away. She was not considered a violent offender—old murders don't do much for your reputation in Reed County. I wondered what it took to get sent to the Morganton Prison, where they kept the lifers and the death penalty cases—probably a conviction. I had an all-new vocabulary after talking to the feds, who said they wanted to help us but were always fishing for details. I still didn't know anything. I kept apologizing for disappointing them.

"I just want you to know—" my mother immediately said when we sat down in front of her.

"Not even gonna say 'hi' first," I interrupted. We'd walked in in a line, strangely able to fit between all of the tables and sofas strewn about the room. It smelled like mouthwash and old potatoes in there. I was in the middle of Peter and Freddy and felt the most conspicuous—this was one of a hundred words I now knew to describe how I was feeling in a whole mess of awkward situations. I'd never felt as out of place in my own skin as I did once I started realizing just how I looked in my skin. I was wearing cutoff jean shorts, which I'd thought would make me look more grown-up and rebellious against my criminal mother, but the shorts did little else than help me fit in at the jail. I was one of several girls wearing a pair.

"Hi," my mother said like she'd been patted on the ass by an unknown hand. "Hi," she said again, more calmly. "I'm... We don't have a lot of time to talk," she said. She took a slow breath and held up her tiny index finger. All I could think about was her drowning Emily Webber with her small hands, those tiny fingers, with a death grip. *Yeah right*, I thought, but it didn't last.

"I...I want you to know that I am very, very sorry for what I have done," she said. "I have had a lot of time to think in here. I know what this has done to you, to your lives, what you will have to live with because of me, and for that, I am truly sorry."

"You had a lot of time to think at home too," I said. "Why's the thinking better in here?"

"I am so sorry for what I have done to you," she repeated before standing up and raising her hand toward the guard who'd brought her in. "Excuse me," she said like she barely knew us.

She turned back for a second, her eyes losing focus. "She made him something," she said like she was talking to a speck of dust flying over our heads. "She wanted to give him a necklace... She was making them..." Her face shook from side to side ever so slightly. She looked at us, then at something beyond us in the dark halls of her mind before looking at me again, like a dart that lost its board. "Excuse me for... I want you to stay away from him."

"Huh?" I said.

"I want you to stay away from him. There was an accident—I know it was an accident. It's not his...I don't care what anyone says. I don't care what they say. No." She was having a conversation with herself. "No. I won't hear it. Leave Andy alone. Please." She walked toward the guard who escorted her back through the door from where she'd come. She did not turn around. We stood together in stunned silence.

"She didn't even try to hug us," I said, close enough to tears that I could taste them on the roof of my mouth. "She didn't even try to touch us." We all stood up as if to follow her but remained next to the table. Her light hair was longer but cut at the end, straight as a line. She looked like she'd gained weight—her face was fuller and somehow brighter. I hated to see her looking so well.

"And what necklace?" I asked. "What the hell was that about? She talked to us for all'a five seconds so she could tell us about a necklace? A necklace and Andy. Jesus bless. Like Dad wants a necklace. Man don't even wear a wedding ring. And who had an accident? Sarah-Anne? How the hell would Mom know?"

"I don't know if she meant Dad," Peter said. "About the necklace."

"And I was the one who thought Andy was so great. Everyone

acts like he's their territory now, but I'm the one who met him. I brought him over in the first place."

The boys both looked at me, each like they were about to say something. They'd correct me in their own ways—making sure I got the memo. Everybody knew Andy before me. He was Emily Webber's son—my mother's murder victim. "Kay," Freddy finally said, but I didn't want to hear him.

"Whatever," I shot back. I was out of words for this life. I thought I might never talk again. I almost prayed for it. I was so tired of going on and on always trying to think of something to say. Words fail when your mother killed Andy Webber's mother. It's a pretty unique situation. There's no good way to talk about it.

"Just forget it," Peter said. "Let's go." We'd all been standing there with our faces melting into our necks, empty heads disintegrating into hollow bodies. Peter put his arm around my shoulder and took Freddy by the hand. Peter had driven us to the station that day. It was his time to be the adult. Someone had to.

"Kinda hard thing to forget." I moved a little closer to Peter and let him get a better grip on me.

"She said she was sorry," Freddy said while we were walking back through the nine locked doors that had led us into the visitation area.

"She's sorry all right," I said.

"Just keep walking, Kay," Peter said.

"Yeah," I answered. I thought he and Freddy were the only

people in the whole world who I could trust. I was lucky they were there.

∾

My mother was convicted of Emily Webber's murder that October. She never spoke to the police and remained silent and stoic throughout her three-day trial. It was my father who gave the most damning evidence against her. When he'd called the police station from the boat dock before he and Nile left on the shrimper, he told the lady on the line a few things only a person with real knowledge of the crime would know. The police took a whole day to verify what he said. Clay Whitaker wasn't taken too seriously in Bledsoe, not then or later. No one rushed to arrest my mother after one conversation with him. Then Sarah-Anne went missing and everybody got confused about what was really going on. But my dad's the one who turned Sue-Bess in, and he's the one who put the nail in her coffin in the courtroom.

He said he was missing some bricks. "I had five bricks in the shed," he said to the jury. "There were four gone." Apparently it was the same kind of brick; they called in a brick expert. I didn't even know that was a real job.

My dad wore a tie and gave testimony on the stand. We were not allowed to go to the trial. We read about it in the paper and heard about it at school. Even the teachers had to look away when we walked into the classroom after that.

Emily had had an affair with my father when I was barely three, after Elizabeth, but before my memory. No one ever told us this directly. It was okay to talk about our mother shoving Emily Webber's face in the water. It was okay to talk about her pressing her knee into Emily's back after she smacked her over the head with one of the bricks that she put in Emily's pockets to help keep her under—but we weren't supposed to know that our father put his tongue down Emily's throat before that. When Peter said he used to hear that Dad was running around with Emily Webber, I wasn't surprised—Peter remembered everything. It did make me wonder why Nile Webber was so kind to our family, what with all we'd put him through. But in the end, he was just like us—between a rock and a hard place. His wife ran around on him. I guess he didn't think that was our fault just like Andy didn't think it was our fault that our mother killed his. All I did was think, all the damn time. I wouldn't have been able to think my way around facts like this if they were about my life. I guess that was one small thing my parents did right. They let us think about the way things were. I don't know if Nile and Andy had that luxury. There wasn't room for thinking at the high-heel house; they didn't even have a pot to piss in.

CHAPTER 27

The first time I saw Andy again—nearly five years later—I was walking a green mile home from work. Heading home always felt like heading to the gallows. I never got a better feeling about Bledsoe or the house on Hack Road; I stayed, but it wasn't out of affection.

I was kicking up dust all the way back from the Walgreens where I worked—and where I'd just been fired for pinching a lipstick. My boss called the police but then called them back and said never mind, misunderstanding. He was a kindly gentleman—Howard. He didn't care about the Revlon; it was just lessons, and I guess he thought I'd learned enough lessons. I was a favorite and had never been busted for taking even a nickel before this. I don't know what possessed me. I didn't care a lick for lipstick, except in that instant.

Bright red with a matte finish. I like a woman with a matte finish. I saw it in a movie. My hand did the talking for my mind—I guess I'd always wanted to take something that wasn't mine.

I was walking with my hands in my pockets, on Gerard Road, feeling like a wrestler in the wrong weight class, fighting my way uphill in the midday heat. I hadn't thought about Andy much in recent years, maybe a little after it happened, but that faded like everything else. He and Nile had moved out just a few months after my parents were convicted of Sarah-Anne's kidnapping.

The Webbers went back to the high heel before Andy moved away to be in a band in North Carolina, I think it was—or some state other than Georgia that didn't seem like much of a place to start a band; I never could remember exactly where. All I knew was that he left Nile there—floating in the water, like the house, like his mama, like a dead fish.

Freddy and I went back to the Branskis' for a long time; then I went home to Hack Road with my dad when he got out of jail. He was only in there for a year and change. It seemed like a person should have to stay locked up longer for stealing somebody's kid, but I guess he got a deal for throwing Sue-Bess to the wolves.

Freddy eventually went away to school in Meridian. Peter was long gone before any of this; he did not have to go back into foster care. There were advantages to being the oldest Whitaker child, the only one who remembered all the bad stuff happening…when it happened.

I stayed right there next to the marsh—same water, same sand, same sad stories with sad endings. I kept telling myself it was because of Elizabeth and not wanting to leave her alone there under the tree, but I knew it was because that place had a hold on me, like a choke chain around a dog's neck. Sometimes I thought maybe I was waiting for Sarah-Anne to come back. I did look out the window every so often and swear to a god I wasn't sure existed that I saw her, on the edge of dry land, waving to me from some place I couldn't figure out how to get to. Sarah-Anne. The name became like a blindfold. I couldn't see right when I thought about her too much.

Sometimes I'd see Nile Webber here or there, walking in town or in his boat rattling up to the dock. Nile wasn't unfriendly, but he acted like he forgot who I was. If I said anything about Andy, he changed the subject or turned to look at the sun, praying for blindness maybe—mine or his. I was used to pretending things weren't there and so was he.

I was in a thick mood walking on Gerard after my near arrest. I wasn't willing to be happy or cordial. I ignored everyone I passed, even throwing up the bird at a pal from school who drove by me and called out my name. He was going downhill, while I was trucking up. I was really in my head, sweating on the outside and rock hard on the inside. It wasn't necessarily the lipstick and getting busted for grabbing it; it was the length of the day. Just the length of a day can really get to a person when they're walking on Gerard Road sometimes. Twenty-four hours seems a little excessive in Bledsoe.

I was on the second of my three-mile walk home before I got up to the stretch by the grocery store and the barber shop. I had about another half mile before I would turn onto Hack Road. And there was Andy leaving the store with his one-tone face and body like a Popsicle stick with a tan. I thought he must have been home visiting Nile. I knew Andy came back to Bledsoe sometimes, but I hadn't seen him.

Andy didn't look much older even though I knew I did. I'd filled out and had shorter hair, cut right next to my chin. I raised my hand to wave, never having been able to stifle my enthusiasm when it came to Andy. He looked directly at me and opened his mouth as if in awe of the past coming back like a fire over a plain. He didn't say a word, just looked at me. I couldn't reconcile the difference in me or him. I thought I was frowning but found my face was serene—I know because I reached up to touch the corners of my mouth—symmetrical and running right with my top lip.

He lowered his head, looking very serious like, shoved his hands in his pockets, and hightailed it away from me without so much as lifting an eyebrow. "Andy!" I said loud enough to be heard but not really all that friendly. He didn't turn around, just kept on, going back in the direction I'd just come.

"Weirdo," I said to myself. I felt a little funny, ugly and repulsive even, the way he was in such a hurry to get away from me. I found I was standing still. All that walking, and I'd stopped. I figured I'd go in the store too. I had enough change for a drink. I could also open one of the refrigerator doors and stand in front of it for a while to cool down. "What a weirdo," I said again as I walked inside Marcia Bullock's store.

I spent the better part of four minutes in front of the Gatorades before grabbing a lemon-lime and walking to the checkout. A guy named Ross was working; I'd seen him before. He was old with gray teeth, and he was always a little too chummy. "You hear?" he said to me like we were old buddies from the train yard.

"I'm here," I said.

"No, did you hear? They found a body in the marsh." His eyes were lit up and gleaming under the dusty fluorescents. "Bones."

"No," I said nervously. I'd given him five quarters and was due some change.

"They're back there now. The police." He handed me a dime and three pennies.

"Okay then," I said. Suddenly the lipstick didn't seem like such a big deal.

"They're sayin' it's a kid," Ross went on.

I grabbed my drink and walked to the front of the store where the sliding doors greeted me with a loud whip, rolling on their tracks like a two-wheeled skateboard over asphalt. I turned back around briefly, about to ask old Ross a question, but went outside instead. I stared in the direction from where I'd come—where Andy went. I could no longer see him; he was gone. Four minutes gone.

She made him something.

~

Earlier that day, Phil Williams, who had been bringing the monkey lady her groceries for fifteen years, went out to deliver her usual order. When she didn't come out to greet him on the stilt house's front deck as she'd been doing for a decade and a half, he went inside to look for her. He found her dead, lying in bed, gray and stiff, still in her pajamas. God's mercy is an old woman dying in her sleep.

Phil called the police, who came to remove the body and make sure everything was on the up and up. She had to be at least a hundred, someone said. It was her time.

One of the officers, Matt Proctor—who'd only graduated from the academy six weeks earlier—saw markers behind her house, small wooden shapes stuck in the ground on sticks. In waders, Matt walked out to investigate. There were three wooden boxes buried in a shallow swirl of water beneath the branches of a mangrove. The sticks were gravestones. The two small boxes held monkey bones. They found Sarah-Anne's remains in the largest box. There was a peony flower carved into the top of her casket. The police ran some tests; Sarah-Anne was about fourteen years old when she died. She'd been dead this whole time.

Phil Williams found something else in the box, along with her warped bones: a thimble on a guitar string, the ends tied in a knot. The police put the necklace in a Ziploc bag with a sticker and sealed it shut.

She was making him something.

It was an accident.

Leave Andy alone.

I never knew her real name.

READING GROUP GUIDE

1. Water is a common symbol and plays an important role throughout the book. Discuss the ways in which water appears throughout the story and its significance.

2. Discuss how Kay's age influences how she perceives everything happening around her.

3. Kay likes to push the boundaries—especially with her father. Discuss the ways in which she does this and the consequences later on in the book.

4. As the youngest child, Kay struggles to have her voice heard

in her family. In what ways do you see this, and how does it impact her behavior?

5. How do you think the story would change if it were told from the perspective of Peter, Freddy, or Andy?

6. In some ways, Kay seems wise beyond her years. But in other ways, it's clear she is still a child. Discuss in what ways this is evident and its impact on the story as it progresses.

7. Peter seems to have the most knowledge of the bad blood between the Whitakers and the Webbers. How does this influence his reaction to Sue-Bess's arrest, Sarah-Anne's disappearance, and their father's reaction to these events?

8. Why do you think Sue-Bess doesn't reveal to the police who is responsible for Sarah-Anne's disappearance?

9. At one point, Kay says, "I pretended to care deeply about the tree; anything to avoid watching my mother have a personality." Do you remember when you first started seeing your parents as people beyond their roles of "mom" and "dad"?

10. Kay clearly has a rebellious streak. Did you ever go through a rebellious period when you were younger?

11. Memory is a tricky thing. How much do you think one's memory can be trusted? How does this play out in the book?

12. What do you think comes next for Kay as she moves on into young adulthood and beyond?

A CONVERSATION
WITH THE AUTHOR

What inspired you to write *The Floating Girls*?

The Georgia coast is a hauntingly beautiful place. Between the beach towns popular with tourists and the more developed cities, on intracoastal waterways and barrier islands, are tiny slices of a life that have largely been forgotten or ignored—places that have failed to keep up with the pace of their better-known neighbors. We have spent a lot of time heading south from our home in Atlanta. I am an avid people-watcher and side-of-the-road observer. I like watching the houses and small, hardly noticed towns slide by the car window. We were on a certain stretch of road not far from Richmond Hill, Georgia, when I saw a house and spot of land that inspired me to create Kay and her family. I could perfectly imagine all that might be happening so close to the water and tucked so far back away from the rest of the world.

Why did you decide to write the book from Kay's point of view? In what ways did this influence how the story developed?

Kay, although unrefined, is very bright and perceptive. I wanted to see the world through her eyes, speak through her mouth, and think with her head. While I was writing, it was almost as though I was getting to know her as the plot moved forward. I made her facial expressions while writing and could vividly "see" her in her dresses, barefoot, fidgeting her way through life, yearning for adventure. This is a book about a family, but the experiences in it are uniquely Kay's. For me, there was only one way to tell her story—let her tell it.

When writing, what comes first to you: the plot of the story or the characters?

For me, definitely the characters and the setting. The plot is like a hovering cloud, and I am waiting for it to rain. Sometimes it comes down in torrents, other times a long, slow drizzle. The plot falls on my characters and their environment and has to be woven into their personality. It can make for tricky editing, but I find it is much more organic to let the characters—once I know them—tell me what happened.

What was your path to becoming a writer? Did you always know you wanted to write novels?

Not really. I had a very fantastical, perhaps naive view of creative people and creative careers before really giving writing my all. It wasn't until after I completed my law degree that I truly grasped how much hard work goes into writing, editing, rewriting, scrapping, and starting over time and time again. I figured if I could get through all of those solitary hours in the law library working on papers and academic articles, then I could do anything. I was a musician in Los Angeles during my younger years, and although I thought I loved performing, I was actually much more drawn to the creative process in the studio and while writing music than I was with the spectacle of live performance. I am a true introvert and thrive when alone and in deep thought—the perfect disposition for a writer.

What is your writing process like in terms of your routine (i.e., when and where you write)? Do you develop an outline for a book first, or do you let the story take you where it needs to go?

I write in my office at home or in local coffee shops, the park, on an airplane, in a hotel lobby, while sitting at a bar in a restaurant, really anywhere. Sometimes I need the solitude of home, while other times I need the energy of people and events around me. I write with headphones on and music playing—highly unusual, I know. I am not really listening to the songs, which are mostly like white noise, but it helps me to get out of one world and get into another if I can't hear anything going on around me. I learned to people-watch with soundtracks of my choosing while living in New York City. It has proven an invaluable skill as an author, because there is no environment in which I cannot concentrate and escape into my story. And no, I do not outline. I have never been able to be that organized about anything!

What are some of the books you've read that have influenced your writing?

Where to begin! I will read anything (including grocery lists) that Joan Didion, Penelope Lively, Truman Capote, or Alice Munro has written. I have devoured much of Margaret Atwood's, Anne Tyler's, and Larry McMurtry's bodies of work as well. When asked my favorite books, I always give the same answer—*A Thousand Acres* by Jane Smiley, *The Blind Assassin* by Margaret Atwood, *The Grapes of Wrath* by John Steinbeck, and *Cold Mountain* by Charles Frazier.

Do books have a designated place in your home? What's on your TBR (to-be-read) pile these days?

Books are EVERYWHERE in our house. I have two young children who are also avid readers, so almost every surface is covered with at least a handful of books. My nightstand is where I keep what I am currently reading and about to read. Right now I have designs on finishing the Wolf Hall trilogy by Hilary Mantel, completing *My Name Is Red* by Orhan Pamuk, and revisiting some Graham Greene classics that I read when I was younger.

ACKNOWLEDGMENTS

Thanks to Alyssa Jennette at Stonesong and Erin McClary at Sourcebooks for making this happen.

Thanks to my family for their unwavering support, especially my mother, who read everything—some of it a few times—and Johan, who kept the ship afloat while I tried.

Finally, I'd like to thank Georgia for being my home, my inspiration, my soul, and a place that's so rich with sentiment, it writes its own stories.

About the Author

Lo Patrick lives in Georgia with her husband and two children.